D1255168

THE SECRET LiFE OF LADY EVANGELINE

EVANGELINE

SECRETS ~ BOOK 1

JAN DAVIS WARREN

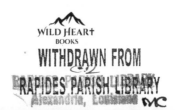

WILD HEAR†
BOOKS

WITHDRAWN FROM
RAPIDES PARISH LIBRARY
Alexandria, Louisiana

Copyright © 2020 by Jan Davis Warren

All rights reserved. No portion of this book may be reproduced or transmitted in any form or by any means - photocopied, shared electronically, scanned, stored in a retrieval system, or other—without the express permission of the publisher. Exceptions will be made for brief quotations used in critical reviews or articles promoting this work.

The characters and events in this fictional work are the product of the author's imagination. Any resemblance to actual people, living or dead, is coincidental.

Unless otherwise indicated, all Scripture quotations are taken from the Holy Bible, Kings James Version.

ISBN-13: 978-1-942265-28-3

To every reader of The Secret Life of Lady Evangeline. Thank you.
May the Lord bless and keep you.

To my sweet husband, David, who bought me my first computer and
insisted I write my stories down.
I know he is smiling down from heaven.

CHAPTER 1

1186
ENGLISH

anger!
Warning prickles burned like hot sparks across Evangeline Stanton's neck and shoulders. Those prickles were never wrong. A memory clawed at her mind, loosing a flash of raw terror of the consequences of a time unheeded.

Her racing heartbeat pounded in her ears. The cold steel of Evangeline's short sword, clutched tightly at her side, helped to steady her. Taking a slow breath, she forced the memories back into the past where they belonged.

"Tweet, tweet, tweet." The gang member named *Sparrow* gave an impressive imitation of a house wren, which was the signal that their quarry approached. The young widow and mother of two was perched high up a majestic sycamore tree to keep watch for travelers on the road coming from both directions.

The rest of the unlikely band of thieves were hidden in the dense stand of trees behind large boulders and thick underbrush along both sides of the road, waiting for Evangeline's signal to attack.

For decades, the original Fox and his gang's murderous history, with their ability to appear and disappear without a trace, had struck fear into the hearts of travelers, both rich and common, throughout England.

That was then. If the truth was known of who now wore the disguise of the Fox...

A chill of apprehension passed over her thoughts. The lives of these brave women depended on her.

The jangle of harness and prancing hooves echoed through the narrow forest passage. Their next victim would soon appear around the bend in the road headed north, toward Brighton Castle or beyond.

"Hoot...hoot...ca-cawl-l." Evangeline could not ignore the dire warning that continued to prickle her skin and repeated the signal to abort. "Hoot...hoot...ca-cawl-l." They wouldn't like it, but it was better than the hangman's noose that surely waited if they attacked this target. Would that hotheaded new member they called *Mouse* stay put or rush out and get them all killed?

Evangeline, the *Fox*, as the gang knew her, pushed farther back into her hiding place, tugging the hood of her tunic closer around the grotesque mask she wore. A gift from her deceased predecessor, the distinctive mask had the tails of three foxes tied by leather strips to the top of the deer-hide bag she wore over her head. Human teeth sewn on in a gruesome smile, small animal's bones, shells, and bits of skin were attached to form a nightmarish monster's face on the worn leather. Holes had been cut out so the wearer could see, and several vertical slits allowed her to breathe and speak, but the smell was intense even after numerous attempts to clean it. The Fox's name, savage reputation, and the mask—all inherited from the real highwayman when he died.

The grotesque image depicted on the mask and its odor

repulsed Evangeline every time she put it on, but she couldn't deny its effectiveness as their victims willingly gave over their goods, usually without more than a fearful whimper of protest. Thankfully, there had been no need to shed blood...so far.

Sweat beaded on her forehead and ran down her neck. Evangeline fidgeted against her confines. It was taking too long for the expected traveler to arrive.

Midday, yet only scattering shards of sunlight penetrated the thick canopy of the huge trees and flickered onto the road.

All would be fine as long as everyone stayed hidden and kept their wits.

The stifling July heat made the scars on her back burn as hot as her memories of the fire that inflicted them eighteen months ago. The stench of burning flesh and guttural cries for help still haunted her dreams.

No more.

At the sound of a muffled thump to her left, she swung around, her short sword raised in ready.

She sagged back with relief. A baby squirrel had fallen out of its nest into a pile of rotting leaves. The small furry creature appeared shaken but unscathed. Taking a calming breath, she watched as its mother's frantic chatter and tail twitching encouraged the baby to waddle to her. Together, they skittered out of sight.

By now, Evangeline's daughter would be walking too...if she'd lived.

Why did she torture herself with such ponderings?

Like her grief, the stench of the mask and heavy wool tunic grew increasingly unbearable. Evangeline fisted the coarse material, fighting the urge to strip it off and run as fast as she could for the cool sanctuary of the abbey.

Too late.

The carriage neared.

Please, pass by in peace. She closed her eyes and concentrated on the birds tweeting, squirrels chattering, and breezes gently teasing the leafy canopy overhead. A whispered plea for the protection of the gang slipped from her lips.

Her heartbeat slowed, but then, so did the traveler.

Why?

Eyes wide open, she scanned the trail, fearing the brush and limbs that they had gathered to block the way had been pulled into place without her signal, but she saw no obstruction. Relief eased the knot between her shoulders. No sight of the other women, but the temptation would be even greater now that their target was near.

Danger was upon them. The prickles increased.

She tightened her grip on the hilt of her sword. A quiver of seven arrows hung across her shoulder, and her bow lay ready at her side. The carriage stopped a stone's throw from her hiding place.

She leaned forward for a better view. A familiar coat of arms decorated the door.

Blood drained from her extremities, leaving her weak and shaken.

A man leaned out of the carriage window. The sight stole her breath.

Her husband, Lord Henry Stanton II.

The crushing weight of regret caught her by surprise. She sagged against the granite that hid her from the man she never expected to see again. Eighteen months had aged his once-handsome face with hard angles and graying temples.

"How much longer must we endure these insufferable woods? My servant is ill...again." His tone dripped with contempt. The sound of someone getting out on the other side of the carriage and retching confirmed his words.

"Not long, Lord Stanton." A guard on horseback halted beside the carriage. "We mustn't tarry here. I was warned that the Fox and his ruthless band of robbers frequent these parts." As if expecting an arrow to fly at him at any moment, the guard twisted from side to side to scan the forest. His mount pawed the ground, sensing the rider's fear.

Evangeline's stomach revolted. Bile burned her throat.

"I will protect what's mine." Henry's tone conveyed death-defying earnestness.

Her scars proved otherwise.

Bitter determination conquered the fear paralyzing her. Slowly she released the breath held captive within her lungs. He couldn't hurt her anymore.

Lady Evangeline was dead.

Her heart thumped out its denial as she touched the locket that hung around her throat beneath her tunic and pressed it against her skin. The intricately etched silver heart, a gift from Henry, contained a wisp of fine baby hair. It was the only connection to survive that part of her past.

Why was Henry invading her father's woods? Was it merely her husband's appearance that had set off her prickles...or something more?

An icy chill licked her spine. She closed her eyes. Definitely something more.

A distant sound drew her attention. She strained to hear over the servant's continued misery. A few seconds passed, and she knew. At least a half dozen soldiers were headed their way. Not even the village idiot could have missed the huff of the large animals ridden hard, carrying their heavily armored passengers.

A small child cried from within the carriage.

"Rebecca, hurry up. My daughter needs tending." Henry's anger sent another wave of regret spinning in Evangeline's midsection. There was a time when his voice held humor...and love.

Wait! *His daughter?*

A whimper of anguish slipped from her lips. She stood, took a step, raising her sword.

An iron grip clutched her shoulder from behind and pulled her back into hiding. Another hand pressed the mask firmly against her mouth to silence her. More hands pushed her down until she was flat on her back. She struggled but couldn't move. Dark-hooded figures, their facial features obscured by streaks of mud and grass, bent over her. Shock and confusion flooded her emotions until she recognized her childhood friend, Helen, known only to the gang as *Shepherdess*. Her friend's eyes pooled with tears of compassion, but the hard line of her mouth warned of her determination.

The distraction and noisy arrival of the soldiers had covered the women's scuffle.

"Get this carriage moving!" The captain of the castle guards slid his horse to a stop near the granite ledge where Evangeline and her captors were hidden.

"What's the meaning of this?" Henry's shout exceeded that of the captain's.

"Sorry, your lordship, but we have information that the Fox and his gang of robbers are near here today. We have orders to hunt them down and hang them." The captain's horse stomped its foot, sidestepped, and shook its head with impatience at being restrained.

"Carry on, Captain. We too have urgent business." Henry motioned for the captain to pass. The slam of the carriage door was followed by the thump of a cane against the roof of the carriage. "Continue, Alfred."

Once the carriage and soldiers had departed, the women restraining Evangeline released her and helped her up. Their lookout chirped out a warning, and they slipped back into hiding and watched the road from behind trees and rocks. Within minutes, five grim-faced men on horseback charged around the curve, as if in pursuit.

The rough looking bunch stirred a shimmer of memory from Evangeline's nightmares. Her pulse quickened, and her fist tightened around the hilt of her short sword. There was something familiar about the leader, with his scarred face and eye patch.

"Brigands, by the looks of them." The oldest member of their gang, a short quick-witted woman they called Owl, appeared beside Evangeline. They watched as the men disappeared from view. "Probably after that carriage, too."

Fear spun a web around Evangeline's middle. Surely the carriage with the child would be fine with the castle guards patrolling and the safety of the castle not far away. Still... She slipped her sword into its scabbard, picked up her bow from the ground, and adjusted her gear for travel.

"Those brigands will have a time of it when they run upon the castle's guards." Helen laid a hand on Evangeline's shoulder as if sensing her intent to pursue. "That should keep them all too busy to bother with us...or the carriage."

Sparrow whistled the all clear before climbing down. The rest of the women came out of hiding, murmuring with displeasure at their close call before they blended into the forest. They knew to scatter and make their way to their camp a mile away.

Evangeline and Helen lingered for a moment to travel together.

"I fear we have a traitor in our midst." Helen took her role as shepherdess seriously. She shredded the leaf she'd plucked from a tree in passing.

Evangeline's mind had been occupied with only one matter, the child. She stopped, tugged off the mask, and glanced at Helen, her brows raised in question.

"Traitor?" Evangeline resumed walking when her friend nodded. She thought back to what she'd heard. "The captain said he had information the Fox would be on this road today."

She and Helen had carefully investigated each member

before accepting any into their tightknit little gang. That one of them could be a traitor was cause for alarm.

Helen twisted and then split the remaining bit of mutilated leaf. Drawing a deep breath, as if a decision had been made, she cast the leaf away, ran her hands down her tunic, and smiled.

"God will reveal our traitor in His good time. All we need to do is have faith and act normally." She touched Evangeline's hand, which had closed over her sword hilt. "No need for that. Promise you'll not glare at our friends as if you suspect them." At Evangeline's reluctant nod, Helen laughed. "Good. Now put on that disgusting mask, and let's hurry lest we be the last to arrive."

Evangeline may have played the role of the Fox because of her ability to plan and fearlessly execute their raids, but Helen was their true leader and spokeswoman when they were all together. Speaking loudly enough to be heard by the group put too much strain on Evangeline's weakened voice. The intense heat and smoke she's inhaled during the fire had scarred her throat and altered her voice, making it raspy and low.

Seven women gathered at the river. Along with Evangeline and Helen, there were Sparrow, the miller's widow, Wren and Lark, both farmers' daughters, Owl, the blacksmith's widow, and Mouse, the newest member, an escaped slave. They waited for the Shepherdess to speak.

"Thanks be to God, the Fox's instinct saved us from capture again. I know—"

"Saved us! The wench almost got us hung." Mouse glared at Evangeline as if she were the enemy.

The Shepherdess scanned the faces of the group. "The heat and injury of an old wound got the best of her." Her soft-spoken confidence reassured the women, expelling the tension among them. "It's never happened before, and it won't happen again, will it, Fox?"

All attention fell on Evangeline. Her lapse of self-control had put them in peril.

"No." Guilt pushed conviction into her reply, which appeared to satisfy the majority, indicated by their reassuring smiles and pats her on the shoulder. Evangeline touched her tunic to feel the locket beneath. Was the child in the carriage her daughter? Some of these women were mothers and would understand her need to find out the truth, but she dare not risk sharing her secret with them to ask for help.

No one was to know the others' true names. The purpose was to protect them if one were captured. Their disguises, donned only for their missions, would remain in place until removed in private. Their real identities were known only to Helen and Evangeline.

"Do not be vexed at this setback," Helen continued. "There'll be other fat pigeons to pluck." She crossed her arms over her tightly bound chest that hid any signs of womanhood, lending to her boyish disguise. "Take care that ye keep your oath of silence. Now off with ye." She stopped Mouse with a gentle touch and dropped a few coins into her hand. "This was your first time, and I know there's need of food at the home where ye are staying. Thank ye for keeping your wits."

The woman grunted her thanks but glared at Evangeline before disappearing into the forest.

Once the women had dispersed, Evangeline and Helen walked down a slope to the river's edge. Hidden behind large boulders, they removed their disguises along with their heavy-hooded tunics and breeches and then loosened their uncomfortable bindings. A brief wash in the river cooled them and removed all traces of the mud rubbed onto exposed skin as part of their disguises.

Clothed only in their linen undergarments, they carried their costumes and weapons along a narrow path up the embankment to the neglected remains of the old mill. Hidden beneath a curtain of moss and vines, the stone structure clung to the rocky ledge, which hovered over the flowing water below. Only a portion of the large water-propelled wheel remained that once turned day and night to grind the abundance of grain grown in the fertile valley.

The same fields that had lain fallow for the last three years Evangeline had been gone, for there was no one to plant nor harvest them. Peasants and gentry alike had fled the region after the imposter, using the name, Robert Greene, the Earl of Evanwood, and his hired thugs had appeared and begun stealing and killing in the name of the crown. Evangeline's ailing father, Lord Mathias Brighton, had been helpless to stop them, for none had remained of his loyal guards, all having died from a mysterious malady or simply disappeared without a trace. In time, they were all replaced with more of the earl's hirelings.

Money to feed and care for the starving children, widows, and infirmed remained a powerful motivation for donning the disgusting disguise of the Fox and taking such risks. She ignored the added satisfaction of outwitting the imposter, Earl of Evanwood, who had plundered the land of anything of value in the name of her innocent father. Was it truly stealing, taking back what was stolen from the people and those rich enough to share their wealth with the less fortunate? That question often worried her conscience.

Helen's groan of pain interrupted Evangeline's troubled thoughts. The threadbare dress she had pulled over her head hung loosely on her slim frame. Her friend grimaced and rubbed her shoulder.

Evangeline had noticed Helen's many bruises at the river. The result of her cruel husband's continued abuse. She'd refrained from commenting then and did so again now. Her protest would be useless as long as her friend was determined to honor her wedding vows to God and the church. There was nothing she could do to free Helen short of running a sword through the wicked man. Helen insisted God had a plan that would make all things right, but her faith had always been stronger than Evangeline's.

Evangeline traded her guise as the Fox with that of a nun's habit. Anger burned through her veins. She was as helpless to fix Helen's marriage as she'd been to fix her own.

Against all odds, she and Helen had grown up as close as sisters. Helen was a third-generation slave. Her grandmother had been captured as a child during a raid by the English into Scottish territory. She and many others were claimed as spoils and sold as property afterward. Evangeline's grandfather bought the captives and put them to work constructing Brighton Castle, which had been built as a fortress to guard the border in a remote wilderness where English laborers were few.

Evangeline, the privileged only child and heir of the third Lord of Castle Brighton, could trace both sides of her lengthy ancestry to kings and noblemen. Yet, for her and Helen, loneliness crossed all man-imposed boundaries. Helen knew Evangeline better than anyone and loved her like a sister, in spite of the trouble Evangeline's more adventurous nature had gotten them into during their youth.

After the death of her mother, Evangeline rebelled against her elderly aunt's cruel determination to take her mother's place and make her a lady, by learning how to use weapons instead of needlepoint. Because of his sympathy for her cause, the captain of the guard had reluctantly agreed to show both girls how to use a sword, daggers, bow and spear. As they advanced in proficiency, so did the intensity of their lessons. Evangeline loved the strategy of sparring, as much as the opportunity to escape the bitter, old woman's domination.

With her peace-loving nature, Helen had been a more reluctant participant in learning the art of war, but she had remained a faithful friend, knowing that being caught would result in severe punishment for all involved.

This time was different.

"I recognize that look of determination." A scowl on her face, Helen stood with arms again crossed, this time with impatience.

"It was a shock to see Henry in that carriage!" Evangeline's once velvet voice, scorched by the smoke and flames that almost took her life, was now hoarse with emotion and barely audible. "You heard the child's cry." She finished dressing and kissed the large cross before slipping it around her neck. Memories of the events surrounding the birth of her child now flooded her thoughts. Those deepest hurts had been too grievous to share even with her best friend. She paced to the doorway of the ruins.

"Do ye think the child in the carriage is yours?" At Helen's touch, Evangeline flinched.

"Yes. I felt it in here." She wheeled around, her fists pressed against her chest. "Her cries tugged at my heart until I feared it would burst from me." She hugged her empty arms around her midriff feeling the painful memories rise from the ashes of her past. "I don't know. I was very weak from the long labor and difficult delivery." She paused to swallow her misery. "It's a blur of fragmented words of overheard conversations. My widowed sister-in-law, Millicent, kept my trusted servants from my bedside after the birth." Evangeline's breath caught. "She told me..." The anguish clawed at her throat. "She told me my baby had died and they were tending to her for burial." The cross bit into her palm. "That woman taunted me for days afterward with dire predictions that I, like my mother, would never give my husband an heir. She said Henry hated..."

Evangeline's hand shook as she positioned the thin veil that pock victims often used to hide their scarred faces. Her face had miraculously escaped being burned, but she needed the protection of the veil to avoid being recognized by many in the castle and region where she had grown up. The changes in her voice kept even her blind father from knowing her true identity.

"Your husband thought you dead. Might he have wed again and the child be of that union?" Helen's voice was soft with reason.

Determination overrode the doubt that plagued Evangeline.

"Millicent lied about so many things." Her gravelly tone deepened with intent. "I shall find out the truth, either through my guise as Sister Margaret Mary, or, if need be, with my sword as the Fox."

CHAPTER 2

*H*enry Stanton cradled his daughter, Sarah, protectively against his chest as the carriage swerved and bumped its way over the badly rutted road. She smiled up at him with emerald eyes that were just like her mother's. Her trust soothed his grieving heart but also stirred up the reminders of the many mistakes he'd made. If only...

A shout alerted him. He looked out of the carriage window, as his guard raced up to ride along side.

"Lord Stanton, I fear we are being chased by bandits. Arm yourself and prepare for battle." The young guard, whose name slipped Henry's mind, yelled up at the driver to flee. The carriage lurched forward and the guard held his mount back in ready to defend his charges.

Henry handed the baby to her nursemaid. They had passed the castle guards a mile back. The captain was berating a farmer as his men ransacked the poor man's wagon. How had the bandits slipped by them?

"We're all going to die!" the young woman screeched. Eyes wide with fright, she clutched the child to her chest. The carriage bounced and tipped dangerously to one side as it made a sharp bend in the road. The nursemaid's whines escalated into screams of hysteria, which started the baby wailing. No amount of Henry's reassurance calmed either. The confined space quickly became unbearable.

"Stop that caterwauling, Rebecca. You are frightening the child." He smacked his sword loudly against the seat beside her. The shocked nursemaid's wails stopped immediately, turning into tear-filled mews. The rocking back and forth of the carriage movement helped his daughter to calm.

"Get on the floor and cushion the baby with your body." He leaned out the window and watched in horror as five armed bandits surrounded the lone guard, separating him from the carriage and bringing him to a halt.

Daniel. Henry remembered his name. The young man's efforts were valiant, but he was badly outnumbered. Daniel fought off two others, but a bandit wearing a black patch over his right eye rode up from behind and, without hesitation, ran him through with his sword. His anguished cry pierced the air, followed by shouts of triumph from the brigands.

Henry's gut soured with regret. He would reward the young man's family generously for his bravery, unless… What if they didn't make it to the safety of the castle? The thought turned his blood cold.

A glance down at his precious daughter ignited the fire of fight through his veins.

How much farther to Brighton Castle?

The carriage again tipped as the driver whipped the horses around another curve, but it righted and kept going.

Was the attack merely to rob, or was there a more sinister plot at hand? There was one way to find out. He pulled out a small bag of gold coins from his pocket. The bulk of the gold he'd brought was intended to help his father-in-law and was hidden in a secret compartment beneath the floor. Inside this one leather pouch was enough gold to pay five men's wages for a year. A cheap price if it secured his daughter's safety.

He opened the bag and grabbed several coins. Without hesitation, he flung them out the carriage window onto the road behind them, then more coins and again until the pouch was empty. Angry shouts drew closer, but the brigands didn't stop to pick up the gold.

He had his answer. This was not a robbery but a kidnapping at best or an assassination at worst. He flexed his fingers before tightening on his sword's hilt. He would fight them all, if necessary, to protect his only child.

"Stop the carriage!" The one-eyed bandit raced up alongside and pointed his sword at the driver.

"Alfred, keep going!" Henry yelled. He turned to the nursemaid cowering on the floor and handed her his dagger.

"Protect my daughter with your life." He frowned at the pale, whimpering woman. Despite the nod, her efforts would be futile, unlike his beautiful Evangeline, who could have fought beside him as his equal to defeat an army of brigands. Regret burned deep in his gut. He would never again let anything happen to those he loved, not as long as he had breath.

The carriage rocked to one side as if being boarded. Alfred's yell of protest was followed by the man's scream in pain. The carriage lurched to the right and stopped. Henry leapt out, sword readied.

"So, Lord Stanton, do you think you can kill us all before we take what we want?" One-eye laughed and rode up to meet him. The loudmouthed leader had a nasty scar from the patch down the side of his dirty, pockmarked face. The man didn't dismount nor come within striking distance of Henry's blade.

"I can and shall dispatch the lot of you." He swung his sword to limber his journey-weary body and prepared for battle. "Go now and live. Or stay and prepare to die." He glanced from man to man, counting only three. Hadn't there been five?

The carriage bounced and brushed against Henry's back with the weight of someone moving on top. Alfred's body landed on the road beside him. Henry leapt back. His driver was dead, his tunic covered in blood.

A sword swung down from above. The smooth, flat side struck Henry on his left shoulder slamming him into the carriage door. The pain burned down his side. Stunned, he fought the darkness clouding his vision. Angry determination kept him standing, his back to the carriage.

"Griswold, don't kill the bugger!" One-eye yelled at the man leaning off the top of the carriage.

Still dazed, instinctively, Henry struck out at the attacker above him, striking the hand of the distracted scarred-faced minion. The bandit called Griswold, yelped and dropped his sword. Blood poured from the wound where two fingers had once been.

"Parker, stop!" One-eye ordered, as a third man, wearing a green coat, rode up to the carriage as if to intervene.

Henry struck the newcomer, slicing deep into the rider's leg. The heavy steel hit with a crunch of splintered bone. The surprised Parker jerked his reins, causing his frightened mount to rear, throwing the bleeding rider to the ground. The riderless horse galloped off into the woods.

The nursemaid's scream of alarm jerked Henry's attention from dispatching the screeching green-coat brigand, writhing at his feet, to rescuing his daughter.

The nursemaid barred the entrance to the carriage. Her eyes were wide with horror. As the dark-haired brigand reached for her, she screamed and stabbed him in the shoulder.

"Fisher, get in there and shut her up!" One-eye ordered from the safety of his horse.

The brigand cursed, punched the screaming girl in the face knocking her unconscious onto the floor and climbed inside.

"Surrender, Stanton and no one else need be hurt." One-eye

yelled, then cursed the man on the ground. "Parker, get up and fight."

One glance at Parker and Henry knew he was no threat. One-eyed remained out of range of Henry's sword. The man on top of the carriage still cursed and moaned over his injury making him no longer a threat, yet there remained a rider that held back, as if reluctant to get into the fight. That left Henry's greatest concern. His daughter remained inside the carriage with the unconscious nursemaid and a wounded, but ruthless brigand.

He had to save Sarah.

"Leave my daughter alone." Henry grabbed the doorframe to pull himself up through the opening.

A blow struck his already injured left arm causing him to release his hold. The pain sucked the air from his lungs. The ground heaved beneath him, and he stumbled backward. He turned and struck out wildly grazing something unseen. A blow to the back of his head dropped him to his knees. Stars swarmed his vision.

"Griswold get that carriage moving!" One-eye yelled at the man on top.

Cursing followed by the sound of reins slapping the team sent the carriage lunging forward barely missing Henry who remained slumped on the ground.

"No! Don't take my daughter!" Blurry-eyed and head pounding, with no strength to get to his feet, Henry watched helpless as the carriage drove away. Then he turned his attention to the brigand responsible, ready to offer him anything to get his daughter back..

"Get up, Parker." One-eye rode up to the green-coat bandit lying on the ground, writhing in pain, and cursed him. With an angry mumble of disgust, the leader did a quick, cold assessment, then leaned down, swung his sword, and slit the man's throat in one swift movement. His gaze darted to the remaining mounted cohort who was also bleeding, but from a lesser wound to his leg that Henry inflicted only moments ago. "How about you, Buttons?"

"I'm fine." The wounded man cursed in French and grabbed the reins of the two riderless mounts belonging to the two brigands now in control of the carriage. Then he rode in haste to follow it.

One-eye glared at Henry.

"I was paid well to let you live." He pointed his sword at Henry's face. "If not for that, I would slit you top to bottom for the trouble you've caused me."

Henry gritted his teeth and glared at his adversary, refusing to cower. He struggled to stand.

"Don't try and follow if you want the child to live." One-eye reined his horse harshly and fled after the carriage.

As if a giant fist squeezed his chest, Henry couldn't catch his breath. He watched helplessly as his carriage and all he held dear disappeared from sight.

"God, you have failed me again!" Bitterness and every vile thought that had festered in his soul since the death of his beloved Evangeline spewed out.

His fury spent, his pain spiked, sending him to his knees. He bowed his head in shame and defeat.

"Oh, God, I'm not worthy, but please save my daughter." His plea sounded pathetic and weak compared to his previous angry rant. Why would God give heed to him?

The sun glinted through the trees onto the ground beside him, highlighting the hoof prints of the runaway horse that had bolted into the forest. Hope ignited like an ember being fanned into a flame. If he could find that horse, he still had a chance to reach the kidnappers before they escaped with his child and her nursemaid. As he staggered to his feet, nausea swirled around his gut. Holding onto a sturdy oak, he waited until the ground steadied beneath him.

The excruciating pain in his wounded shoulder rendered his left arm useless. His head pounded with the intensity of a battle-ax banging against a warship's hull, but his life wasn't worth living if he couldn't save his little girl.

With the rough condition of the road and the threat of bandits, it was unlikely another traveler would show up this late in the day to help him. That runaway horse was his only hope. With a steadying breath, he pushed away from the tree and kept his eyes on the tracks in a determined pursuit.

The heat and injuries produced a mammoth thirst, which he tried to ignore, thinking of what could happen to his daughter if he didn't hurry. Why would hired murderers want a helpless child and her nursemaid?

As ransom from my father-in-law for his only grandchild?

The nearly blind, bedridden old man had no means of raising such funds. Besides, the thugs had ignored the coins thrown from the carriage. No. These brigands were hired to kidnap his daughter and her nursemaid, and leave him alive, but why? Surely the person responsible knew that he would not stop hunting for his child.

The attack made no sense.

His pounding head warred against clarity of thought. It took all of his concentration to put one foot in front of another.

The ground became rocky and uneven. Exhaustion and thirst took its toll as the rapidly fading sunlight muddled the ground until the hoof prints disappeared, along with any fledgling hope. He should have never made this journey to Brighton, no matter how desperate his father-in-law's request had been. What could he do for the lord of Brighton Castle now? The money hidden in a secret compartment deep within the carriage would be safe unless they took apart the conveyance piece by piece. Even if the gold remained hidden, it was still as good as gone unless the carriage was recovered.

Henry swiped blood and sweat out of his burning eyes. He would be no help to anyone in his present condition.

Leaning against a sturdy tree, he closed his eyes.

A portion of a scripture that Evangeline loved to recite flitted through his mind.

He that dwelleth in the secret place of the most High shall abide under the shadow of the Almighty. I will say of the Lord, He is my refuge and my fortress: my God, in Him will I trust.

"No!" He'd begged God for a second chance to prove his love, but He had not saved Evangeline from that fire, and now their child was in peril.

Vengeance is Mine, saith the Lord.

"Not if I reach them first." He'd personally see to it that any who survived that encounter would hang for what they had done.

The tinkling sound of a brook teased his consciousness. He pushed away from the tree and stumbled around a large outcropping. Was it a mirage? Dropping to his knees, he stretched out onto his stomach at the water's edge and ducked his face into the brook, drinking his fill. After quenching his thirst, he sat up and cleaned his head wound as best he could. It had stopped bleeding, but now the water washed away the crusty scab, allowing the blood to drip down his neck once more. He tore a large piece from his tattered tunic and tied the silk fabric around his head to cover the wound.

A large shadow moved over him, blocking the last of the waning light where he knelt. Heart pounding, he fell back, fumbling for the missing dagger.

When he looked up, standing over him, was the very horse he'd sought. It whickered a greeting before dropping its head to take a long drink from the brook.

Was it a figment of his addled brain?

Henry ached down to his weary feet. His head and wounded shoulder throbbed from the movement, yet he had to know if the horse was real. Using a broken limb for a cane, he stood and reached out to touch the animal. The horse twitched, but remained steadfast, drinking as deeply as Henry had just done. He rubbed his hands over the mare's neck, murmuring words of comfort as much for his sake as the horse's. He inspected the saddle and found a leather bag tied to the back. Inside were a dry shirt and a small linen pouch that contained roasted corn enough to satiate his hunger and renew his energy for the pursuit to come. It also held an empty silver flask that reeked of ale and a small tin of salve, which had the strong odor of camphor, a good ointment to put on his head wound. The last item in the bag, tied with a strip of wool, was a rolled-up map. The name and location of the Black Swan Tavern was drawn on the parchment with a crude sketch of Henry's family crest, which was painted on the doors of his carriage. Crossed swords of valor with a war horse in full armor on one side and an eagle clutching arrows on the other painted on a black background with a gold cross in the center representing faith and honor.

Fear warred with anger as the realization seeped into his weary mind. Who hated him so much to plan this attack? He rubbed his thumb over the letters on the parchment. There was something familiar about the scrolling loops of the handwriting, but with his throbbing head, he couldn't place it. When he remembered, he would know the identity of the person who had hired those murdering cutthroats. He returned it to the bag for safe keeping as proof when the time came.

Its thirst quenched, the horse wandered to a nearby patch of tender grass. Assured that the horse would graze for a while, Henry rinsed and filled the empty flask with water. When he rubbed the grime off the silver, a faint etching appeared on the front. Tilting it to catch the light, he read, "To Lord Henry Stanton for valor on the field of battle."

Lord Henry Stanton.

Henry had been named after his grandfather. The flask

conjured up childhood memories of trips to the hunting lodge. His grandfather had been an elderly man with laughing eyes who often sipped from this same flask to ease his gout. He'd stored it high upon the fireplace mantle after he caught Henry with it.

Henry's grandfather had passed away six years ago and eighteen months ago the lodge had been burned down with his wife inside leaving nothing left to bury. How had this brigand acquired the flask if not by murder?

Henry walked to the horse and slipped the water-filled flask into the bag, vowing to make sure the murderers told everything they knew about the death of his wife before they died.

By the position of the sun, even with a rested horse, it would take another miracle to track down the kidnappers before evening. Urgency overrode his doubts. He picked up the fallen reins and drew the horses' head up from grazing.

It took all of his strength to pull himself up onto the saddle. The effort increased the pain until it blurred the ground beneath him. Sweat beaded his brow, but determination to save Sarah overrode his physical misery.

He pointed the mare in the direction he hoped would take them back to the trail of the carriage, and let her pick her way through the thick underbrush. When they broke free onto the dirt road, two evenly spaced grooves of carriage tracks stood out in the waning light. He urged the horse into a gallop, which tortured his aching body and threatened to spill him onto the dirt. At the fork in the road the tracks kept to the right.

He had a vague memory of the tavern keeper at the Black Swan telling his driver, Alfred to keep to the right at the fork in the trail, which led only to Brighton castle. The left fork led to the coast and a small fishing village.

Were Lord Brighton's captors also accomplices in the kidnapping waiting for the brigands to bring his only heir to the castle as a pawn in their lethal game?

CHAPTER 3

*I*n her haste to get to Brighton castle to see the child, Evangeline had to go by the abbey to gather herbs and supplies to doctor her father. Fresh herbs would give her, in disguise as Sister Margaret Mary, a reason to appear two days earlier than her regular twice-a-week scheduled visit. The fake heir, going by the name of Richard Greene, the Earl of Evanwood, would have her murdered, too, if he suspected she knew he was an imposter and was plotting his demise.

Every visit allowed her to help determine his and his hireling's weaknesses. It wouldn't be long before she knew all of his secrets, then they would pay dearly for their deeds.

Henry and the child would be safe enough at the castle, for the earl would not be so stupid as to threaten them during their visit. Even he dare not harm the king's favorite son-in-law.

She stopped at the garden on her way and hastily gathered several medicinal herbs, both fresh and dried. Many different herbs hung, curing on the fence. The variety would treat several maladies. She also grew lethal herbs to deal with vermin and would gladly use them on the evil earl, but he made the servants taste all of his food and drink before he consumed it.

She went inside the abbey to gather the other herbs and oils she'd put aside to take with her. Urgency pressed her to hurry.

Why had her husband come? Was the child that stirred the longing inside her indeed her own?

She longed to take her sword in case of trouble, but it was not possible to conceal. Patting her side, she confirmed the dagger hidden within the folds of her nun's habit and the smaller one concealed within her cross. She would have to hurry to make it to the castle before nightfall.

"Sister! Help me, please." A frantic voice called from outside. "My baby...he cain't breathe."

Evangeline hurried out to see a young peasant running up the dusty path toward her. The girl held a small naked child, not more than two years old. The babe dangled limp as a rag doll and had bluish tinges around his dirt-crusted mouth.

Evangeline ran to meet the girl and grabbed the child. Opening the little boy's mouth with her thumb, she cleared it of dirt as best she could then held him upside down and slapped his back soundly. Nothing.

"Oh, please God, save this child." She righted the thin youngster and squeezed him. Air escaped with a gurgling noise. Again she held him upside down and thumped him firmly between the shoulder blades. This time, a small stone flew from his mouth. He gasped and started to wail. The young mother pulled the child into her arms, weeping as she rocked him in her arms.

Relief flowed over Evangeline like an ocean wave crashing against her body, and her legs would no longer hold her. She sank onto the tree stump at the end of the garden. Her hands shook with relief until the anger sat in.

"Why is this child's mouth filled with dirt?" Indignation scorched her voice into a low gravely whisper.

"My milk dried up over a month ago, and the watery gruel we make from the wild onions and roots don't set well with him. He's always hungry." The mother wept and continued to rock the screaming toddler.

"He needs milk. Have you sought a wet nurse?" Evangeline waited for her extremities to gain strength so she could stand.

"No one will help me for fear they will dry up too." The young woman drew a ragged breath. "The taxes have left us naught to buy food or milk but even so there be no farmer willing to sell, lest he be punished for stealing from the crown." Barely into her teens, the maiden had a pale haggard appearance, evidence of a hard life with too little to eat. "Lord Brighton demands our entire harvest for payment. Tis no food left to eat."

"It was *not* Lord Brighton who caused this injustice." Evangeline barely held back the fury that brewed within her to defend her gentle and kind father.

"I knowed that it is the fault of the Earl of Evanwood, though if he be gentry my Aunt Essie be the King's mum." The girl gave a stone an angry kick. "But only Lord Brighton has the power to stop him, and he's naught done it."

According to the rumors, a stranger had appeared two years ago claiming to be her father's long lost cousin and next of kin. There was a battle within the castle. Afterwards, her father had been locked away, and the "earl" took over. He had demanded outrageous taxes in the name of her father, claiming his kinship. Evangeline knew from her years of studying her family lineage that no such person existed on either side. In fact, because of war and pestilence, her father and mother's entire bloodline rested solely in her. The King of England would appoint another Lord over Castle Brighton when her father died, unless Evangeline came forth with her husband.

An impossibility. He thinks she's dead and even if she made herself known, betrayal isn't something easily overcome in a marriage. A deep ache stirred within her with that thought.

"Our prayers will soon be answered, Sister. The Fox will dispose of the lot of 'em." The girl shifted the child in her arms.

"Where is your husband?" Evangeline needed to change the subject. Heavy regret weighed her down. For the immediate present, the Fox's reputation far exceeded her small band's abilities to fulfill the hope of freedom. Evangeline turned her thoughts to the fretting baby. There was something familiar about his features and his lazy eye.

"I ain't got no man." Tears ran down her cheeks. "Is this God's way of punishing me, Sister, for getting a baby when I weren't married, even if it weren't my fault?" She stopped rocking and stared at Evangeline, fear and truth evident in the young girl's eyes.

"Of course not. God is love. He punishes only the wicked." She brushed a tear from the child's gaunt cheek. "It was He who saved this precious life, not I." She pointed to the bucket she used to water the garden plants. "Wash his hands and face. Make sure you clear his mouth." She smiled to soften her words. "Stay here until I return."

Evangeline walked to the crumbling abbey and to her room in the back. She wiggled loose a stone in the wall and pulled it out. She reached inside and tugged out a small leather pouch of coins. She removed some of the few remaining, enough to purchase a milk goat. She returned the bag to its hiding place and replaced the stone to cover the hole. With her shoe, she swept away the loose dirt and pebbles made by its replacement. On her way out she took her last bit of bread and cheese and wrapped them in a cloth.

The girl remained where Evangeline had left her, rocking her sleeping child, who now had a clean face and hands.

"Here." Her throat ached from so much talking. "This should be enough to buy a milk goat. I know a farmer that might be willing to sell you one." She offered the coins to the girl, but the young woman stepped back and shook her head.

"No good will come of me having coins. Da will take them and beat me for holding out. He has a powerful thirst for ale." Sad eyes looked at the coins with despair. "He boasts of the fine goat herd he'd buy with the reward for catching the Fox, but not he nor any peasant would do such a thing, even for so great a sum as forty gold crowns."

She'd known there was a bounty for the Fox, but it had doubled since last she'd heard. Hunger could cause even an honest man to betray his dearest friend if the price was right. Had one of the gang also decided the reward was a better choice than hanging if they were caught?

"What are your names?" Evangeline waited as the girl shifted her stance again. Even so small a child would soon weigh heavy in her thin arms.

"I be Anna and this here is Angus." Anna gently touched her child's face.

"Well then, Anna, I find I have need of a milk goat." Guilt for stealing these coins from a drunken, potbellied tax collector, scratched at her conscience only for a moment. "Come here every morning to milk the animal and feed the babe." Evangeline dropped the coins into a small cloth pouch tied at her waist.

"Truly?" The girl's eyes lit with excitement and then narrowed with suspicion. "Why would you do that for me and my babe? I can't pay you back." She raised her head with pride. "I cain't take charity from the church."

"The milk is part of your wages for tending the animal and help with the garden. I know little about goats." Evangeline watched hope again light the young woman's countenance.

"I knowed all about them. We used to have over fifty before the earl's marauders stole 'em and broke my da's leg for standing up against them. He turned to drink to ease the pain, but it's been over a year, and his leg still hurts him fierce." Pride stiffened her stance. "He was once a good herdsman...and father."

"I'm sorry for all you've lost." Evangeline handed her the bread and cheese. "This is for you to eat now. You need strength to carry your son. Once you've finished eating every bite"— she smiled as the girl hesitated only a moment before accepting the food—"I want you to go to the back door of the Black Swan." She waited until the girl devoured the food and drank her fill of water.

Anna shook the crumbs off the cloth and handed it to Evangeline.

"Keep it and use it to wrap Angus." She smiled as the girl fashioned the cloth into a nappy and tied the corners on each side to keep it in place.

Evangeline retrieved a coin from her purse and pressed it into the girl's palm. "Tell the mistress at the Black Swan that I sent you. She will sell you enough fresh milk to satisfy Angus's hunger for today." The girl frowned, but Evangeline continued. "This is payment for your promise to help me. Say nothing to anyone about our arrangement."

The young mother nodded and tucked the coin inside the top of the nappy. "It be safe in there. No man would chance a look inside." She grinned and hugged her son.

"Off with you. With brigands and the earl's guards wandering about, you don't want to be late getting home." Evangeline smiled at the happiness that lit the girl's blue eyes, giving a glimpse of the beauty that lay hidden behind the despair. "I'm needed at the castle and may not return before you come tomorrow. I trust you to keep your promise."

The girl nodded and hurried down the path with more enthusiasm than Evangeline felt.

Helen would care for the poor thing and her babe, but she would be far less sympathetic towards Evangeline for making such a commitment when the Fox could be needed at a moment's notice. The arrangement would have to work out, for she couldn't let the girl and her child suffer.

The Fox needed to break the strangle hold of the impostor who called himself the Earl of Evanwood before the whole land rose up to hang her father for the terrible deeds he had been powerless to stop.

Tugging her nun's habit straight and dusting off the dirt, she picked up her basket of herbs.

First, she had a goat to purchase. She'd received cheese as an offering to the church from a farmer who still had livestock not confiscated by Evanwood's hirelings. He'd remained isolated from the marauders by destroying all evidence of the road that once led to his place. The farm was hidden in a lush valley not far from the abbey. The walk took her only a little out of her way.

Her short detour was well worth it. By the generosity of the man's devout wife, Evangeline was able to buy two milking goats and a few chickens with her small sum. The farmer had a son old enough to deliver the animals and build a pen to make sure the creatures were safe and secure at the abbey. There was an old shed in the woods that would make a good hen house, with a little work. The area was heavily wooded to keep them safely out of sight of the earl's henchmen and tax collector.

Arrangements were made and the purchase complete, leaving her little purse empty but her soul satisfied that she had done the right thing. At her refusal to stay for a meal, the farmer's wife insisted she take cheese, bread, and bit of smoked sausage to eat along the way.

The urgency to get to the castle quickened Evangeline's pace. She needed to reach the keep before dark.

The Fox needed more funds to feed the poor who were hungry and in desperate need, like Anna. The money stolen from travelers was split equally among their group with the promise to share their portion with the needy. The peasants were a proud lot and wouldn't take charity, but she had faith that God would find a way to bless them with honest work, by bartering goods and services until the enemy is vanquished. With more money, she could pay to have the abbey repaired and a number of other chores completed. Her mind spun with the possibilities.

"Dearest Lord, I need wisdom and enough money to accomplish these lofty goals." A whispered, *Amen,* and her burden seemed suddenly lighter.

A glint on the badly rutted road caught her eye. She stopped and picked up a gold crown. It was the fastest answer to prayer she'd ever received. She spotted another coin, then another. Would there be more? Hope filled her heart, as she gathered more coins scattered about, as if flung aside. Who would do such a thing? Maybe another of the earl's drunken tax collectors?

Her pouch was soon bursting at the brim with gold enough to help many families. How was it possible that the coins had been untouched? More than likely, travelers and villagers had been warned that the castle guards were hunting for the Fox today and would stop anyone they found on the road. Questioning by the guards usually ended in being falsely accused of one infraction or another and fined, arrested, or killed. For whatever reason the gold remained on the road, she was truly grateful.

Overhead, a hawk squawked from the dense forest canopy. Fear made her clutch the newly acquired fortune tightly to her chest. She would need to keep these funds safe from the imposter's hired henchmen, who would not think twice about robbing a nun.

Helen told her that the death of the abbey's elderly priest, Father Andrew, had been caused by those same henchmen when he tried to stop them from stealing from a farmer.

Evangeline would need a better way of hiding this blessing.

Pressing the last coin into the overflowing purse, guilt overburdened her conscience. A lifetime ago, she'd frivolously spent funds equal to and greater than the amount she'd just collected, often in less than an hour. Surrounded by bodyguards, she had roamed the weekly markets with her handmaidens and bought trunks of useless trinkets along with anything else that had caught her fancy. She still remembered the vivid colors of the exotic silks, from the orient, that were soft as butter to the touch.

She smoothed the rough cloth of her habit. With a murmur of repentence, she clutched the basket tighter, tucking the coins beneath the herbs. Such shameful waste was in the past. Every coin she could get her hands on now meant the difference between life and death for the hungry it would feed. If the child, with Henry is truly hers, if given the chance, she'd raise her to value people more than things. She pressed her hand against the locket beneath her habit.

An empty pouch lay in the road ahead. Just what she needed. She stopped to pick it up, eager to transfer the coins to this larger, more secure purse. It had two long, leather cords, which would allow her to tie the pouch at her waist and be hidden beneath her habit. She stopped long enough to transfer all of the money into the larger purse and tugged the cord tightly so none could slip out. There was a deeply embossed pattern embellished on the side of the leather. A close examination left her breathless. It was unmistakably the Stanton family crest.

Realization hit like a punch to the stomach.

If the coins were from Henry, then there must have been a good reason he would have thrown them out.

Her heart sped up. She gathered a handful of her heavy habit, and the basket full of herbs, and began to run. The gold in the leather pouch hit against her side with every stride.

If those hard-riding brigands she'd seen earlier on the road had ignored the coins being thrown from the carriage then...

She stumbled to a stop and stared in horror. Two bodies lay in the road.

"No!" Her breath escaped in a ragged gasp of dread.

As much as she hated Henry for his betrayal, by abandoning her for Millicent, she didn't wish him dead. Who would protect the child...her child? A feeling she couldn't ignore.

By the signs, the carriage had stopped and a battle had ensued. Her heart pounded, as she drew closer to the bodies.

A sword and the dead men lay on the ground nearby. The stench of death and dark splotches of blood soaked the dirt road. Unexpected relief flushed her skin as she realized neither person was Henry. The older man she recognized as the carriage's driver by his livery. The other body was one of the brigands who had ridden past her earlier. There was no sign of Henry or his guard. Had they escaped with the carriage?

Was Henry injured? And what of the child? Her gut soured with what she might find next. She scanned the road. It appeared as if a lone horse and someone on foot had headed into the forest. She paused to listen and hoped the man chasing the horse would not reappear. With an anxious glance around, the silence confirmed that no one lurked in the deepening shadows.

Prayers for the dead had become far too numerous of late, yet her conscience dictated that she spare a moment to make her plea for the dead men's souls. Unfortunately, the scent of the dead bodies would draw predators during the night, for there was no one to bury them.

Her Christian duty completed, she picked up the dead brig-and's short sword from the road and swung it, testing it for balance. Satisfied that she could handle the weight, she glanced around for more clues to where the carriage went. It was easily followed, because its tracks were distinctive in the depth and width of the wheels.

The daylight was almost gone, meaning she would not make the castle before nightfall and she didn't want to be anywhere near this place lest she become another meal for the hungry wolves that roam the land.

Retrieving the herb basket in one hand, she kept the sword ready in the other and continued her journey at a slower but steady pace. She'd need somewhere safe to spend the night. Only one place came to mind.

A half-hour later, the sound of something large crashing through the brush ahead startled her to a stop.

CHAPTER 4

*F*ollowing the tracks of the carriage in the waning light, Henry pushed his mount ever harder to gain ground on the kidnappers. Dark thoughts of what could happen to his little Sarah tormented his thoughts. The pounding pace had taken a toll on both him and the animal. The pain from his multiple injuries grew intense, and he could no longer feel the fingers on his swollen left hand.

The mare stumbled.

"Easy, girl." Fearing she would fall, he pulled back on the reins until the horse slowed to a walk, a welcome relief for both.

Fresh horse droppings he'd spotted a few minutes ago confirmed he had closed the gap. If he could locate the brigands before their tracks were lost, then he could seek help, but who could he trust?

The sunlight gone, the forest lining the road thickened until only spotty moonlight slipped through the dense canopy, made any signs of the carriage nearly impossible to see.

Pressing on to a clearing, where the full moon lit the ground. He pulled the bay to a halt. Acres of timber had been eliminated on either side of the road for farming leaving room for the moon to highlight the terrain. No crops grew in the dark loamy soil. He had seen similar barren fields after a war, burned by the invading army to starve any survivors, but why here and why now?

A chill of dread tugged out memories best forgotten of his first experience with war. He had run away at the young age of seventeen to fight. The enemy had been a small raiding party of less than fifty seasoned soldiers spying out the land. No amount of practice and drills had prepared him for the thunderous roars of armored soldiers charging one another.

His father's guards had found him injured on the battlefield that evening and taken him home. The battle's stench of death and the screams of the dying had faded during his short marriage, but once again tormented him in his sleep since Evangeline's death.

He cleared his mind to resume his search for signs the carriage had passed this way. The mare hung her head. Her sides heaved, as she drew in deep gulps of air. Guilt pricked Henry's conscience for riding her so hard.

"You're a fine mount." He patted her sweaty neck. "We'll rest here a moment before we continue." It would be easier if he could examine the road up close. Weariness checked him before he swung off. If he dismounted, in his weakened condition, he may not be able to pull himself back up onto the saddle.

He rubbed his eyes to clear his vision, then leaned over to examine the marks in the dirt. Dizziness swamped him. He threw his arms around the mare's neck to keep from falling off. Drawing a deep breath, he stilled until the disorientation passed.

Slower this time, he clung to the saddle for balance before he leaned over to search the ground. By the dung and sharp prints in the dirt, he could tell that a herd of goats or sheep had passed this way not long before. Bleating could be heard in the distance. Their passing had obliterated any remaining evidence of his quarry's tracks.

"Should I continue on toward to the castle or backtrack until I find the trail again?" Speaking his thoughts and stroking the mare's neck helped him ignore the pain shooting through his body.

He would backtrack a short distance at a slower pace. Perhaps he had overlooked something in his haste. With increasing effort, he straightened in the saddle and turned the horse around to retrace his path with methodical precision. He sought the last sign of the carriage tracks, fearing it could be a waste of precious time.

What if he had lost them?

"Lord, I need Your help." His words came out ragged as his waning hope.

A few yards back, the bright moonlight revealed the distinctive grooves left by the carriage.

"Thank You." His words came out barely above a whisper because of the overwhelming flood of gratitude. Weariness was the only possible excuse for how he could have missed such blatant tracks the first time. The driver had veered off the road onto a dusty path barely wide enough to navigate the carriage and a team of horses. Broken branches of the low hanging limbs and thick overgrowth that lined the trail confirmed their direction.

With hope ignited again, Henry turned the suddenly skittish horse onto the narrow path. The mare snorted, balked, and fought his effort to continue on the trail. The struggle for control strained Henry's wounds and stiff joints, but he held fast.

"Easy, girl." Wanting to rant at the animal for the delay, which would only further frighten the already agitated beast, he softened his voice and spoke reassuring nonsense while urging her down the path. "Nothing is going to harm you."

Wham!

A heavy limb slammed into Henry's side, knocking him off the horse and flat onto his back on the hard ground. The mare wheeled around, barely missing his crumpled body as it escaped back the way they had come.

He should have listened to the beast.

His lungs burned with need, but he couldn't draw a breath for the pain.

"That be for cutting off me fingers." The angry voice of his attacker bellowed like a wounded bull, low and dangerous.

A blurry face hovered over Henry before the darkness sucked him into a void of nothingness.

~

*H*enry's shoulder and side burned like a hot poker jabbing into it. His left arm was swollen and stiff. The loud pounding in his aching head made it difficult to understand the words coming out of the person leaning over him.

"Wake up!" A menacing voice ground out close to his ear.

Henry's shoulders were lifted and shaken then dropped. His head hit hard against the dirt floor, sending fiery sparks shooting through his skull.

"Oh-h." A groan was the best he could manage in response.

"You better be glad he's not dead."

"He deserved the thrashin' after what he done to me." This angry voice was from a different man, who spewed vile curses followed by a vicious kick to Henry's leg.

Strange. Henry didn't feel the kick, though his mind told him it should have hurt.

"Stop! You idiot. His high and mighty Lord Stanton won't be worth a shilling if he dies." The sound of a door slamming shut. "Since his lordship refused to heed my warning not to follow, I will make use of his stupidity and send a ransom demand to his cousin the king."

Footsteps receded. He dared to open his eyes, but even his eyelids hurt. A flickering glow teased his senses from a gap under the door. Only able to take small breaths, the earthy damp smell and coolness of his surroundings reminded him of a cave he once explored. He didn't like it.

"Go find someone to doctor his lordship. I hear there's a nun who can heal the sick. You better hope she can, for if he dies, you will, too. But instead of burying, I'll turn your dead rotting body in for that hefty reward I saw posted on that London tavern wall." A cackle of sardonic laughter was followed by loud protesting curses.

"Non! Her ladyship, she'll no like that his lordship's been harmed." The heavily accented voice of a third man joined their conversation. "She no pay unless he lives."

"The ransom will be requested by a local thief, the Fox. Nothing will tie the kidnapping to us. Besides, after the king has paid and his lordship is returned alive, I think her ladyship will hand over whatever I say when I go to collect the balance promised, or risk being revealed as the person who hired us," the first man boasted.

Henry turned his head. Under the large gap at the bottom of the door, the feet of three figures shifted in the glow of their torches. An uneasy feeling persisted that he'd overheard something important, but his weary thoughts refused to sort it out.

"A shame about that pretty green eyed-mother-of-gentry. Parks, rest his miserable soul, told me how ye thought her weak as a kitten when she wielded that dagger of hers like the king's guard and plucked out yur eye like a ripe grape off the vine." The second man snickered. "Does it still pain you much?"

A bellow of outrage erupted followed by the thud of fists hitting flesh. The scuffle of grunts and cursing disappeared with the sound of another door slamming shut. They took their torches with them, which plunged his earthen cell into an inky void.

Justice and honor demanded retribution for their murderous deeds, but Henry's pain-filled body refused the call to battle. A vow to avenge those wronged settled deep within his heart.

First, he must survive.

Thirst parched his throat. Maybe they left some water. He tried to sit up. Excruciating pain from his ribcage sucked the air from his lungs. Unconscious oblivion would be welcomed to escape his misery, but no relief came this time. Every regret of his past ran through his mind, each more torturous than his physical pain. None greater than his current failure to rescue his daughter.

"Please, God. Help us."

CHAPTER 5

*T*he coming night drew dark shadows on the road. Twigs snapped with the approach of something large. Evangeline held her breath and listened. Could it be the missing man and horse?

A panting stag crashed from the underbrush. In two leaps it disappeared into the thick forest on the opposite side. Fear raced along Evangeline's spine. The frightened animal was being pursued by a predator, be it man or beast. Before she could decide whether to hide or fight, a lone wolf leapt out onto the road and stopped. The scraggly predator's eyes glowed amber in the moonlight, and it glared at Evangeline as if to assess an easier target. With a yell, she set down the basket, raised her sword, and took a defensive stance. The animal turned toward his previous quarry and disappeared into the woods. Wolves usually hunted in packs. Thankfully, this one appeared more interested in chasing the fleeing deer than confronting a stubborn human with a weapon. She'd heard tales of a wolf chasing its prey into the trap of his waiting pack. A chill followed at the possibility that more wolves lay in wait. To her relief, there were no sounds of more predators, but she would not tarry to find out.

Evangeline hurried onward. She preferred not to spend the night in a tree.

As much as she wanted to continue on to the castle, the last two miles were the most treacherous, with far more dangerous predators than hungry wolves roaming freely. The earl's hirelings attacked any who strayed outside the castle walls especially after dark.

She remembered an abandoned farmhouse around the next bend in the road. Old Farmer Danby and his family used to live there. They'd sold their produce at the village market every Thursday for as long as she could remember. She and Helen had accompanied Helen's mother, the head cook, to the open air market when they could escape the watchful eye of Evangeline's aunt. The always-jovial elder Danby would give them an apple or one of his wife's home-baked sweets.

The girls had spent many hours arguing over which of the farmer's two elder sons was the most handsome with their work-honed physiques and lake-blue eyes.

Those happy memories gave way to sadness. According to village gossip, the farmer and his two older sons had died a year ago when their burning barn collapsed on them while they tried to put out the blaze. The fire was started by the hired thugs of Lord Evanwood because the farmer had complained that their demands for more of his harvest didn't leave enough to plant for next year, much less enough food to feed his family over the winter. The henchmen had emptied the barn and pens of livestock and put a torch to it.

Evangeline winced as the scars on her back ached with the ever-present reminder of what it felt like to be trapped in such an inferno.

The farmer's widow had fled that night to save her remaining two children, a daughter and son, abandoning the farm and leaving everything behind. It was said, that in her grief, she cursed the men and any evil-hearted person who would take anything from her home or try to possess their land. Two of the five men who'd been responsible for the deaths of her husband and sons had taken up residence, determined to claim the farm for themselves. One had been found dead in the middle of the road within the week, fear frozen on his lifeless face. The other had disappeared, never to be seen again. The rest of Evanwood's henchmen involved in the farmer's death died within the month. Had their deaths been merely bad luck, or were they the victims of the widow's curse? The locals believed the latter, for any who tried to claim the abandoned farm fled with tales of avenging ghosts.

A chill of apprehension for her own misdeeds burrowed into Evangeline's conscience. Though her intent was noble, was stealing in order to do good still a sin? Did that make her evil, too?

More thoughts flashed into her mind, thoughts of Evanwood's cruelty, each evil deed committed in the name of the crown fed the fire of revenge, like kindling thrown on the embers of injustice, which burned within her soul.

Until help arrived, the *Fox* and the brave women of her gang would have to continue to do their best to stand against the evil men who had invaded the land. Justice must prevail before they stole everything of value from the realm and left her father accountable. Evanwood and his greedy cutthroats would pay for their reign of terror with their lives.

The sword had grown heavy in her grip. She swung it to limber her tired arm.

Lost in thought, it took a few moments before the quiet alerted her senses. The night sounds of the forest had ceased. An ominous silence surrounded her.

A prickling sense of danger rose with the hair on the back of her neck. She stopped, dropped the basket of herbs, and placed both hands on her sword, waiting and listening.

Snap! A twig broke, and another. Leaves rustled to her left. This time, there was no mistake. The heavy tread belonged to the two-legged variety of predators. She edged closer to a large oak and slipped behind it, every muscle tense and ready to spring into action. The bulky habit she wore, and the heavy pouch containing the gold, would be a hindrance, but with God's help, she would manage.

"I told you we'd be too late to catch up to her." Barely visible in the moonlight, a dark figure stepped out of the forest and onto the road, followed by another, a bit taller.

"There be no way she could have passed us with the shortcut we took." The young men argued back and forth.

"We did our best. I wish we had a few farthings so we could stop at the Black Swan for a pint of ale before we go home."

"If you're goin' to wish, why not wish for food to fill our empty bellies, you fool."

"Anna'll be not happy that we failed."

That young mother had betrayed her? Why? Disappointment, like the foul smell of death, sent a wave of revulsion through Evangeline.

"I ne'er seen her so pushy."

"We promised to protect the nun to the castle, but if we naught can find her...wait. What's that?"

The young men stopped.

Relieved that Anna had only wanted to help, Evangeline stepped into their view.

The two startled youth filled the air with high-pitched yelps and an outburst of curses.

"That belongs to me." Her tone was light with humor, because the dark habit she wore must have appeared specter-like in moonlight. "I'm Sister Margaret Mary." She picked up her basket of herbs.

"Sorry, Sister." The shorter of the two stepped closer.

"We thought the ghost of old Farmer Danby or one of his sons had come to slay us." The taller youth's unexpected honesty and nervous chuckle sent mirth bubbling up within Evangeline. She coughed and cleared her throat to hide the laughter that would have surely offended him.

"I heard you coming and decided to hide until I knew if you were friend or foe." She stepped closer and softened her hoarse voice with a smile. "I am Sister Margaret Mary." Keeping the sword hidden in the folds of her garment, she reached out her other hand to the nearest of the two. The moonlight shone brightest in the spot where they stood. Obviously the young men had forgotten the need to keep into the shadows to avoid the earl's henchmen patrolling day and night.

"I be Hank, and this be my twin brother, John." The shorter brother hesitated before he took Evangeline's fingertips and kissed them as if unsure how to address a nun. "Our sister Anna sent us to protect you."

"It was very kind of her to think of my safety." Evangeline grinned at his earnestness, although, if such an occasion arose, it was far more likely she would need to protect the boys, who were barely in their teens.

"We passed the earl's marauders on our way here. They be coming up the road, not far behind." Hank was obviously the leader of the two. He had long dark hair tied in the back and was thin like a beanpole where his brother, John, was stockier with broad shoulders and at least three inches shorter than his sibling, with light, short cropped hair. They looked nothing alike in physical appearance or mannerisms.

"Here, carry this for the sister." Hank handed John the basket before he took Evangeline's arm.

"There's a shortcut to the castle, but it be rough. We'll get ye there, but don't know how to get ye inside the walls until daylight when they open the gate for the merchants." Hank led the way into the forest. The young men had either the night vision of owls or were very familiar with the rocky path, for they slowed only to help her over a fallen tree.

"Just lead me to the castle. Once there, I know a place where I can hide and wait until morn." Evangeline didn't mention she knew a secret passageway into and out of the solid stone walls. She had used it countless times to escape lessons or boring visitors that she'd been expected to entertain.

The forest grew ominously silent. Danger. She tugged her hand out of Hank's grasp and stopped to listen.

He groaned in protest.

"Shh!" She raised her hand for silence. The boys pressed closer, one on either side and she could feel their tension, perhaps still shaken with the thoughts of ghosts wandering through the woods. They didn't have long to wait to find out what had alerted her instincts.

Loud, drunken voices and a horse's grunts of displeasure at being handled roughly came from the direction of the road. The glow of torches passed, throwing ugly shadows on four men on horseback headed toward the castle. An uneasy feeling remained. Someone or something still lurked nearby.

"We need to hurry if we want to avoid meeting any more like them along the way." Evangeline kept the sword hidden within the folds of her bulky habit. Her eyes had adjusted to the darkness, and the sporadic opening in the forest canopy allowed the full moon to light their way.

The ground was uneven and steep in places, laced with fallen limbs and boulders, but their pace remained steady. Lost in her thoughts, recounting today's events, she stumbled over an exposed tree root. She swung the sword out to keep her balance. The blade struck the stony ground with a metallic clang.

"Where'd that sword come from?" John reached for it.

"I found it on the road." Evangeline was impatient to get to the castle, but the weariness in her limbs demanded a brief rest, and she sunk down onto a fallen tree. "Here." She handed the sword to the young man to examine and then rubbed her aching shoulder. "It's very sharp. Careful how you handle it."

The highly polished steel glinted in the moonlight as John swung it in a clumsy arc from side to side.

"We found three dead men on the road on our way to find you." Hank watched John handle the sword. "The first one was a royal guard by the looks of the fancy shield lying by his body. He might have had a sword, but there were three castle guards picking the body clean of anything that could be used or sold." He grabbed at the sword, nearly getting cut in the process.

John used his stout body to foil his brother's attempts to snatch the prize.

Dread filled her at the thought of the guard dying and leaving Henry and the child without protection. Had they made it to the castle?

Evangeline reached out. "I'll take that now."

John relinquished the weapon, which she held against her side to keep them from further horseplay and possibly being injured by the finely honed blade.

"One of 'em dragged the bodies off of the road, but the likes of them don't report deaths." John moved to Evangeline's right side and focused on the sword resting there. "The wolves will take care of the rest." His voice had taken on the matter-of-fact tone of one who had seen worse. "The Fox and his gang are ridding the land of the o-o..."

"Oppressors." Hank pushed past his brother and reached for the sword. "Don't you think I should carry that for ye, Sister?"

Evangeline stepped out of reach to protect the weapon.

"I'm taking it to the castle to turn it in and report the dead men, as someone from the village should have done. It's the least we should do for those poor souls." She was disheartened to realize how these desperate times had stolen even basic Christian values from those who needed them most. "The dead men deserve a decent burial, no matter what they've done."

"But the sword be too heavy for a nun." Hank reached out to take the weapon again, but she slapped his hand.

"Enough! It's not too heavy for me." She tightened her grip on the hilt. The feeling of danger still prickled against her neck. They were being watched. Man or beast, she couldn't tell. "We must go or risk running into the marauders...or worse."

A glint of fear passed between the boys as they peered into the dark recesses of the woods. They hastened along the path, keeping close to Evangeline.

"Do you think there be avenging spirits wandering the forest, sister?" John moved close enough to Evangeline so she heard the fear in his whisper.

"Ghosts won't bother us 'cause we're helpin' a nun, right, sister?" Hank also moved closer, until Evangeline thought she would step on them.

"No one ever has to fear anything from the dead when they are doing a good or noble deed." Evangeline wanted to explain to them that there was no such thing as ghosts, but setting them free from ancient superstitions would take more time than she could spare at the moment.

The sound of twigs snapping on the trail behind them, stopped when they stopped, confirmed Evangeline's feeling of being stalked. Be it man or beast, it left no doubt that whoever or whatever was following them was of this world.

Within the hour they arrived unmolested by men, beasts, or ghosts, at the clearing near the castle. She stopped, still hidden from the castle within the tree line, not willing to risk the boys learning the way to the secret entrance.

"This is where we part." She retrieved the basket from Hank, removed the cloth bag that held the bread, cheese, and sausage, and handed it to John. "Inside is a little something to thank you for your protection. Not even the King's guard could have done a better job." While John opened the bag, she turned to Hank. "And thank your sister for me, for thinking of my safety. God will bless her, and you, many times over."

"Food!" John tore off a large piece of the bread, hesitated then offered Evangeline the first bite.

"I'm not hungry." Evangeline's stomach rumbled in protest. The boys were starving, and she could find something to eat once she was safely inside.

John handed the bread to his brother, who grabbed it and shoved it into his mouth in one bite.

"Shouldn't we wait to protect ye?" Food muffled Hank's words. She would love to have rewarded each with a gold coin, but she couldn't risk them telling who had given it. Besides, Anna had warned that their father would spend the money for ale.

"It will be safer for me if I remain alone," she said. "I know a place to hide." The moonlight became spotty as clouds slid by. She waited as the two devoured bites of bread, cheese, and sausage, moaning with delight. The moonlight made a brief appearance, and she noticed Hank's attention drawn to the blade glinting at her side. "I'm sorry that I cannot also give you this fine sword, but it is illegal for you to have it in your possession. You know the law. If a castle guard or nobleman saw you with it, they would execute you on the spot."

The boys mumbled a reluctant agreement. They finished the portion in their mouths and John closed the sack.

"Can we save the rest for our family?" Hank's concern for his siblings warmed Evangeline's heart. The Fox must prevail to rid the land of those responsible for their hunger.

"Certainly." She stepped away. "I only wish it were more." Weariness slowed her speech and stirred up desperation to be alone. All she wanted was to escape inside the castle, and slip into her old room to sleep. "I'll be safe. Go with God. Leave now, before the moon comes back out and someone sees you." She watched as the youths jogged back toward the path they had just left and disappear into the forest. With a tug at the leather pouch that had rubbed her waist raw from the weight of the coins, she adjusted her burden. The pain was well worth it. Others would soon have food to fill their empty bellies.

She crept along the ridgeline toward the castle wall to the one blind spot hidden from the sentries watching from above. Clouds still covered the moon, reducing her visibility and anyone else's who might be lurking about. Though they had traveled some distance from the road where she'd met the brothers, she still couldn't shake the feeling of being watched and paused to listen. Hearing nothing, she continued on. The entrance was a mere stone's throw away.

Heavy footsteps sounded behind her. Heart pounding, she flattened against a small mound of earth, blending into the terrain, making sure the sword was covered by her habit to hide it from the moon's reflection, yet easily accessible dare she need it.

Eager to reach the secret passage, and too consumed with her dread of seeing Henry again, she'd failed to heed the tingling prickles that zinged along her neck.

"This is far enough away from the castle and its spies. We can't be seen here," a man with a gruff voice whispered nearby.

How many others knew about the blind spot in the castle's defenses made to cover the royals' exit from the keep?

"*W*hat's so important that you had to drag me out here to tell me?" That came from the whiney voice she recognized as the fraudulent Earl of Evanwood. "I was about to retire and surprise another unsuspecting serving wench with my prowess." He chuckled.

The image of the man and his lazy eye came to mind. She guessed that he had fathered Anna's child, certainly not consensually. Anger, so intense it made her body tremble, filled her being. The need for justice over his soiling the weak and innocent was restrained only by the weight of exhaustion that slowed her reflexes and the greater need to hear more.

The evening breeze carried the acrid scent of unwashed bodies and the equally unpleasant odor of soured ale.

"The arrival of Lord Henry Stanton-n should-d be enough reason to meet. I figured you'd be clamorin' to know what to do next." Buford Oxley, known only as Ox, had a slight stutter making him easy to recognize. He was the fat, lazy owner of the Black Swan Inn—and Helen's despicable husband.

"Lord Stanton? Coming here? When?" The so-called earl's whiney voice shrilled with fear.

The blood in Evangeline's veins ran cold. Henry and the child hadn't made it to the safety of the castle? Her hand tightened on the hilt of the sword. She prayed the ale would keep their tongues wagging a little longer to reveal Henry's location.

"What? He ain't at the castle?" Ox bellowed then followed with a string of curses. "His carriage should have arrived hours ago, unless-s…"

"I need to leave the country now! He will cut me down, or have me hanged. You have my share of the money. Give it to me!" Evanwood's whine turned into a high-pitched panic, followed by the sound of a scuffle then a sharp slap.

"Get hold of yourself-f, or I will kill you-u." Ox's threat ended with Evanwood's whimper followed by a slap, much louder this time. "Listen you fool-l. If his lordship hasn't arrived, then something must've delayed him-m. Perhaps the carriage broke down-n or…" He paused. "Maybe those brigands I saw ride by the inn-n caught up to him-m. There must have been a battle. Maybe they took him captive." Ox clapped his hands "Perfect! I wondered where that fancy armor came from-m, that was brought in for trade-e."

"Stolen armor?" Evanwood grew bolder. "I want my share."

"The trade goods-s that you took from that rich merchant last week as tax, in the name of the crown, should fetch a tidy sum-m." Ox ignored the demand. "I have a buyer who'll be here to take the livestock and the bulk of the grain and goods-s next week. We'll both have enough money to live like kings-s."

"I want my share now. I have plans that will take me far from this awful place. Too many people want to kill me. Even my own men..." Another slap interrupted Evanwood's gathering tirade.

"I have plans-s, too, which don't include my uppity, too-good-to-wipe-my-shoes-s wife. She is always sneakin' off when she ought to be workin'." His chuckle held no humor. "I plan to be a widower again very soon. I have something special planned for that skinny wench, far more creative than the others-s. Then I'll be free to live the rest of my days-s some place warm. I'll live in luxury with plenty of servants-s." Evanwood and Ox's voices faded as they walked away.

Shock paralyzed Evangeline until realization roared in her gut against the threat she'd heard. She stood, sword in hand. Fury blazed through her veins. Ox was the one behind the appearance of the fake Earl of Evanwood and his hired thugs. Between the two, they had caused untold suffering and death. Now Ox planned to kill Helen, too.

She wanted to race out and dispatch both of the men, but, unlike them she was not a murderer. She would see them tried and hung for their evil deeds.

Picking up the basket of herbs, she continued to the secret entrance. Ox was right when he said the castle had many ears. It was time she found out what the gossips knew about why Henry was late getting to the castle.

It had grown too late to question anyone, and she needed rest. Weariness made every step a determination of her will. Helen needed to be warned. Evangeline would send a loyal servant from the castle with a secret message only Helen could decipher. One consolation was that Ox wouldn't carry out the murder before he had the rest of their ill-gotten money, which, according to him, wouldn't be for at least a week. Since he was too fat and lazy to do the work to keep up the inn, he wouldn't kill Helen until he was ready to disappear.

Helen was smart. She'd know what to do to protect herself from the fiend. Even as a child she had caught on to the tutor's lessons faster than Evangeline. Helen had a knack for learning, which had annoyed Evangeline's aunt and tutor, the elderly Sister Agnes. She'd been raised by a string of hired nannies, which spoiled her, and instilled the belief that servants should remain ignorant to keep them in their place.

Fortunately, Evangeline's father did not hold with that notion, and even encouraged Helen to teach any of the staff who wished to learn basic reading and math, as long as it was done discreetly.

As Evangeline's constant companion, Helen's thirst for knowledge had spurred Evangeline to try harder to keep up.

When Helen reached seventeen, Buford Oxley had approached her mother for Helen's hand in marriage, though he was old enough to be her father.

Ox had been widowed twice, the second wife had been buried only two days before. Helen had flatly refused. Not only was she repulsed at very thought of Ox, who had ogled her for years; she was deeply in love with one of the castle guards, Armand Degraff. If it had not been for her mother's plea for freedom, which Ox had promised if Helen married him, she would not have married him. He had freed her mother only to murder her a month after they were settled into the inn.

Helen and Evangeline were close as sisters, but to Evangeline's regret, during that time when Helen had needed her most, she was in London where she met Henry and was soon wed. It was not until after her return, disguised as Sister Margaret Mary, that she heard the horrid details of Helen's marriage. Ox's treacherous cruelty had scarred her friend, as much as the fire had etched Evangeline's back and soul.

Helen had encouraged Evangeline with prayers and insisted God had a plan. As the innkeeper's wife, she could ferret out information without people realizing they had revealed their secrets.

Surely Helen knew that her husband was up to no good. Did she also know he was involved with the imposter claiming to be Lord Brighton's cousin? If so, why hadn't she mentioned her suspicions?

Evangeline reached the entrance and set down the herb basket. The heavy door required both hands to release the latch. She leaned the sword against the wall and pulled aside the thick ivy, her fingers searching for the cleverly hidden lock. The earthy smells of the vines mixed with the moss-covered stones stirred up memories of past excursions, making her eager to be inside.

A pebble hit her shoulder, and she wheeled around, scooped up the sword and took a fighting stance.

Fog rose from the ground encircling the lower portion of a ghostly specter in a dark hooded cape, which gave it the appearance of floating above the ground. A sword glinted at the specter's side.

The boys' talk of the avenging ghosts elevated her fear until all she could hear was the blood pounding in her ears.

"I have not been given a spirit of fear but of power, love, and a sound mind." She mumbled the holy words she'd memorized while living with the nuns and squeezed the hilt of her sword tighter. The cold metal cut into her palms.

The cloaked specter moved toward her, parting the fog in a swirl of motion.

CHAPTER 6

"*E*vangeline."

The ethereal whisper of her name backed Evangeline farther into the thick ivy. A flush of childish terror stirred up old nightmares of the castle's own avenging spirits.

She couldn't escape. The door pressing against her back was hard to open. Dropping her sword to free her hands to work the mechanism was not an option. Her breath came in shallow gasps. She drew in a deep breath, to calm her frantic thoughts, and straightened with determination. Murmuring every Holy Scripture that came to mind, she waited to meet the apparition with the sword of the Spirit and the sharp edge of her blade.

"Evangeline, tis only me." The specter came closer and pushed back the hood of her dark cloak.

"Helen!" Evangeline dropped the sword and rushed to her friend. They hugged as if they hadn't seen each other in decades, but a lot had happened since that morning.

"T'was you watching us in the forest?"

"Aye, I needed to speak with ye, and knew you'd be headed to the castle, but the boys found ye first."

"Did you hear Ox and Evanwood just now?" Evangeline wished she could see her friend's features, but the darkness of the alcove and the thickening fog made it impossible.

"Aye, I heard." Her voice held a weary resignation. "I've known for some time of Ox's acquaintance with Evanwood, whose real name is Urso Hemming."

"When did you find out?" Evangeline kept her words low, but she wanted to shout at her friend for withholding this vital information.

"Today, after I returned from the mill. Ox was in his cups and plying a passing traveler with ale. Too drunk to walk, he demanded I fetch his special brandy. He threw me the key to his room, which he always keeps locked. The space was filthy and the stench overpowering. I tripped over discarded clothing and fell against the fireplace. A loose brick fell out. Hidden in the hole, I found a small pouch of gold and some papers, one of which was a wanted poster. Leaving the rest, I took the poster and replaced the brick. After I delivered the brandy, I slipped away to read the parchment. It had a good likeness of Hemming's face on it, along with the amount of a hefty reward. Ox had written the details of Hemming's crime on the back." She tugged her cloak tighter to ward off the chill. "Hemming was once a tutor for the children of the king's chancellor until he was caught in the act of forcing himself on his employer's fifteen-year-old daughter. He barely escaped with his life." Helen's voice relayed her disgust. "Ox must have spotted him as a guilty man with a secret the first night he showed up at the pub. His typical way to extract information is to get his victim drunk and then pry the details from his loose lips."

"Why didn't you tell me Ox and Evanwood, I mean Hemming were in this together?" Evangeline's exhaustion made it hard to talk but her disappointment was evident.

"Forgive me, but until I knew for sure I couldn't risk telling you knowing you might do something you might later regret." She took a deep breath and released it. "I had my suspicions, but no proof Ox was behind Hemming's treachery until now." Her voice cracked, revealing her grief. "Nor that he had succumbed to such greed as to starve and murder innocent folk." She touched Evangeline's shoulder. "I'm glad that the truth is out in the open so justice can deal with them accordingly, but." She paused. "I have graver news to relate."

Her weariness hung as heavy as chains and filled Evangeline with dread.

"What could be worse than this?" Then she knew. "Henry!"

"Aye." Her friend lowered her voice.

"How? Where?" Evangeline fought the panic that rose within her.

"Wren reported that she heard about a carriage that veered off the road and headed down the overgrown lane toward the Danby's farm. Since no one goes there, she went there to find out why. Just as she arrived, a horse and rider appeared. The gent was knocked off his steed by a man using a limb to erase the carriage tracks."

"Henry was the rider?"

"Aye."

"Was he hurt? Did she see the child?" Evangeline's voice became deeper and more gravelly with every question. "What—"

"Stop." Helen sounded as weary as Evangeline felt. "All I know is that he was captured by the brigands who passed us on the road. He, the child, and nursemaid are alive, but held prisoner."

"I should…"

"You're trembling with exhaustion. You must go inside and rest. I'll pray and ask God for wisdom and a plan. You do the same, and we'll see how best to go about saving us all."

"You're right." As much as Evangeline wanted to rush to the farm to free the prisoners, she knew her strength was too far gone to risk a battle she could not win in her present condition. "Won't you come with me? We've always worked better as a team." She paused. "And it's too dangerous to go back to the Black Swan since we know of Ox's plan to murder you."

"I'll be safe tonight." She chuckled. "I took the horse he left tied in the forest. He'll have a long walk back. With his gout, it will take him all the night and part of the morning. I'll bolt the inn's doors against the blackheart and rest easy. Tomorrow, he'll be in a foul mood but will want only his bed and enough ale to ease his pain. I'll slip him a draught. While he slumbers, I'll listen to the gossip of the inn's patrons for any further sightings or rumors of the brigands, *Lord Evanwood*, or any who might hinder the rescue of Henry and the babe." She helped Evangeline disengage the latch and open the door then picked up the sword and the basket of herbs and placed them inside the tunnel. "In with ye. Can ye find the candle and flint?"

The dank smell of the narrow space had always filled Evangeline with the dread of being trapped. Her hands shook as she searched the darkness, touching the mossy walls to find the ledge and the earthen bowl and a tallow candle she'd left behind years ago. She'd used the passage to escape after her aunt demanded Evangeline leave the castle and go to London to be presented at court. She'd hid in the forest until her father found her. Only after he agreed to accompany her did she submit to her aunt's plans. She met Henry in London at the king's ball.

Brushing away thick spider webs that touched her face, she tried not to think of what else may have taken up residence in the tunnel since last she'd gone this way. The sticky webs clung to her hands. She scrubbed her palms against the rough texture of the rock wall and located the stone outcropping.

"Yes. Here they are." She worked the flint several times over a small bowl of dried moss. A spark settled, and a flame took hold long enough to light the candle. A cool breeze flowed through the open door behind her and threatened to blow out the fire. She turned to protect the flickering light with her body. The door shut firmly behind her and the flame steadied. Her friend was gone.

CHAPTER 7

*E*vangeline climbed the back stairs and slipped unnoticed into her old bedchamber, hoping the familiar surroundings would ease her exhaustion, both physical and emotional. She opened the leaded glass window to air out the musty room and then tugged off her clothing. To keep the sword within reach, she hid it among the heavy fabric of the canopy that hung in thick folds at the corners of her bed. She untied the leather strips of the pouch filled with gold from her waist, she almost cried with relief. The heavy load had rubbed her skin raw. Released from her burden, she shoved the pouch under her pillow. She climbed onto the feather mattress and tugged the down-filled blanket over her. Her father's room was on the same floor as hers making it easy to slip out in the morning to see him.

She yawned and turned to her side, then her back, unable to find a comfortable position. After so long sleeping on grass-woven mats on the hard floor of the old abbey, since she'd returned, the feather mattress refused to comfort her. Frustrated, she pulled the blanket to the floor, stretched out and fell fast asleep.

~

*T*he early morning sun shone on her face through the opened window. She awakened with a start. A complaint when she was young, the sunshine now served her well. Rising, she searched her wardrobe and found a strip of lamb's wool once attached to her hunting bow as a sling. She tied the wool around her tender waist and secured the gold around her midsection before dressing. She kissed the cross and settled it about her neck with a whispered thanks to God. Once again being safe within the keep and near her father were reasons to be grateful. Rather than turn the sword over to be used against innocent folk, she tucked it in the wardrobe behind the silks and brocades of her past life, she remade the bed to eliminate any sign of her presence.

If her aunt were still alive, she would have been appalled and lectured Evangeline for at least an hour for doing a servant's tasks. It had happened too many times to count.

As a child, Evangeline had shunned the bitter old woman who didn't know how to give comfort or receive the love of a grieving ten-year-old. A prideful woman, her aunt had been left at the altar. Humiliated, she escaped to London and joined a convent. Unlike the kind and giving nuns who had saved Evangeline's life, her aunt had found no solace in her vows, holding on to her anger and pain. She never forgave the man who drove her away from her highborn life. Over thirty years after the wedding that wasn't to be, still miserable living a sacrificial existence as a nun, she had eagerly accepted Lord Brighton's request to serve as ten-year-old Evangeline's tutor. Once again in the castle where she'd grown up, the old nun ran the household and young Evangeline with an autocratic iron fist. She died a month before Evangeline's return home from the convent where she'd been living, while the nuns healed her burns.

Evangeline sighed. After being taught the use of medicinal

herbs to heal and ease pain, she regretted not returning in time to help relieve her aunt's suffering and tell her she forgave her.

More regrets to add to the long list she kept in her heart. She knew now how bitterness and betrayal poisoned the soul. God's love and forgiveness were the only antidotes, but first one had to want the freedom. He brought more than the promise of revenge.

In her childish rebellion against the strict dictates of her aunt, she'd found her revenge by learning the use of weapons of warfare, taught by the captain of the guards. Captain Ezra Browne was an experienced soldier and friend of her father who had taken pity on a grieving child that wanted an escape for that grief. The more dangerous the exercise, the harder she trained. First, because the old nun would have forbid it, then later because she loved the strenuous activity and the strategy of combat. There was great satisfaction in finding the weakness to best her opponent.

The past was unchangeable. Evangeline must put her mind to besting the evil men ravaging the land. Forgiving her aunt had come in time, but those who harmed the innocent didn't deserve God's mercy.

With renewed determination, she picked up the basket of herbs and checked the corridor to make sure it was empty before she made her way to her father's chambers down the hall.

Quietly, she opened the heavy door and slipped into his room. The familiar smells surrounded her with peace and happy memories of her childhood. The scents of leather from the two large hide-covered chairs that faced a big fireplace blended with wood smoke that permeated the space. The huge hearth crackled with a fire, warming the room even on a summer's day because of her father's frail health. White hair like wispy goose down, framed his head and pillow. His eyes opened, but a milky film hindered him from seeing. He turned toward her.

"So, Sister, you've come to check on this old man?" He smiled when she stopped. "I know your tread, and you always bring the smell of herbs and sunshine with you."

"It is I, Lord Brighton." Her grief made the burden of truth harder to conceal. She hurried to his side. "How are you feeling this glorious day?" Her voice was husky with emotion and a sudden need to feel her father's reassuring arms around her. She wanted to confide everything and beg him for advice, but her need to protect him from the criminals around him was greater. They would kill him and her if they knew she lived and could spoil their ruse with legal action and the king's army. According to the servants, her father had remained cooperative, because of the so-called earl's threat to murder every servant and villager if Lord Brighton gave them any trouble. But her father would have a plan to rid himself of these murderers.

"Better now that you are here, my sweet Evangeline, or should I continue to call you Sister Margaret Mary?"

She gasped, and he laughed.

"You know?"

"I've known from the beginning. The reason for your disguise and allowing everyone to think you dead, now those are questions that have caused me many sleepless nights." He struggled to rise in the bed. "However, I've played along with your ruse believing you must have a good reason. Every visit I had hoped that you would trust me with the truth."

Evangeline brushed aside the veil covering her face and leaned near to help him sit, tucking pillows behind his back.

"From your letters, I thought you and Henry were happy. What happened?" He patted the bed beside him. "It is time you tell me, daughter. All of it."

She threw herself into his arms. Tears clogged her voice as she told him her sad tale, sparing only her guise as the Fox.

"Henry and I were very happy, even more so after we found out I was with child." Evangeline cleared her throat. "Henry's parents, our friends, and even the servants were thrilled to know there would soon be another generation of Stanton's in resident, especially since the death of Henry's younger brother. Our lives were blissful until the day Millicent arrived acting the grieving widow. Within a week, she had the entire castle in an uproar over the seeds of lies she spread. She set friends against friends among the servants and guards and soon after, Henry against me." Evangeline brushed an unexpected tear from her cheek, surprised the old hurt had surfaced with her tale. "He ignored the truth of the matter and my pleas to send her away."

"Because he felt to send his brother's widow away would dishonor his brother's memory." Her father patted her hand.

"Yes, that was his excuse, but I felt as if he were choosing her over our happiness." She straightened and leaned against the pillows. "Her lies spread doubts in Henry's mind over my fidelity until one evening just as we retired he demanded to know the name of the father of my child." Her tone rose harsh with anger. "That is when I asked him to leave our chambers and sleep elsewhere."

"You did what that evil woman could not by barring Henry from your presence." Lord Brighton's tone was soft but his words hit hard.

"As it neared my time, I had a hard time resting. One evening someone knocked at my door, I thought it was the servant who had gone to fetch me some warm milk. I opened the door and found Henry. I had missed him and hoped he'd come to tell me the wicked wench was gone. He appeared worried and wanted to talk. Before I could let him inside, Millicent walked up behind him and put a possessive hand on his shoulder, which he ignored. With a wicked smile of a tormentor, that harlot let her robe drape open to reveal she had nothing on beneath. I slammed the door and bolted it. Henry pounded on it for several minutes until the servants came and ushered him away." Evangeline twisted the corner of the comforter into a sharp point wishing it were a dagger in Millicent's heart. "I went into labor that night and for two days my sole thought was to have my baby and leave that place." She smoothed the comforter flat again. "I was too weak to protest her appearance after I delivered my baby, I barely remember the midwife tell me it was a little girl before Millicent sent everyone out. She told me the baby had died and my servants couldn't attend me because they were tending to the baby's burial. I was devastated but that wasn't enough for Millicent. She told me because my mother couldn't have more children and give you an heir, I would never be able to give Henry a male heir."

"My poor baby." He hugged her tight and released her. "There is no reason that you cannot have many healthy children." He patted her shoulder. "I assumed you knew that your mother's problem with carrying a child was not a weakness passed on from her ancestors but from an unfortunate accident." He slumped back into the pillows and took a deep breath and released it.

"Our parents betrothed us while we were still children. By the time we married, we were very much in love. We were wed only a short time when she realized she was with child.

His grin stirred up a memory of Henry's similar expression of joy when Evangeline had told him of his impending fatherhood.

"I was the happiest man in the kingdom. All afternoon we laughed and talked of our wondrous future, full of plans and expectations." Sadness replaced the joy on his face. "Three months later we went to a large open market. She'd insisted she needed to purchase more items for the baby." His voice lowered until Evangeline had to lean in to hear. "I'd stepped away to check out a vendor selling new weaponry and to visit with some old friends."

Evangeline took his hand, and he squeezed it.

"I heard the screams of warning, but I couldn't push through the wall of frightened people. A team of runaway horses dragged a broken wagon through the crowd like a scythe through a wheat field, cutting down everything in their path. In their wake people lay injured and dying. By the time I reached your mother, it was too late." He rubbed his hand over his face, as if trying to remove the image. "Her injuries were severe. By God's grace she lived, but we lost the baby. The physician told me that she might never be able to bear a child again." He cleared his throat. "Yet here you are." He patted her hand. "Now, that's enough sad tales of the past. What else has happened to fill your voice with such sadness?" He stroked her face and dried her tears with the long sleeve of his nightshirt.

His love and warm hug melted away the sorrow of their mutual losses, filling the void with his all-will-be-well assurance. As a child, she had believed he could fix anything wrong in her little world. His reassuring presence still soothed her fears, but she knew better. Only God could cure the evil that had invaded their lives and their land.

She told him of the dead bodies she had found on the road, but not of seeing Henry. Was her father well enough to hear even more bad news?

"I'll have my servants search for the men to assure the dead receive a Christian burial." He patted her shoulder. "What else? I sense there is yet more heavy news to share."

"I found out today that Ox and Urso Hemming, representing himself as Robert Greene, the Earl of Evanwood, have been using your name and the crown to murder and steal."

"I'd heard of the stealing and murders but didn't know that Ox was connected to our fake earl." Lord Brighton adjusted his pillows to sit up straighter. "After my attempts failed to imprison the imposter, which cost the lives of six brave guards and eight faithful servants, I realized I have traitors among my staff. I dare not risk more lives when I had no idea whom I could trust. Not even Elsa has been able to ferret out the spies, so it was time to enlist some help. Two months ago I sent secret missives to the king and your husband, asking for their assistance." His voice was once again strong.

She slid off the bed to pace the room. His requests for help were a well-kept secret indeed, if neither she nor her friends had heard wind of it. Since Hemming and Ox now knew of Henry's arrival, her father's life could be at stake. How would she protect him?

"I have had confirmation from each. I heard that a fine carriage with a guard was seen traveling toward the castle. It could be that Henry chose to come immediately, not waiting for the king's troops." He shifted to draw the covers closer. "And now it's your turn. What more have you to tell me?"

Not wanting her father to know of things that would evoke a scolding or worry, she'd avoided mentioning her reason for being on the road that day.

"I was in the forest near the place where Henry's carriage stopped. I saw him clearly but he did not see me. I heard a child's cry come from within the carriage before he drove off." To ease the knot of fear in her chest, she walked to the portico. Dawn's early light shone on the activity in the courtyard below. Children played tag and mothers bent over wash tubs as they gossiped and kept a close watch on their brood. How could life appear normal with so much evil in their land?

She turned toward her father.

"I know deep within my heart that the child I heard is mine." Her suspicion that her sister-in-law had hidden Evangeline's child from her and the many other lies Evangeline had caught the woman in during her stay at the castle had spilled out in detail and brought forth sudden clarity of Millicent's motive.

The evil wench wanted Henry for herself.

A memory stirred of meeting Henry for the first time at the

king's ball. Seventeen-year-old Evangeline had been flattered by the devoted attention of the very handsome and dashing twenty-one-year-old Henry. Their instant attraction kept them on the ballroom floor excluding all who might be tempted to intrude. A blonde woman with menacing dark eyes, wearing a beautiful green gown with a lower-than-proper scooped bodice, pushed through the crowded dance floor and tried to step between Evangeline and Henry. The brash blonde demanded he dance with her. He pried her fingers from his sleeve and quietly, but sternly rejected her. Adding insult to injury, Henry drew Evangeline away and introduced her to the king as his future bride. The spurned woman made such a scene with her tantrum that the king had his guards escort the woman from the castle with orders to keep her out.

Evangeline realized that woman had been Millicent.

"Come." Her father patted the side of his bed.

Evangeline returned to stand by the bed near him. She knew he couldn't see her but his hearing was astute.

"Even as a child you had premonitions that came true. At three, you cried and refused to go to the stables to visit your pony, which you loved. You insisted a bad dog was there, though all of the dogs were friendly. A fox, sick with rabies showed up at the stables that same day and attacked a stableman who barely avoided being bitten before putting the poor beast out of its misery. The next day you were happy to go to the stables." Lord Brighton smiled. "I learned to listen whenever you mentioned a vision, dream or a warning."

"Then why didn't I know about the brigands who tried to burn me alive in the lodge?"

"Perhaps you did but in your grief you couldn't hear the warning." Lord Brighton smiled. "You have a gift from God, Evangeline, but you must keep close to the Lord to hear His whispers."

A cold chill stiffened her with resolve. She needed to get

back to the abbey. It was time for the Fox to intervene. She had stayed too long, the morning was slipping away and there was much to do.

"I received word that Henry and the baby might have been captured by brigands and could be at the old Danby farm." She drew a deep breath. "His delay may be nothing more than a problem with the carriage. I must go and see if the report is true." She pressed a kiss on her father's forehead.

A soft knock on the door sounded a moment before it opened.

Evangeline tugged the veil into place to hide her face. Their trusted servant, Elsa, stepped inside.

"Sister." She bobbed a curtsy and came toward Evangeline with a welcoming smile. "I didn't know you were in the castle. My spies are getting slack." She chuckled, but Evangeline doubted that much got past their faithful servant, with the exception of the traitor who was passing on information to the *Earl of Evanwood*. The sad fact was that some people were willing to do anything for a few coins. No matter how clever the traitor thought they were, the truth would prevail. Evangeline had known Elsa most of her life and the elderly servant heard of everything that went on in the vast castle, village and surrounding farms. She sat down a tray of food for Lord Brighton.

"Elsa, I'm sorry I can't stay and visit this morning, for an emergency has arisen and I must return to the abbey." She handed the basket of herbs to her and snagged a warm breakfast cake to satiate her hunger. "By now, you are as well versed in using these healing herbs as I." She hurried to the door. "I'll return with more as soon as I can."

"Good bye, Lord Brighton. I'll return soon." With Elsa there, she couldn't say more.

"Good bye, Sister. I look forward to our next visit. God go with you." Concern blanketed his words.

Taking a seldom used passage, Evangeline avoided the fraudulent *Earl of Evanwood*, his men, and the servants who roamed the castle. She slipped from the castle through the same tunnel she'd taken to enter.

~

*T*he walk to the abbey was long, though she knew she'd made it in far less time than it usually took to travel the distance to the castle and back. Freed of the burden of deceiving her father, her body was energized by the knowledge that her dear father knew the truth and still loved her unconditionally.

When she arrived at the abbey, Anna was milking one of the two nannies in the newly built pen. The young mother spoke soft and encouraging words, coaching the goat to give more. Little Angus fussed beside her.

"I'm almost finished, babe." Anna patted the child then resumed her chore with joy in her voice.

Not to be hindered with questions, Evangeline skirted the yard and kept out of sight until she reached the edge of the abbey, then slipped inside unseen. A far cry from the castle, the abbey was a modest structure of three rooms. A large stone fireplace covered one wall to her left and was once used to heat and cook. With the fear of burning the structure to the ground, she'd avoided using it since her one attempt to use it to cook a meal resulted in filling the abbey with smoke and sparks. It was far safer to cook outdoors over the stone fire pit.

To the right, a small doorway led to the prayer chamber, but rotting roof beams had collapsed months ago, rendering that room uninhabitable. The remaining thatched roof over the main room had huge holes that let rain and creatures in, but the back room where she stayed was still mainly dry and safe. She opened the heavy wood door, stepped inside her chamber and waited until her eyes adjusted to the dark interior. Thick stone walls held up heavy beams which angled down until the thatched roof almost touched the ground, forming a lean-to at the back of the abbey. Light through the opened door allowed her some visibility. The almost cave-like windowless chamber had sparse furnishings. A small rickety table held the chipped water pitcher, a tallow candle and her Bible. It was a dungeon compared to her airy bedroom with the high ceilings and large windows in the castle. Everything appeared untouched. She hid the gold in the hole in the wall and replaced the stone. Confident it was safe, she cleaned up the dust left behind on the floor then washed her face and hands. She tugged the veil in place and smoothed her habit.

A screech of alarm sent her running to the door. She clutched her dagger and wished she'd kept the short sword she'd left in her room at the castle.

One of the brigands she'd seen pursuing the carriage held Anna with a blade against her throat, another waited on a horse nearby.

"What is going on here?" Evangeline held the dagger at her side, the other hand readied to free the blade concealed in the large cross she wore around her neck. A touch would release the mechanism that would separate the blade from the holder. She held it at ready.

"So you don't know where the Sister is, huh?" The man shoved the girl away and she rushed to her squalling child. Picking Angus up, she hurried to Evangeline's side.

"I didn't know you were home, Sister." Anna glared at the man who had accosted her. "Tis the truth."

"I just arrived." She patted the girl on the shoulder and turned toward the two men who waited in the yard. The man on horseback had a bound leg. He held the other man's horse.

"You the nun who heals?" The man on foot had a dirty

bandage around his right hand. With a menacing look of determination, he stalked toward them.

Evangeline whispered to the girl, "Take your child into the
forest and don't return until these men have gone." She stepped
in front of her, to cover her escape.

"I can't leave you alone." Anna's courage warmed Evangeline.

"God is with me. Protect your child. Now go!" Evangeline
waved her hand behind her back for her to leave.

Before the girl reached the trees the brigand on horseback
cut her off, and the one on foot rushed forward and grabbed her
by the hair jerking her to a halt. She struggled against his hold
to maintain her grip on Angus.

"I didn't say you could go, little girl." The man pulled Anna
toward Evangeline.

"Release them at once!" Evangeline prepared to strike. Her
anger made the words hoarse and terse. With a swift glance at
her two opponents to assess her options, she readied to do
whatever was necessary to keep the girl and her child safe.
Drawing a calming breath, she searched her thoughts for a way
to free Anna and best these marauders.

"I am Sister Margaret Mary." Appearing helpless would give
Evangeline the element of surprise and supply her with a
certain advantage, so she relaxed her stance.

"Then it's you we've come to get." The man on foot
continued his approach, dragging the terrified Anna behind
him, making her struggle to remain upright while keeping the
screaming child tightly within her grasp.

"Let them go, and I will discuss the matter with you." Evangeline raised her voice to be heard over the wailing.

"I give the orders here. Come with me or watch these two
die before your eyes." He stopped in front of Evangeline and
grinned, showing rotting teeth and a glint of blood lust in his
eyes. Jerking Anna to his large barrel chest with his bandaged
hand, he again pressed a knife against her throat with the other.

"Stop!" Evangeline commanded with a regal tone of one used to being obeyed. She stepped forward. The hilt of the dagger bit into her fingers. With her training, Evangeline had the skills to disarm the two injured brigands. She took a stance ready to do what was necessary to protect Anna and Angus. *Save us Lord from the evil ones.*

"S'il vous plait, Sister. Please. His Lordship's very ill. If you no want him to die, you must come now." The man on horseback rode closer.

His mention of Henry stayed her from lunging forward to free Anna by plunging her dagger into the brigand's arm.

Until the king's soldiers arrived, she was Henry and the child's best chance of escape. To free them she needed these men to take her to them without delay, but she wouldn't allow them to hurt Anna or her baby.

"Griswold, release ma fille and her bebe." The Frenchman ordered. "We must hurry to avoid the castle guards patrolling the road."

The man with the bandaged hand grumbled in protest but released the young mother and her child. Anna again rushed to Evangeline's side. They appeared physically unharmed.

"Go! Hide in the woods until we've gone," Evangeline whispered before she turned and stepped toward the men waiting in front of her.

A quick glance behind her confirmed that Anna had used the crumbling abbey for cover and made her escape unhindered.

"Let's go." The one called Griswold grabbed Evangeline's arm in a punishing grip.

"First"—she jerked free—"I need to gather my healing herbs." Grabbing a large basket from the end of the garden, she released the dagger and let it remain hidden in a secret pocket in the folds of her habit. She used the garden knife she'd left inside the basket to cut the fresh herbs and plucked dried ones from the fence where they were hung.

"Why take the dried up ones?" The man called Griswold hovered by her side.

"Because drying concentrates the potency and makes them able to be ground into a fine power to make a poultice or for drinking." She headed toward the abbey to fetch her bag, which contained clean linen for bandages and the items needed to sew up wounds.

A rough hand on her shoulder halted her steps.

"Enough." The brigand's unwashed body and foul breath made Evangeline's stomach revolt in protest.

"Unhand me." Royal indignation rose in her voice. She slapped the man's injured hand with the flat side of the garden knife. He yelped and released her. Regret was immediate when she saw a murderous anger fill his eyes and flush his face.

She shoved the knife into the basket of herbs, stepped back, and raised her empty hand in surrender. "If you want me to tend to your wounds as well, I must fetch my travel bag, which contains the necessary supplies." She edged toward the abbey's opened door. "It's just inside the doorway."

He stomped close behind her.

"Here." She grabbed the leather bag and shoved it into his chest, making it necessary for him to grab it. "You can carry it."

He backed out of the way while she pulled the heavy door closed, allowing her to take the lead toward the man on the horse.

Griswold hurried up from behind, pushing her forward with his elbow. When they reached the mounted rider, Griswold handed up the basket and bag before turning toward Evangeline. Without warning, he grabbed her by the waist and threw her onto his horse, then leapt up behind her. He grabbed the reins and kicked the animal into a gallop, making Evangeline, riding side-saddle, cling to the horse's mane to stay on. The breeze from the ride kept a certain amount of the man's stench at bay.

She felt the brigand lean against her. Thankfully, her habit kept a barrier between them.

"Maybe you got something in that bag to keep that tot from squalling, too."

A whispered prayer of thanksgiving shot up to the heavens. The child was alive. With an urgency to see for herself, she willed the horse to go faster.

The jarring trip seemed to take forever before they turned down an overgrown path and she knew where they were headed. As Wren reported, the prisoners were being held at the Danby Farm. The place she had thought to stay the night before the twins showed up on the road to lead her to the castle, God's divine intervention, no doubt.

Remnants of the burned out barn, like a charred skeleton, stood a hundred paces from the vine-covered, abandoned farm house. A sound, like a whispered moan, moved through the tall trees surrounding the property and sent a chill down her spine.

The men pulled the horses to a halt. Griswold jumped down and pulled her off the horse with an iron grip.

A frequent nightmare washed over her. Panic stole her breath. Something about the familiarity of the scene stirred old memories of her near death by the hand of just such brigands. The remote surroundings, the blackened remains of a fire that had taken the lives of good men, the foul smell of her captors and their bruising treatment—all were part of her horror.

"Unhand me or face the wrath of God." Anger rose up and overrode the fear. She elbowed Griswold hard in the ribs, slapped his injured hand, and jerked away. Taking a defensive stance, she fumbled to free the dagger hidden within her habit.

"You little—" Griswold cursed and raised his hand to strike her.

The Frenchman, still mounted, spurred his horse forward and pushed between Evangeline and the cursing brigand. He shoved the basket of herbs and bag down at Griswold and reached for the reins of his partner's horse. "Take the nun to our guest immediately." He turned to Evangeline. "Sister, he'll not harm you." Spoken as if an oath, he glared down at Griswold. "For it is not only God's wrath he should fear if he strikes a servant of the church." The Frenchman led the horses away to the pen where the carriage horses wandered around.

Perhaps she had an unwilling ally in the Frenchman. A shove from behind pushed her toward a large mound of earth at the east end of the farmhouse. Likely the family's root cellar dug deep into the earth to store food and grain. Had Henry been imprisoned in that forbidding place?

CHAPTER 8

*E*vangeline scanned her surroundings. Henry's carriage, battered and scratched, stood abandoned in the yard. The occasional snuffle of restless horses came from the pen, but there were no other typical farm sounds, not even a birdcall, only eerie silence. Once-majestic oaks that had shaded the tidy farmyard in the past were now charred skeletons. Moss and vines hung from their barren limbs, like the shroud of a ghostly apparition, giving no relief from the oppressive heat. No breeze ruffled the tall weeds engulfing the once happy, pristine home of her memory.

"About time you got back." A short and stocky, black-haired brigand met them.

"Fisher, you're a…" The already ill-tempered Griswold didn't appreciate the snide remark. He shoved Evangeline forward and loosed a string of curses attacking the other man's parentage and his manhood, and then added a mumbled reference to donkey dung.

Wedged between the two bickering brigands, she was pushed past the farmhouse toward the structure. An open door that led into the root cellar and total darkness.

She hadn't seen nor heard the child since her arrival. Worry churned within her and increased her pace.

～

"*W*ake up!" A shout and the screech of rusty hinges troubled the recesses of Henry's sleep.

He dismissed the demand, for he and his beloved Evangeline rested in their bedchamber enjoying their private time.

Entwined in each other's arms, they lingered, discussing the day's events. He loved the way her mind worked. She gave a unique insight and clarity into problems he'd once wrestled with for days. Inhaling lavender, roses and her special womanly perfection, he relaxed, savoring his time with her. The numbness in his left arm was unrelenting. He tried to shift his position without releasing Evangeline, never wanting to let her go again. This time he would keep her safe.

"I told you to wake up, fancy pants." Rough hands shook him. "You got a visitor."

"Ugh-h." Anger scratched Henry's parched throat at the intrusion and made his protest weak and garbled. The diversion tore away the remaining image of Evangeline. An unmerciful and pain-filled reality emerged in her place.

～

"*G*et in there, Sister." Fisher, the third of her unwashed kidnappers, pushed her into the dark, earthen room. "There's your ailin' patient."

"Ailin'? Not near what he deserves for this." Griswold shook his bandaged hand at Henry's body lying in the dirt. The vile names he spewed were followed by the same vicious curses that he'd just proclaimed over Fisher.

As if he evoked an evil presence in the confined space, a chill spread through the room stayed only by the dim light of the torches.

"Enough." Evangeline cleared her troubled thoughts and spoke in her most demanding voice, a hoarse imitation of her aunt's commands. "No one deserves to be treated in such a manner, no matter what they've done." A quick perusal of the confined space confirmed the child and nursemaid were not here.

She knelt beside Henry. He was barely conscious, dirty, and, by the sounds of his groans, in considerable pain. The anger she'd carried for his neglect and betrayal these last eighteen months had hardened into a wall of bitterness after the fire. The time spent with the nuns at the convent as they'd ministered to her burns and broken spirit had mellowed those feelings into cold indifference. Or so she'd thought until yesterday when Henry leaned out of his carriage and spewed his haughty diatribe about protecting his own. A reserve of hidden resentment had burst into a flame of full-blown hatred quenched only by the sound of the child's cry. A total contradiction to the alarm she now felt. Left in this filthy, dark and dank place, he would surely perish.

"He must not remain here." She straightened to her full height. "If you want my help, then this man must be taken to the house and put in a clean bed."

Something moved in the dark recesses, stirring up an eerie stench of decay. Evangeline suspected a rat. One glance at the fear she saw in her captors darting gazes, and she knew what to do.

"Did you hear that?" She crossed herself and kissed the cross now clutched in her hand. She lowered her voice to a husky whisper. "I heard rumors that the owner of this farm, and his sons, all good men, were murdered defending their home. They say their spirits roam here hunting the evil men who took their lives and any others with malice in their hearts." She paused and crossed herself again. "Surely men of the world such as you can feel this place is haunted."

The men grumbled a muddled protest of disagreement, but their eyes grew large. They searched the space around them as if they too had heard the scratching and felt the chill enter the darkened cellar. They turned toward the open door as if to assure a way of escape if necessary.

While they were distracted, Evangeline sent a stone flying into the side of a wooden crate with the toe of her shoe. A large rat darted out, dislodging a bundle of straw leaning against the wall. The men turned back in time to see only the straw falling —for no apparent reason. Eager now to leave, with a man on each side they picked up Henry by the arms and dragged his limp body toward the house. Evangeline followed them, eager to check on the child.

The heat slammed into them as they left the clammy gloom of the old root cellar. The men bickered back and forth, each voicing his disbelief in vengeful spirits but hauled the unconscious Henry inside the house. Their complaints increased every step it took to reach the third floor attic. They put him in the larger of the two rooms under the thatched roof. It could have housed one of the older sons by the size of the extra-long bed. Bird and rodent droppings littered the area, but the holes in the thatched roof also allowed light and air to circulate. Not ideal, but, once cleaned, the space would be a healthier environment than the rat-infested earthen dungeon. Evangeline set her bag of healing supplies on a wood crate by the door and stepped out of the way.

Her captors dumped Henry onto the bare bed, sending up a cloud of dust, and headed to the door.

"Wait." She did a quick evaluation of Henry's injuries. There was bruising around his ribs and a large bump on the back of his head. She touched his forehead and flushed cheeks. He had a slight fever. She could do a more thorough exam once he was washed. "I need hot water to bathe his wounds and bring me a broom and scrub brush, if you can find them. This whole room needs to be swept and cleaned immediately."

"I also need clean straw for the bed and blankets from the carriage." She softened her tone when she saw their rebellious expressions. "After I've seen to his Lordship, I will tend to your wounds, also."

Fisher and Griswold grumbled but moved Henry to the floor before they left. The bed's old cloth ticking was torn and had become a cozy place for mice to live. While the men were gone doing her bidding, she dragged the old bedding to the window and pushed it out. She did a quick cleaning of the area as best she could. After the men returned with the items she requested, she covered the fresh straw, the men had piled on the bed, with a woven blanket of fine fabric taken from the carriage. When Fisher returned with another pail of the water, she had him help her get Henry onto the bed.

"You need more fetching, you do it." Fisher gave Evangeline a menacing glare and stomped off down the stairs.

She stripped off Henry's dirty, bloodstained clothing to further assess his injuries and cleanse his wounds. A groan escaped when she washed his neck and shoulder.

An unexpected wave of emotions and memories rose like a tidal wave within her. She knew his body almost as well as her own. She had surprised and delighted him with her curiosity and questions as they had unashamedly explored each other.

How easily he had abandoned her when she'd needed him most. He moaned and pulled away from the tight hold she had on his bruised shoulder. She released him, appalled at the fresh hurt the memory had loosed within her.

After a few cleansing breaths, she resumed her exam. She ran her fingers over the dark bruising over his ribs, relieved they didn't appear broken. He had lost weight to the point of being gaunt, though his muscles remained firm and well defined, as if he'd spent many hours sparring. She touched a small scar on his chest, an accident caused by his younger brother, Robert. Henry had regaled her with hilarious stories of his childhood growing up with such a mischievous younger brother. His stories had only confirmed her conviction that she wanted many children. Growing up as an only child was not a fate she'd wish on anyone.

Helen had been as close as a sister, but the difference between servant and royal kept a barrier between them not of their making.

Henry had been crushed when the news of his brother's death had reached the castle.

Regret settled into a pool of mourning within her soul at what she'd lost that day. She and Henry had been blissfully happy until then, especially with the news of her pregnancy only days before. After the news of Robert's death, the castle's populace went into mourning. Henry and Evangeline had spent many hours consoling each other within their bedchambers.

Warmth flushed her face when she realized her train of thought and how easily she'd found solace in touching her husband. Taking a deep breath, she stood and poured the pail of dirty water out the small attic window, replacing it with clean water from the pitcher. She wished she could get rid of her hurt as easily, but she was no longer the innocent she'd been back then. Betrayal and nearly burning to death had seared more than her flesh.

Determined to keep her emotions and memories in check, she pushed back the veil to see unhindered and returned to her task. She rubbed crushed lavender over his numerous cuts. The deeper wounds she smeared a mixture of herbs boiled down earlier at the abbey to make a poultice and wrapped each place with clean linen.

Her emotions tormented her, from fury, at his betrayal to fear for his life. She fought for control while she finished washing her husband's battered body and completed her examination. In spite of the anger that rose from the ashes of her grief, his weakness stirred up compassion that she justified by her time spent in the convent.

Forgive us our trespasses as we forgive those who trespass against us. She prayed the Lord's Prayer every day. *Why, Lord, must forgiveness be so hard?* Tears came unbidden for the man she'd not long ago wished dead for the misery she'd endured. Now...

She stood, stretched, and took a deep breath to calm her wayward emotions. She needed to remember why she was here. *Focus.* She must finish doctoring Henry, locate the baby, then figure a way to free them all.

His groan drew her to his side, and she bent over him. With a light touch, she wiped his face with a damp cloth that she'd soaked in lavender water. The large knot behind his right ear concerned her most. It did not bode well if he remained unconscious for long. She dabbed the wound with camphor, the strong scent lingered in the space. Packing the area around the wound with dried herbs she'd combined with more camphor would help reduce the swelling. She then wrapped a linen bandage around his head to keep the poultice in place.

She mixed a combination of fever and pain-reducing herbs for him to drink. Seeing him injured and helpless was hard enough, but holding him close to administer the medicine evoked a deep fear that he might suddenly awaken and see through her disguise. She wished she'd tugged the veil down to cover her face.

"No." Henry mumbled and pushed at her hand that held the cup.

Tears of relief blurred her vision. His resistance was a good sign, even though his eyes remained closed.

"You must drink this." She knew her voice was far different since the fire, but still he might recognize her. The passion they'd felt at first glance had never gone away. Could he feel it too?

"You've come back to me." He blinked and smiled up at her, his voice a husky whisper that stirred a familiar longing. Shock that, even in his dazed and fevered state, he too felt their connection intensified her hold, pressing against his injured shoulder. He groaned, pain furrowing his brow. Immediately she relaxed her grip.

"Don't leave me-e." His words slurred, and his feverish gaze dulled. He slipped back into unconsciousness. She shook him.

"Henry, you need to swallow all of this to get better. Do you understand?" Cradled against her like a child, she supported him with one arm and tilted the cup containing the herbal draught to his lips with her free hand. He accepted the drink this time but grimaced at its bitter taste.

"I know it's unpleasant but it will help with the pain." She eased him back, but he grabbed her arm.

"I'm sorry." Tears pooled in his eyes. Gone was the arrogant aristocrat, but for how long? His grip tightened. "I-I love..." Though she longed to hear the rest, his voice faded.

"Rest." She set the cup down and smoothed his hair away from his face. He relaxed, his hand dropped to his side. His features smooth. The draught was working. He would sleep for a few hours, until the next dose of medicine.

Heavy footsteps stomped up the stairs. She stood and tugged her veil back into place.

"Come down and doctor my hand, Sister." An angry Griswold stopped at the doorway and waved her to the stairway. "Now."

A young child's cry echoed from below. Grabbing her bag and basket of supplies, she followed Griswold down to the first floor, excitement thrummed within her. She would finally get to meet the child and question the nursemaid about many things, including the child's parentage.

CHAPTER 9

*G*riswold stopped Evangeline with his beefy grip before she could search out the child.

"I need to tend to the..."

"You need to fix me hand first." He tugged her into a small sitting room to the left and shoved her toward one of the two oak armchairs and dropped into the other. With the audacity of a bully used to getting his way, he extended his arm on the table between them.

"Get to it."

She could barely concentrate for the loud wails coming from the room across the hall. The child's distress and Evangeline's need to intervene grew more intense by the minute.

With little care for the pain she must inflict, she stripped away the brigand's nasty bandage, which had stuck to the wound in several places.

"Aargh-h!" He jerked his hand back and glared at her with murderous intent, uttering a string of threats and curses for the pain she'd inflicted. The missing bandage revealed two missing fingers. Losing the index and middle fingers on his sword hand would certainly hinder his ability to continue his life as a mercenary.

"It had to be done quickly. If you wish, I can leave it untreated, but I warn you that you'll not live out the week by the looks of it." She leaned back and crossed her arms. "Your choice."

"Fix it." He shoved his mangled hand back at her. Fear had won out, but by his mumbled complaints and scowl, it angered him more by the weakness his acquiescence had revealed.

There might be a human hiding within that angry exterior after all. She almost laughed at that thought.

The big man wore a filthy, sleeveless tunic covered by a stained leather vest and equally worn and stained boots. Whatever the color of the original cloth tunic, it was now a faded gray with blood stains, dried black and crusty. His bare face, neck, arms and hands were littered with scars revealing a harsh existence.

A sharp sword had removed the digits as smooth as a surgeon's knife. The wound was red and swollen, making it impossible to stitch the cuts close. All she could do was clean the area and pack it with a poultice made up of a mixture of herbs and dried garlic to help ward off infection. The bandage should be changed often, a chore she didn't relish, considering his foul mouth and angry threats, which had continued throughout the bandaging process.

It was a good thing that thoughts were not daggers or this brigand would be dead. In her opinion, he deserved to die for his part in the kidnapping and murder. Fortunately for him, her greater concerns were seeing the child and assessing their best way to escape.

She tied the last knot of the bandage and put away her supplies.

"Go! Do something to shut up that caterwauling, or someone

else will." Griswold stood, drew his dagger with his left hand, and waved it in the direction of the child's distress.

"I suggest you put away that knife lest..." She stood and walked away mumbling the rest of her tirade out of his earshot, knowing her words would reveal her grievous lack of Christian piety where he was concerned.

She crossed the hall and into a large open room filled with furniture. A huge stone fireplace filled one end of the space. The great room must have been the family's favorite, by the care that had gone into the fine wood and stonework.

Movement drew her attention to a disheveled young woman of slight build pacing back and forth in front of the hearth. She carried a red-faced toddler, who pushed and squirmed against the nursemaid's hold. The child's angry cries were interspersed with the toddler's demands. "Down!"

As Evangeline drew closer, she noticed the nursemaid's smudged and filthy dress had a large tear at the shoulder.

The girl turned and saw her.

"Sister, I'm so glad..." She hurried over to her. "Please. I can't..." Her words dissolved into sobs, and she shoved the child toward Evangeline, who dropped the basket to grab the baby. The little girl reached out for Evangeline and clutched her neck. Her green eyes were puffy and her cheeks were flushed from crying. The toddler shoved the middle-two fingers of her left hand into her mouth and cuddled closer to Evangeline, quieting immediately, except for an occasional hiccup from crying so long.

The distraught nursemaid sunk to the floor and rocked back and forth covering her face with her hands. Her loud sobs echoed through the low rafters.

A quick perusal suggested the disheveled girl was in a state of nerves with no apparent wounds or injuries. Evangeline turned to Griswold who stood in the doorway, cursing at the young woman to be quiet.

"Fetch me some fresh water from the well, and I'll mix a draught to quiet her." Evangeline rocked the toddler in her arms.

He hesitated.

"Or you can continue to listen to her distress."

He glared at the distraught woman with his hand on his dagger. With a permanent scowl etched into his hard features, he turned and stomped out the door grabbing an empty bucket on his way.

With him gone, Evangeline seized the private time to study the little girl in her arms...her little girl. She'd recognized the truth the moment she'd looked into the child's eyes. The child snuggled against her side and quieted, though it was obvious by the stench she needed to be changed. Finding a clean nappy was another matter only accomplished after the nursemaid finally responded to Evangeline's plea and pointed to a woven hamper in the corner. It contained nappies, towels, soap, lotions, and other basic necessities. Being a child of the realm, no doubt more elaborate attire was packed into a trunk somewhere.

As Evangeline gathered what she needed from the basket, the brigand returned. He set the bucket on the floor with a thump hard enough to splash water on the floor, then stood with arms crossed, defiance etched on his face.

"Thank you." Evangeline barely contained the rebuke boiling up within her. She blew out the breath she held. With the baby on one hip, she mixed the draught needed to quiet the nursemaid.

Only because of Griswold's threat to cut her throat did the nursemaid finally drink the liquid down. Although the fuss she made about its taste, one would have thought she was being poisoned.

A short time later, blessed silence reigned. The herbal mixture did its work and the girl snoozed, prone on the floor in the corner near the fireplace.

By the stench and the dirt covering her face and hands, the child needed a bath. With Griswold as her shadow, she found the attached kitchen and searched the cupboards for a large washtub. A quick glance outside the window revealed a summer kitchen, which would have been used to cook on during the hot days to keep the heat outside, but it was in shambles and unusable.

A fire burned in the large kitchen fireplace, and a large iron pot hung on a swivel hook, with water boiling. The kitchen was tidy and ready for use. She had a hard time believing one of the brigands had done this. Who else might occupy this home?

"What's you goin' to cook?" Griswold stared into the pot of boiling water.

"Fetch more water." She dipped enough water out of the iron pot to warm the small wash tub she found hanging on the wall. She needed to cool it with water from the well. "First, I need to bathe the baby." She turned and held the empty bucket out to Griswold, ignoring his howl of protest. "Or you can hold the child while I fetch the water."

"Bathin' leads to consumption. You don't want the little tike to die...or starve to death, do ye?"

She tapped her foot and motioned for him to take the empty bucket.

"Donkey dung." He growled but took it. A few more of his favorite curse words accompanied his trek out to the well and back.

Evangeline added more kindling to the dying fire, which increased the heat in the kitchen, making her wish she could remove at least her veil, but she dared not.

"I'm done being your servant. If you need more water, fetch it yur-self." Griswold set the empty bucket down and stomped outside.

She placed the washtub on the large oak table. After cooling the heated water with the well water, she stripped the baby and placed her inside.

The toddler loved the water, splashing Evangeline and the floor, though she was not as thrilled to be scrubbed clean.

"No!" Apparently that was the child's favorite word, which she'd already used with authority of someone used to getting her way.

Evangeline's examination revealed a small, red strawberry-shaped birthmark on the little girl's left shoulder just like she remembered seeing on her baby at birth. The size and shape of the birthmark were exactly the same as Evangeline's and her mother's. In fact, all of the women in her lineage had this same mark in the same place. According to her mother, it was a sign of her royal bloodline, a lineage that could be traced back to the conquerors and monarchy of England.

The wave of elation that her baby had not died was closely followed by the fear that she would somehow fail to protect her from these brigands. With God's help she would find a way to free them all.

The little girl tugged on Evangeline's habit smiling that she had gained Evangeline's full attention. The toddler's eyes were the same forest green as her own, with the exception of golden specks in the center, which were just like Henry's.

The golden specks in his brown eyes changed colors with his mood. She quickly shoved away the memory of their molten color of passion.

Bathing the child filled Evangeline with unexpected motherly emotions. She still had no idea what to call her.

The nursemaid could sleep for hours with the level of her emotional exhaustion and the sleeping draught.

During Evangeline's pregnancy, she and Henry had argued good-naturedly over what to name the baby if it was a girl, but he had insisted it would be a boy. Evangeline smiled at having been right all along.

Evangeline cuddled her little girl, who was now clean, dry, and dressed in a nappy and cotton cover. Sarah had been Evangeline's mother's name and had been her choice if the baby had been a girl. Had Henry remembered?

"Is your name Sarah?" Evangeline scooped up the little girl and cuddled her.

The toddler smiled and cooed.

The matter was settled in Evangeline's heart. Sarah it would be.

"Sister." The Frenchman hobbled into the kitchen with a pail of garden vegetables. "I see you have a way with *se bebe, oui?*"

"Buttons, get that food cookin'. I'm starved," Griswold yelled from the doorway. He glanced over at the toddler, who smiled, waved, and babbled something that sounded like *bear*. He gave an answering grin and waved back then grimaced, as if appalled at being caught. He wheeled around and stomped back out the door.

"Let me save some of this hot water for cleaning before you use what you need for cooking." Evangeline dipped out a pitcher of hot water and set it on the table.

The Frenchman prepared the vegetables and made soup in the remaining water. Soon, delectable odors filled the room, and a hungry, little Sarah became fussy.

Nothing could hurry the cooking process, so Evangeline bounced Sarah on her hip while she assisted in the meal by scrubbing the table and searching for dishes and tableware. By the time the soup was ready, the child's cries had grown loud and demanding.

"Have patience, little one." Evangeline giggled as the little girl shoved handfuls of the cooked and mashed vegetables into her mouth before Evangeline could feed her.

Food was smeared on Sarah's face and surroundings, including the large apron Evangeline wore. She'd found it hanging behind a cabinet door. It was large enough to protect her habit and was still damp from the bath. Now it was also adorned with splatters of carrots and green beans. Tummy full, the toddler could no longer fight sleep. Though she was content for now, the babe needed milk to grow strong. After they were freed, she would have all the milk she needed.

Reluctant to put the child down but knowing it would be cooler for her, Evangeline laid her on the floor near the sleeping nursemaid. She surrounded Sarah with two chairs, turned on their sides, to keep her from getting away if she awakened before the nanny.

The savory scent of soup drew Evangeline back to the kitchen.

The Frenchman stirred the contents of the large iron pot, glancing up at her entrance.

"Sit. I will get you something to eat." He used an iron hook to swing the steaming pot out of the fireplace and filled her bowl.

Evangeline sat at the table. She brushed her hand over the rough, hand hewn surface. Not as large as those at Brighton Castle, yet the length would have easily accommodated the farmer's large family and a few guests.

"Sorry, Sister, there is no fine china in which to serve you." He set the wooden bowl before her.

"Thank you, but nuns have very simple needs. This is lovely." She bowed her head and thanked the Lord for the food and asked a blessing over the hands that prepared it.

The man mumbled something. Evangeline looked up and saw him cross himself before he turned away. His show of a religious upbringing made her wonder. If she could gain his trust, would he aid in their escape?

Griswold and the man they called Fisher gathered in the sitting room to eat their meal. Their loud arguments, over being left behind guarding prisoners until their boss returned, filtered into the kitchen. Evangeline ate in silence, her mind cluttered with how best to deal with these cutthroats to escape. Should she put a sleeping draught in their water, escape, and go for help? She could take her child, but her conscience balked at leaving Henry and the nursemaid behind.

Each hour brought a greater chance of being discovered by the patrolling guards, but could she keep little Sarah safe if a battle ensued? Did this Frenchman know who hired them? Could she get him to tell her?

The Frenchman leaned on a crudely fashioned crutch to stabilize him while he stirred the pot then added a pinch of herb or two after every taste.

"This is very good." She savored another bite. "With your cooking skills, you could work for royalty and live a far less dangerous life. Why are you running with this gang of cutthroats?"

He glanced toward her. Heat flushed his face, or was the cause anger, or maybe guilt? He'd turned away too quickly to tell.

"I was once in charge of the whole kitchen for a very rich man. But his daughter and I..." He shrugged. *"Amour."*

"You fell in love?"

"Oui." He glanced up, suspicion in his eyes. "You speak French?"

"Oui." The rest of their conversation was carried out in French with low tones that would not carry to the other room.

"These men call me Button, but my real name is François Burdo." He limped to the table and eased into a chair across from her, pain etched on his face. He swiped his forehead with his sleeve.

Even with all the doors and windows open, the heat from the fire made the kitchen almost unbearable.

"You must let me care for your wound." Evangeline noticed the swollen leg, and the bandage could not hide the blood that had seeped through. Not a good sign.

"I am a dead man no matter what." He shrugged with indifference. "Deverow will kill me if I'm not able to travel when he returns. If I'm caught, I'll be hanged."

Having finished her soup, Evangeline pushed away from the table and knelt before him to examine his leg.

"I must soak this with warm water to remove your bandage."

He barely winced as she did what was necessary.

"How did this happen?" She studied the deep cut about half the length of his calf. The area was inflamed and tender to the touch. She unlaced his boot and removed it, revealing swollen toes.

"His Lordship struck me with his sword." Francois winced as Evangeline examined the wound, which should have been doctored and sewn together within hours, not days. Francois would have an ugly scar...if he lived.

She knew all too well about the scars of survival.

"During the battle and kidnapping?" She retrieved her basket of herbs and bandages.

"I had not intended to hurt his Lordship, but only to aid another. I rode too closely and..." He sucked his breath when she packed the mixture against the wound and wrapped a cloth tightly around his leg.

"You need to keep off it as much as possible to allow the poultice to work." She finished then rubbed freshly peeled garlic over her hands to cleanse them and rinsed in hot water before returning to her chair. At the convent, Sister Agnes had insisted garlic was a gift from God with its heavenly properties that repelled disease and had numerous other benefits if used properly.

"You haven't answered my question. Why do you stay with these...?" She waved her hand toward the other room, where the men continued to argue with raised voices.

"Murderous heathens?" His tone hardened with conviction, as hard as the look he now gave her. "Do not let my skill with the cooking fool you, Sister. I am a warrior." He produced a dusty wine bottle from under the table and offered her a drink. "I found this while looking for the spices," he whispered. His glance darted to the other room. Obviously, he had no plans to share with the others. When she declined, he took a long drink, then another, though the wine did not lessen the anguish that marked his features. "I fled to this country because of my love for a beautiful young woman, and her vengeful father who put a price on my head." He rubbed his face as if to erase the memory. "I escaped to England where I ran into Deverow and Parker. They invited me to join them." He shrugged and took another long drink. "He said he had been hired for a job that needed more men, and I was hungry, so…"

"Where are Parker and Deverow?" Evangeline needed to know exactly how many more brigands she had to deal with.

"His Lordship mortally wounded Parker when we stopped the carriage." The Frenchman stared out the open door as if more memories needled him. "Deverow finished Parker off to keep him from talking." He drew his finger across his throat with no show of emotion. Parker's death explained the presence of the other dead man on the road with Henry's driver. What kind of men could kill with so little feeling of regret?

A chill skidded down her spine. How little they valued human life, not even one of their own.

"And Deverow?"

"He's gone to meet someone." By his constant shifting and his downcast eyes, it was easy to tell he was hiding something.

"You are sworn to keep secret what I've told you, yes?" He searched her veiled face until she nodded. "Good! Now we must only speak English lest we draw undue attention." With a shaky hand, he finished off the wine and swiped his mouth.

"Do you know who paid to have the nobleman and child kidnapped?" She walked to the table where a large wash tub was now filled with dirty dishes and added her empty bowl to the stack.

"Only Deverow knows. We were ordered not to harm the man, to only take the child." He turned away from her.

"And?" Evangeline touched his shoulder, so he would face her. "The truth."

"We were hired to kill the little girl."

At Evangeline's gasp, he shook his head. "No worry, Sister. She will be kept safe and well treated. She's to be sold to a wealthy merchant for his barren wife."

"Sold?" Anger filled her voice, as she touched the dagger hidden in the folds of her habit. No one would sell her daughter, this she vowed.

"At least she will live. If she's returned, the person who hired us would simply hire another to end her young life." He shrugged.

"Button. Stop yur gabberin'." Griswold appeared in the doorway. Had he overheard?

Evangeline didn't wait to find out. Too angry to speak, she put away her herbs, grabbed an empty bucket, and walked outside.

Griswold appeared in the doorway behind her.

"Where do you think yur going?"

"I'm fetching more water to wash the dishes." She turned toward him and held out the empty bucket to him. "Unless you'd be a gentleman and do it?"

"Me? A gentleman?" His laughter held no mirth. "Don't try to escape. You'll be watched." He disappeared back into the house.

At the well, she loosed the rope and dropped the bucket into the inky depths. Before she could draw it back up, a pebble landed at her feet. Startled, she released the bucket and whirled around.

Helen stepped out from behind a large elm at the edge of the clearing. The muted greens and browns of her livery helped her blend into the landscape.

After a quick glance at the house, Evangeline motioned her back into hiding. The Frenchman limped outside onto the step.

"Sister, would you check the garden for anything edible that I can add to the soup?" He grimaced and leaned against the door frame. He spat on the ground then loosed a string of curses in French disparaging his fellow brigands as being too stupid to know the difference between asparagus and milkweed.

"Oui." With a nod, she drew the water bucket up and set it on the ground. A glance behind her confirmed no one followed as she headed to the garden.

Helen would make her way around the house and the burned-out remains of the barn without being seen.

Evangeline pulled away the vines that partially hid a large woven basket hung on the fence. She paused at the crooked gate to view the overgrown garden. It was as if visiting the neglected grave of a loved one. It choked her with sadness.

So different now from the last time she had seen this once pristine acreage. She was fourteen and her father had sent Helen's mother, the head cook, to the farm to buy something special for an unexpected royal guest who had a fondness for roasted peacock. Evangeline had begged to be allowed to go and, to her surprise and delight, her father had agreed.

The garden had been beautifully cultivated without a weed or blade of grass within its borders. Four years later, mere days after the wheat harvest, the farmer and his oldest sons had been murdered and his wife had been forced to flee with her remaining two other children. It was rumored that the distraught widow had cursed any with evil hearts who would take anything from the farm. Rumors abounded after sickness plagued those who had taken the opportunity to steal the abandoned garden's ripening vegetables. The garden had soon gone to seed with none but the beast of the forest enjoying the fruit of the farmer's labor.

Evangeline spotted a noxious weed growing among the

volunteer vegetables that had gone to seed and reproduced. If any of that weed's leaves or seeds had been gathered and cooked with the produce that might explain the rumors of illness and violent distress of any who ate it.

She smiled and gathered some of its seeds, hiding them in the empty coin pouch she carried. As soon as Henry was able to travel, *the curse* would strike again. With the brigands ailing, she and the hostages could escape without hindrance.

As she waited for Helen, she gathered onions and garlic, which had thrived in the neglect. She used her dagger to cut the last stalks of asparagus and dug up a small bunch of potatoes and deposited it all into the basket. There was plenty of edible produce hidden within the dried overgrowth, as if planted this season—evidence that someone lurked nearby.

When she heard Helen's whisper, she tucked her dagger back within its hiding place. Working her way to where her friend hid behind the charred remains of the old garden shed, Evangeline stayed within sight of any watching her from the window. She spotted several vines of climbing peas growing up a broken fence, near where Helen waited.

She reached the peas, turning her back to the house, so she could work and talk without drawing attention.

"I decided to check to see if Henry and his party were indeed here." Helen kept her voice low, but her eyes held concern. "You're well?"

"Yes." Evangeline pulled her veil aside. "My daughter lives." She struggled to keep from shouting her news.

"And his lordship?"

"Henry's injured, but most of his wounds are not severe, though I'm concerned that a blow to his head has left him in and out of consciousness." She cleared her throat of the emotion that clouded her words. "I can't leave until he can travel."

"I see." Helen stared at Evangeline, as if searching for more information.

"What?" Impatience lowered Evangeline's voice to a gravelly tone.

"Nothing important." Helen stepped closer but remained out of sight of the house. "Have you found out who hired these men?"

"A man named Deverow is the only one who knows." Evangeline straightened and clenched her dagger. "He's gone to make a deal to sell little Sarah." Fury enflamed her at the very thought of such an arrangement. "A deal that will never take place."

A rat chose that moment to wander out into the open in front of her. Evangeline unleashed her anger with one swift throw of her dagger.

"I detest vermin, be they man or beast." She bent down and retrieved her dagger wiping the blade off on the grass before putting it away.

"Speaking of vermin, how many brigands are there?"

"Three. A Frenchman with a bad leg wound. A brute of an Englishman called Griswold who lost two of his fingers during their battle with Henry. And a short, ill-tempered man they call Fisher. He has a minor cut to his shoulder and is perhaps the most foul of the bunch. Fisher must be from around here, for he led them to this place. Strangers would never know of its existence." Evangeline turned to glance behind her to make sure no one headed their way. "If you get a chance, see if you recognize him."

"Why not take the child, escape, and send help back to free Henry?" Helen stepped closer.

"The Frenchman warned me that if the child were to return home, she would likely be killed by another hireling. She will not be safe until the person who hired these cutthroats is exposed and dealt with." She added the peas to the basket at her feet.

The helplessness of not knowing who wanted her child dead stirred up such anguish, Evangeline abruptly changed the subject. "Would you check on Anna and her child? She's at the abbey taking care of the goats and chickens I purchased." Evangeline crushed a peapod in her fist wishing it was the throat of the person responsible for hiring the brigands. She stooped over and picked up dropped peas. "While you're there, I could use some milk for little Sarah, if you could find a way to bring it."

Helen smiled and handed Evangeline a large goatskin flask with a carved wood plug in the end.

"Milk?" Evangeline's excitement overrode her caution. The snap of twigs behind made her jump and turn. Griswold. His grumbling and stench was unmistakable. A quick glance back assured her Helen was again hidden from sight.

"Wha' milk?" He lumbered up and snatched the goatskin. "Where'd this come from?" Turning from side to side, he searched their surroundings for intruders.

"I found it here. A villager must have dropped it off for the baby." She tugged the flask from his grasp before he spilled its contents by his reckless handling and walked toward the house. "If you want another meal, I suggest you bring those vegetables I gathered."

"Wait, what villager?" He grabbed the basket and followed. "How'd they know there was a babe 'ere?"

"The woods carry sounds a long distance. I assume someone heard the child crying." Without slowing her pace, she continued to the house. "As poor as they are, I'm grateful that they are willing to share what little they have." She reached the open doorway and hurried inside. The thick stone walls of the larder would keep the milk cooler, so she hung the goat skin on a peg to keep until little Sarah awakened.

Griswold dropped the basket of vegetables on the table with a loud thump and rushed into the other room. Minutes later, another loud argument erupted among the three brigands. By the snippets she gleaned, Griswold wanted to abandon the captives and escape before the captain of the castle guards appeared with soldiers and hung them. Fisher wanted to kill the captives before they left. The Frenchman argued that they would not be paid if they harmed them or left before their leader returned.

With the threat of being murdered, Evangeline knew she needed to step into their conversation. She patted the dagger at her side, and walked into the room where the men argued.

"Please. There is no need for further violence. You are in no danger from the peasant who left the milk. They hate the castle guards more than you. There'll be nothing to fear from them... as long as you do no harm to anyone here."

A sudden gust of wind rattled the windows and slammed the open kitchen door. The old house groaned as if issuing its own warning.

Silence filled the room. The men's expressions flashed with fear. The Frenchman crossed himself and mumbled a child's prayer of protection in Latin. Griswold swore then wiped his mouth, as if to erase his hastily spoken words. Fisher remained silent. He fisted his hands, but not before Evangeline noticed them shaking.

"That was surely a warning. Purge any thoughts of evil doing while you're here or suffer the widow Danby's curse." She turned before her smile ruined the threat.

"Wait, Sister. Bless us and ask God for protection against that foul curse." I-don't-believe-in-what-I-can't-see-Griswold surprised her with his urgent request.

"Why should I? You murder, maim, and kidnap." She faced him resisting the urge to call God's wrath down on the lot of them for the harm they had caused Henry and her child. "Until you repent of your wickedness and choose to serve God by doing good, then there's nothing either He or I are obligated to do on your behalf."

A baby's wail interrupted further discussion. Evangeline skirted Griswold on her way to little Sarah. Her conscience nudged her with the knowledge that she should have given the distraught man a word of instruction on how to repent and find God.

The wails grew louder and more demanding as she reached her child and found the nursemaid also awake.

The nursemaid's arms were wrapped tightly around her legs and hugged against her chest. She must have overheard the men's argument. Her eyes were wide with fright, as she rocked back and forth, ignoring the toddler's demands.

After a quick change of little Sarah's wet nappy for a dry one, Evangeline gathered up the child and hugged her to her side. She patted the nursemaid's shoulder.

"Try not to fret. With God's help, everything will be all right." Evangeline glanced down at the nursemaid and saw only despair. It would take more than words to prove to her their plight was not as hopeless as it appeared at the moment. "What is your name?"

"Rebecca." The girl's reply was barely above a whisper.

Evangeline went into the kitchen and fed the hungry babe with the goat's milk until she was full. The whole messy feeding experience enthralled Evangeline. Every moment with her child brought her both joy and a fierce concern for her safety. Tummy full, yet the little one again grew fussy shoving her fist into her mouth and drooling.

"Tis, her teeth." The Frenchman limped into the kitchen and settled onto a chair.

"What?"

"I come from a large family. As the eldest, I saw this many times. It's when the teeth break through. My mother sometimes gave the babe a boiled chicken leg bone stripped clean and smooth to chew on." He shrugged. "Alas, we have no chicken to boil. Perhaps you should pray and a neighborly peasant will miraculously provide one?" His tone and pointed stare left no doubt of his suspicion.

"God provides the needs of the faithful." She examined the baby's mouth. Her gums were indeed swollen and tender where a tiny white tooth pushed upward.

"I'm hungry." The nursemaid walked into the room, her eyes red from crying. She walked over to the fireplace and stirred the contents in the pot. "Is this vile soup all there is to eat?"

"Watch the baby while I fetch more water from the well." Evangeline set the fussy Sarah on the floor.

Rebecca nodded but turned her attention back to the contents of the pot.

Evangeline would prepare a mild drought that would ease little Sarah's pain, but it would make her sleepy again. Sleep may not be a bad thing if the wails now emanating from the house were any indication of what the day held. With the brigands on edge, she needed to keep Sarah quiet. Evangeline prayed for wisdom for what to do next.

Her thoughts turned to the herbs she'd need, as she picked up the bucket she left at the well.

At the sound of hooves hitting the hard-packed earth, headed toward the farmhouse, the bucket slipped from her fingers and spilled out its contents.

Had the guards been alerted after all? She hid behind one of the heavy posts that held the roof over the well. She watched as a lone rider galloped into the farmyard. Even in this heat, he wore heavy chain mail. A sword rested in its scabbard within reach. He dismounted and tied his horse to a sagging rail of the pen then headed toward the house.

As he walked closer, Evangeline paled. Her heart began to pound. She grabbed the oak post for support. Her knees threatened to buckle.

"Butcher!" A strangled cry escaped in a raspy moan of horror.

This was the man who had killed her servants and guards then ordered his men to trap her inside the hunting lodge and set it on fire. The scars on her back burned. The sound of the inferno roared in her ears.

She shoved a shaky hand into the pocket of her habit and found her dagger. Her vow of revenge spoken that day, as she'd clawed her way out of the inferno, would finally be fulfilled.

Her fingers closed around the hilt. The blade was free.

His every step brought him closer to fulfilling her vow. The patch over his one eye and long scar were the result of Evangeline's weakness, for if she had been stronger he would have not recovered from the wounds she had inflicted in her defense that day.

He hadn't expected resistance. The stench of his body pressing her against the great room wall… His touch… Even now the memory filled her with rage. He had been as surprised as she at her strength and determination to thwart his attack. A dagger of finely honed steel had rested on a stand within her reach. She'd grabbed it and struck blindly, hitting the assassin's face. Blood everywhere…

Evangeline gulped air like a drowning person until she regained her focus.

A nightmare relived. He was back. This time she was not weak from childbirth and grief. Just a few steps closer and she would end his miserable life. Her only regret was never finding out who had hired him to kill her.

Her muscles tensed.

"Sister! Come quick!"

Evangeline jerked upright.

"Please. The baby is ill." The nursemaid grabbed Evangeline by the arm and pulled her toward the house.

CHAPTER 10

*R*aised voices stirred Henry awake. He strained to make out the words.

"Imbecile" was easily discernible, which was followed by "Imbeciles, imbecillus, imbecille," spoken in French, Italian, and Latin. He smiled.

Evangeline had often switched languages using the same word when she was vexed beyond measure. Angry, her emerald eyes would sparkle with the fire of battle.

Regret, more painful than his wounds, nettled his mind. He should have found a way to make her understand why he couldn't do as she asked and send his brother's widow away.

Rumors had spread throughout the castle that Evangeline had taken a lover. Even now the thought enraged him. From then on seeing the glow of happiness whenever she spoke of the unborn child had inflamed him with jealousy. He'd feared the baby was not his.

Guilt burned his conscience.

Their last angry encounter, he had demanded to know the name of the father of the child she carried. Why had he listened to gossip? Millicent had insisted the rumors were true, but the look of hurt in Evangeline's eyes told him the real truth. It had not been his wife who'd betrayed him. Before he could apologize, Evangeline's expression had turned to alarm. The pain of labor tore the breath from her.

He was shooed away from her...*their* chambers by concerned servants. The labor had taken two long days. He couldn't eat or sleep for fear he would lose her and the child.

When he thought he couldn't take another moment of her suffering, the groans were interrupted by the cry of a baby. Boy or girl, it no longer mattered.

He knew his daughter's cries. The thought of Sarah jerked his eyes open. Where was she?

His body was uncooperative and his eyes refused to focus as he turned his throbbing head in search of a servant to help him up. Too blurry-eyed to see, he couldn't make out his surroundings and his throat was too parched to demand attendance. His daughter's wails stirred up fear for her safety. He couldn't wait for help. She needed him.

Weak and trembling, he struggled against the sagging bed to sit up and drag his legs over the side. Pain struck him from his shoulder and ribs, sucking the breath out of him and dotting his already impaired vision with black spots. Using the large log bedpost, he pulled himself to his feet. The room tilted beneath him. He fought to stay conscious, but the darkness overpowered him.

~

*D*ispatching her enemy would have to wait. Voices of the brigands gathered in the other room rose then dropped beyond her hearing. She had no time to waste on them.

Evangeline gathered the child to herself and held her firmly as the babe wretched again and again as if poisoned. Evangeline wiped the toddler's face with a damp cloth and rocked her.

"What have you done?" The raspy tone of Evangeline's voice didn't diminish the fury.

"I was only trying to help." The nursemaid whined and handed her a jar of powder. "I gave her this."

Evangeline smelled the contents then confirmed her guess by tasting a tiny bit of the powder then spit.

"This vial contains a mixture of crushed alder berries, which causes convulsive vomiting. In a child as young as Sarah it could have killed her."

With the toddler's tummy full of milk, the potion had triggered an instant and violent reaction, but the goat's milk had also coated her stomach. The vomiting freed her of the toxin, though she would need plenty of water to dilute any still in her system.

The child's tears turned into angry wails of protest when Evangeline tried to get her to drink more water, something she adamantly refused to do after throwing up again.

She warmed the last of the goat milk, and after much consoling, was able to get her to drink a small cup full. The milk soothed her daughter's stomach, and the fussing stopped. She rocked the exhausted baby in her arms.

"Why would you try and kill the baby?" Evangeline glared at a tearful Rebecca, who sat at the table wringing her hands.

"I swear, I dinna know the potion would 'arm her." It was obvious she was hiding something. The young woman stood and paced the length of the kitchen, then heard the voices in the other room. She hurried back to the table.

"What aren't you telling me? Confess the truth and know peace." What Evangeline wanted to do was put a knife to the foolish woman's throat until she told her all.

"I was told it was a tonic to settle the baby's stomach for the journey. She rather liked the jostling, so I drunk the potion." Her eyes shown with a brief reflection of guilt then hardened. "Why not? I needed it most." The tone again turned whiny. "The motion of a carriage made me dizzy and sick." She dropped into a chair. "But the remedy didn't work. I felt worse than before."

The memory of the coach stopping and the girl retching gave credence to her story, yet Evangeline could tell by the girl's nervous manner there was more than she had yet revealed. She was far too high-strung to be a nursemaid. Why would Henry trust such a person to care for their daughter?

"You are not skilled at caring for a child nor able to tolerate travel, then why would you agree to such a trip?" She glared at the girl.

"I... I..." Wide-eyed with fear the girl jumped up from her seat.

Thump.

It came from overhead.

Henry!

Evangeline hugged little Sarah to her side and raced up the stairs followed by Griswold, who cursed every step of the way for being bothered.

Henry lay still as death in a crumbled heap on the floor.

"Get him back in bed." Evangeline stepped out of the way.

Griswold let loose another string of vile words but grabbed Henry under the arms and heaved him onto the bed like a sack of potatoes. He grabbed Henry's feet and legs and none too gently shoved them onto the disheveled bedding.

"I'll need more water." Evangeline righted the wood crate used as a table and picked up the now empty bucket. She held it out for Griswold to go and fill.

"I ain't your servant." He added more colorful words for emphasis and crossed his arms in defiance. "Tie him down. I ain't pickin' 'im up again." Griswold scowled at the whimpering baby. "And quiet the babe 'fore someone who 'ates noise comes up 'ere and does her harm." When Evangeline did not flinch, he grabbed the bucket and stomped back down the stairs. His thunderous voice reverberated up to the attic room, as he spewed his anger at the still blubbering Rebecca. "Shut up, wench, or I'll lock you in that haunted cellar and let the rats feast on your face."

The nursemaid quieted, but, after what she'd done to little Sarah, Evangeline felt the cellar wouldn't be punishment enough.

She put Sarah against her father's right side and the baby snuggled up to him cooing, "Da, da, da."

Henry groaned as Evangeline checked his ribs. The bandage around his head had blood on it. No doubt his fall had reopened his wound. The dressing needed to be changed and only then could she assess the damage.

Even unconscious, he patted the child and smiled.

A wave of compassion morphed into anger for the lies that had cost her time with her baby.

Four days after the birth of her child, thinking her baby had died, she was sent off to the hunting lodge to heal. Another two days passed without a word from Henry, and, in her disappointment and weariness, she'd ignored the prickles of danger. A memory full of regrets was forever burned into her mind, as were the scars that etched her body.

She put a fresh bandage on Henry's head wound and tried to ignore the loud voices coming from below.

"Oh, she'll pay more after the deed's done." The voice belonged to the man in her nightmares. "Doing her ladyships' bidding has cost me aplenty."

Evangeline's hands shook and she covered her ears.

"Burn, wench! You've cost me aplenty." The memory wouldn't stop. As if caught in a rogue wave, it dragged her under. She couldn't breathe.

Sun barely up, with a thunder of hooves, the hired assassins arrived, which stirred her from her breakfast of tea and toast. Battle cries of her guards echoed through the clear morning followed by the clink of swords. Her handmaiden, Dorcas, had hurried out of the room to lock the front door. Dorcas screamed then only silence. Evangeline looked out a window. Her stomach roiled at what she saw.

Three brigands stood over her dead guards.

"Lady Stanton? Come out." The brigand's demand left no doubt why he had come. By the blood lust in his eyes, this was not to be a mere kidnapping.

"I can handle her ladyship." The leader pushed through the door and signaled the other two men to remain outside "She's pale as a lily. You'll be no trouble, will you Lady Stanton?" He edged toward Evangeline slowly as a predator stalking a deer.

"Who hired you?" Her question was more to distract. Frantic, Evangeline sent forth silent, desperate prayers for help. The larder had a heavy oak door which could be secured on the inside in an emergency. She edged her way to the doorway.

"Someone who wants you dead, m'lady." He leapt in front of her, grabbed her by the waist and slammed her into a heavy log table. A dagger with a deer horn handle tumbled from its stand.

Anger filled her with strength, as the brigand pinned her against the wall and pawed at her bodice.

Her fingers closed over the hilt. She swung it up with a vicious swipe, cutting his face, taking out his eye.

"Arrgh!" He knocked her to the ground and staggered away, stumbling to the front door. "Help me, you fools!" Amidst his curses and screams of outrage, his cohorts pulled him outside. "Burn the wench to death!"

Smoke quickly filled the rooms. They had set the lodge on fire.

Flaming embers fell on top of her and set her clothing on fire. She tore off her burning outer garments. Debris fell like punishment from hell. The smoke-heated air scorched her throat.

The roar of the fire was deafening as it growled and spit flames *around her, a monstrous dragon that grew more ferocious with every hiss, consuming all in its path.*

Climbing over burning rafters that had fallen in her path, she made it to the larder only to find the roof there also on fire. Defeated and resigned to her fate, she lay on the stone floor.

A mouse ran over her hand and she opened her eyes in time to see it disappear into a hole in the wall. She reached out a hand. The log wall crumbled beneath her touch. Turning her focus again to her escape, she clawed at the rotting wood until the outside air flowed in without restriction.

Fresh air brought renewed strength to survive.

Flaming debris dropped all around her. An iron pan fell at her side. She used it to pound against the exterior making the hole larger with each blow.

Blazing timber from the roof fell, igniting the space all around her, portions hit her back. Excruciating pain. Her clothing was on fire. She couldn't wait any longer.

The opening was barely wide enough to escape.

Her heart pounded, and her breath came in ragged gasps. Reliving that moment made every scar burn with fresh intensity.

Those brigands had been nowhere to be seen when she collapsed outside in a smoldering heap, but she'd never forget the man who had caused her such pain.

Her hand clutched the heavy cross that hung around her neck. One-eye would be dealt the cold blade of hot revenge before the sun set on this day.

Forgiveness is always better than revenge, Evangeline. At the convent, Sister Katherine had counseled her daily during the times she doctored Evangeline's burns, an excruciating ordeal. *Revenge is Mine, saith the Lord.*

Henry moaned drawing her attention back to her task and she finished replacing his dressing.

"Where am I?" He grabbed her wrist and pulled her close.

Thankfully, he appeared to have trouble focusing. She pulled loose of his hold and tugged her veil back in place.

"You and your daughter are being held hostage by a band of brigands." She watched as he tensed and tried to sit. She pushed him back down.

"Get out of my way. I need to get to Sarah." Panic and determination creased his features.

"She's right there beside you."

He twisted until he found Sarah's sleeping form by his side. With a heart-wrenching sigh, he relaxed, encircling his daughter protectively with his arm.

"Who are you?"

"I'm Sister Margaret Mary. I was brought here to minister to your wounds." She walked to the doorway and listened to the rumble of an argument from below. She crept back to the bed to stare down at Henry. "We need to escape. These men are murders and thieves. They were hired to kill the child but now they plan to sell her." Her voice lowered, edged with the steel of purpose. "I will not let that happen."

"They cannot." His voice sounded weary but determined.

Footsteps coming up the stairs made her jump.

"Sh-h. Pretend to be sleeping." Relieved he did as she bid, Evangeline moved to the window and glanced down. Was that Wren standing by that large oak on the edge of the yard?

"I've been sent up here to fetch you." Rebecca appeared at the doorway, her voice tearful. Through a tear in her sleeve, Evangeline saw a purple bruise and some scratches on her arm.

Concern made Evangeline reach out to the young woman.

She raised a hand as if to ward off a blow and stepped back unsteadily, dangerously close to the stairway.

"What happened to you?" Evangeline tugged her forward and away from the stairs.

"Nothing that hasn't happened before." She swiped away her

tears on the tattered fabric and grabbed the doorframe to keep from falling.

"Who did this to you?" Evangeline fingered the dagger hidden at her side. Her anger made her tone low and her words raspy.

"Someone who I ne'er 'oped to see again." Her body shook as she stepped inside the room. Rebecca dropped down on the only other chair in the room as if her legs had suddenly refused to work.

Evangeline handed her a cup of water.

The nanny's hand trembled, requiring both palms to steady the cup enough to drink. Her eyes held hatred. "I will have my revenge when he least expects it."

"I assume you haven't always been a nursemaid?" Evangeline watched as the hatred left her eyes, and she blinked back more tears.

"You cain't tell nobody, 'cause you're of the church, right?" The girl dropped her voice and her gaze darted around the room as if searching for a listener. Henry's eyes were closed and a slow, steady rise and fall of his chest made him appear as no threat.

"Yes, nuns are required to take vows to protect the person's confidence whenever they hear confessions." Which was true, real nuns are required to take such vows. It was a hair she'd split many times over the months after coming to her father's realm. Since her persona as Sister Margaret Mary represented the only member of the church around, she'd been forced to hear many confessions and give advice. She'd simply repeated the wise answers given by the nuns whom she'd overheard during her stay at the convent.

"I shouldn't have believed 'er." Rebecca pushed the fallen strands of hair from her face. More tears filled her eyes and slipped down her cheeks. "I was born and raised in a brothel. That's where I first met the monster downstairs." She swiped the tears and ground her palms against her dress. "I escaped and found work at the castle of a rich merchant named Bellachia, as a scullery maid." Her head came up and pride lit her eyes. "I was good at my job and free of my past." A hint of a smile came and went.

Evangeline didn't try to hurry Rebecca for fear she'd shut down.

"The old merchant was dead, but his daughter, Lady Millicent lived there with her 'usband. She approached me one evening as I was emptying chamber pots."

"And what did she want with you?" Evangeline couldn't keep the disdain from her voice.

"At first she only wanted me to do a few extra chores for her personally. She gave me gifts."

"Such as?"

"One time she gave me a fine dress which only needed a bit of mendin'. She promised to learn me to be a lady's maid." After taking another sip of water, Rebecca set the cup down. "Once 'er ladyship gave me time off to visit my friend in the village when she found out Mimi grew herbs. I was to buy some for her, but had to keep it secret." She fidgeted gazing at the floor. "Nightshade is poison." Glancing up, she pursed her lips, and her expression held guilt. "But she assured me it was to kill the castle's rat population." The girl grew more confident as she spoke, though she twisted then smoothed her dress and repeated the gesture several times, evidence she was troubled by something. "Sir Robert died two days later." Her eyes again pooled with tears as she looked up at Evangeline. "Does God blame me for 'is lordship's death because I provided the poison?"

An angry groan came from Henry, and the girl jerked toward him. Evangeline stepped between her and the bed to block her view of him. He was hearing the truth for the first time. How it must grieve him that he had protected his brother's killer.

"You're sure it was the nightshade that killed him?"

"Aye. I seen a cat what's died because it ate a poisoned rat. His lordship looked exactly the same, all gray and..." Rebecca rubbed her eyes as if to get the image from her mind. She stood and paced to the window. "He didn't deserve to die like a rat." Her voice lowered. "Lord Stanton was always nice to the servants, not like her ladyship who went out of her way to be mean to those who had to serve her."

"How is it a scullery maid was sent on this trip with He..." She almost said Henry. "His lordship and the child?"

"I tried to hide but 'er ladyship sent the guards to fetch me to her." Rebecca went back to the rickety stool and sat. "One look and she could see I knowed what she'd done with the poison." Rebecca worried the torn sleeve until it came off in her hands. No emotion crossed her features at the mutilated garment. Absently, she smoothed the fabric with her palm. "She threatened to tell everyone I had poisoned his lordship if I didn't do as she said. Next she wanted the name of a cutthroat who would do anything for money. I gave her Deverow's name and where to find 'im, but I wasn't privy to their dealin's. I was a feared she planned to sell me to 'im, but a week after 'is lordship's funeral we left to go to Castle Stanton." Tears again ran down her face. "I did all manner of spyin' for her. I was there when she lied to Lady Evangeline that her child 'ad died." Rebecca glanced up at Evangeline. "'ow can God let someone so evil live and take the life of someone so good?"

Evangeline looked down at her clasped hands and shook her head. Not only did she not understand the plans of God, but knowing the deeds she'd done in her guise as the Fox, she was far from being innocent and therefore certainly not good in God's eyes.

"Her ladyship made sure the girl's nanny was too ill to make the journey to Castle Brighton so I would 'ave to go in 'er place." She drew a labored breath as if resigned to telling it all. "Lady Millicent read books on plants and herbs, and I saw 'er mixing potions. She could cure certain maladies and told me the potion she'd sent were to help calm the child during the long journey." Sorrow furrowed her brow. "I'm sorry I caused 'arm to the child. Truly I am, I denna know." She stood again and walked to the stairway and leaned over the stair rails before she came back and sat down, her voice again lowered to a whisper. "I know'd she was the one who hired these brigands. I seen 'er talking with a man with an eye patch in the stable several times. I denna know until today that it were Deverow. The bad scars on his face and eye patch changed his appearance but not him."

"She hired these kidnappers? Why?" Evangeline stood, her hands fisted. Millicent would someday face the king's executioner.

"I overheard 'im talking to the others after you went upstairs. They were paid to kill everyone on the carriage but Lord Henry. Deverow say he knows of a rich merchant whose wife is barren and desperate for a child." Rebecca waved her hand in the direction of little Sarah sleeping next to her father. "I'm to be part of the deal." Her expression grew hard. "I ain't goin' to be sold into slavery to no foreigner." Her lips pinched into a hard line of determination. "You're here now to protect the babe, so I can flee." She stood and straightened her dress. Her gaze narrowed at Evangeline. "You canna tell anyone my plan or suffer whatever curse comes on those who breaks a holy vow."

Evangeline's emotions swung from laughter to outrage at the bravado of the scullery maid's declarations. No one was selling Sarah, and any who tried would pay with his rotten life.

"Here, take these rags, wash them and hang them by the fire to dry." The anger won out. Evangeline's tone brooked no back-talk. "Do it now, before it gets dark." She noticed the rebellion in the young woman's stance. An idea came to mind, a way to keep the girl in line and stir up the men by planting seeds of fear. "The avenging spirits of old farmer Danby and his slain sons are upset by the evil in these men's hearts. Those spirits do their worse at night, so I wouldn't try to escape until morn's first light."

Rebecca's rebellious stance was replaced by sagging shoulders of defeat. With a huff, she gathered the soiled rags and hurried down the stairs. Orders shouted at Rebecca demanding one thing then another when she appeared downstairs then an undistinguishable rush of high-pitched whine of Rebecca as she repeated Evangeline's warning about the threat of avenging spirits. A hush fell over the downstairs after that. But for how long?

"Is she gone?" Henry shifted to his side so he could watch Evangeline. The baby lay content against him. "I assume we are not waiting to escape until daylight?"

"We need to leave, but I fear you would not get far in your condition."

"Then you must flee and take my daughter. Go to Brighton Castle and send help. I will be fine until the castle guards arrive."

"There will be no help coming from the castle. An imposter has taken over and there are no loyal men left to protect us." She walked to the stairway to make sure none were there to overhear their plans. Voices speaking in tones so low she couldn't hear the words meant they were too busy to bother with the captives upstairs. She walked back to Henry.

"Lord Brighton mentioned in his missive that the castle was under sieged but surely there are a few good men who could help us." Henry rubbed his eyes as if to clear his vision.

"I have a friend who can help me escape, if I can slip from the house without being seen." She ignored the rush of love that flowed through her at the scene of Henry as the protective father she'd hoped he'd be. They were all in danger as long as they remained in the house. All that was in her bade her take baby Sarah and disappear, but she couldn't leave Henry behind.

She had seen the blood lust in Fisher's eyes when he spoke of eliminating the witnesses and escaping. He had the same look in his eyes as those who killed her servants and locked her inside the lodge to burn to death. The certainty of his intent chilled her bones. Fisher would not hesitate to kill them all when he had a chance.

Henry groaned as he moved his wounded arm then settled once again. His color was better, but was he strong enough to escape?

The sounds of an argument rose louder.

Warning prickles strummed along her neck and spine. She listened but couldn't make out the words. Unrest brewed in the men. Having stirred their superstitions, the tension was thick and their tempers short. She had mentioned the curse with every groan of the house or tree branch that scratched at the roof. If she could get them to turn on each other, getting Henry, Sarah, and Rebecca safely away from the brigands would be possible.

Griswold stomped up the stairs, his accompanying curses as vile as ever.

"Come with me, nun, and bring the brat." He waved his bandaged hand at her. "Now."

"But I just got her to sleep." Something about the way he refused to look at her or the child set her senses on alert. With one glance down at sleeping Sarah and Henry pretending sleep, fear tried to strangle the breath from her chest. She stumbled to the bed determined to stay calm and keep her wits. The fear must not win, if she wanted to save their lives.

"Yeah, well, I do as I'm told, so git." He stepped into the room and headed toward the bed.

"I'll get her." Evangeline leaned down and reached over

Henry to pick up little Sarah. "Don't move. I'll take care of her." She whispered. He frowned but remained still.

Never opening her eyes, the sleeping child snuggled into Evangeline's arms, loosening a fierce determination to protect her little daughter with her life if necessary.

If only Henry were well. The two of them fighting together could have defeated a small army, but her alone? God help them.

CHAPTER 11

"*A*bout time you got down here." Deverow turned to Evangeline making her tense for battle. "Is she sick? She looks flushed."

"'Tis warm in here." Evangeline's voice growled, withholding the anger seething within.

Deverow glared at Evangeline but turned his anger to Rebecca, who stood wide-eyed with fear. "Get ready to travel. We leave within the hour."

"It will be dark soon. The castle's guards and vengeful ghosts roam the forest at night." Evangeline had hoped to have more time. Her mind whirled with her need to escape. She edged back toward the kitchen but when she turned, found her way blocked by Griswold, his arms folded and his feet planted.

"Where you going, Sister?" His voice filled with unspoken accusations.

"To get the child ready to travel." Keeping her voice low and firm, she hoped to disguise her distress.

"Good!" Deverow waved his hand in her direction to proceed. Evangeline controlled her impulse to run. She walked towards the kitchen while listening to Deverow's elevated voice behind her.

"A lackey I paid to warn me of trouble met me on the trail with dire news. He'd passed the King's guards as they rested their mounts at the Black Swan. We have to leave immediately. According to him, they should arrive by morning."

Evangeline stopped near the doorway and listened. Help was on its way to the castle, and would pass right by them. All she had to do was to find a way to divert the soldiers here first and keep her charges safe until they arrived.

"Don't bother with the carriage. Saddle the horses. Take only what we need. We must make it to the coast within the next two days, before the Spaniard sails home. We can sell the brat for enough to disappear without a trace."

"What'd we do with the nun and his lordship? They know who we are." Fisher's words left no doubt of his intent.

"Let her stay and tend Lord Stanton. He ain't in no shape to follow." Griswold's comment surprised her. "We'll be long gone before they can do us any harm."

"Fine." Fisher may have agreed, but Evangeline had no doubt the man would find a reason to slip back into the house and kill them before he left.

With a wave of his hand, Deverow dismissed the men to saddle the horses.

"I ain't goin'." Rebecca screamed. She ran past Evangeline and out the opened kitchen door. Fisher started after her.

Evangeline stepped aside but kicked an empty bucket in his path, which caused Fisher to stumble.

"You did that on purpose! I'll deal with you when I get back." Cursing, he ran out the door after the girl.

Evangeline took advantage of the mêlée to also slip out of the house. She had to get Sarah somewhere safe before she could return to help Rebecca or Henry.

"Where you think you're goin'?" Griswold stood in her path, his arms crossed.

"I must save the child. Please let me pass." She shifted the child to her left hip to free her right arm to fight, if necessary. "God will count letting us pass as a good deed on your behalf."

"Truly?" Griswold's expression of hope stirred her conscience.

"Yes. And by doing a good deed, the Danby curse will not harm you." Relief swooshed over her as he stepped aside.

"Hurry, Sister. Save the little one. The boss won't be far behind." He reached out a hand and stopped her. "Pray for me."

"Of course." She hurried past him and slipped into the shadows of the burned out barn then into the forest hoping that Helen or Wren were nearby to help. Hopefully she would meet one of her gang as she headed toward the mill.

A woman's bloodcurdling scream stopped Evangeline only for a second. There was nothing she could do to help Rebecca with Sarah in her arms, but once she found safety for her child, then she would return with a sword as the Fox. A rush of pent up anger and a vow welled up within her. The long awaited revenge against the man hired to kill her would soon be fulfilled.

CHAPTER 12

*H*enry listened to a commotion in the distance. Men's shouts and a woman's loud wailing stirred him with fear. Sweat poured off of him with the effort it took to push up to a sitting position. His head pounded, and every muscle protested in weak submission.

"God help us." His throat dry, his voice sounded more like a frog's croaking. A gaping hole in the thatched roof let in the last of the waning daylight as he sought his boots. He rubbed his eyes to clear his vision, and finally spotted his clothing beside the bed. He pushed up to a standing position. The room spun. He reached out and grabbed onto the sturdy bedpost until the spinning ceased. Every movement slow and determined, he dressed then bent down to fetch his boots. It took a good portion of his strength to tug them on. Sarah being in danger kept him going. Taking a deep breath, he stood again. He barely made it to a primitive chair near the door before his legs buckled.

He could not remember feeling so weak or helpless. The pounding in his head increased as he fought to stay focused. He reached for the water bucket that sat on the table nearby and dipped in the hollowed out gourd and drank deeply from its contents.

Another scream. The nursemaid.

He dropped the gourd.

Panic shoved him forward to the stairway. Pausing to get his breath, he braced against the wall and listened to the voices that echoed up from two floors below.

"What do you mean she got away? How could a nun carrying a babe outrun you?" The sound of flesh hitting flesh carried up the stairs.

"I saw the direction she took before I caught up with this wench." A man's voice full of anger. Furniture scraped, and then more wails of the nanny, Rebecca.

"Looks like this little serving girl fought like a lion from them scratches on your face, Fisher." The croaking voice again.

"Griswold, shut up and go saddle the horses. I don't have time for this. Fisher, find the brat and bring her back here unharmed. She's worth her weight in gold. I don't care what you do to the nun."

The nun had escaped with his daughter? Determination pushed Henry to the top of the stairs. The distance down was steep and daunting. One slip could cost him his life. His hand shook as he clasped the railing. Leaning heavily on its support, his progress was as excruciatingly slow as it was painful. His aching head and body protested every step.

"Move, wench. Help the Frenchman pack up the food and..." The voice faded as the man walked away.

Halfway down the second stairway, Henry froze in place. His legs threatened to forsake him. He sank to the stair tread to rest, releasing the breath he held when the man with an eye patch passed by the stairway. Thankfully the brigand had been too focused on berating the girl to glance Henry's way.

Rebecca. By her all too familiar high-pitched whimpers,

Henry recognized the nanny as she passed by. She was disheveled and once again near hysteria.

Henry wiped the sweat out of his eyes and sucked in a deep breath. One thought drove him past his pain. Save Sarah.

Standing, he continued his slow journey down the stairs until he made it to the bottom. His breath came in gulping gasps, and his heart pounded from the exertion. How was he going to escape if he could neither run nor fight?

With no time to entertain such doubts, he determined first to escape the house. *One foot in front of another.* Focus. He saw the open window and headed toward it, away from the murmurs he heard from the other room.

Footsteps headed his way, propelling him forward. The window was almost as large as a door, allowing him to sit down on the frame and swing his legs over the edge while holding onto the sides. His wounded body protested as he eased down to the soft ground beneath and waited. He dare not move while the person was in the room, lest he be discovered. He was impatient to be off, but his weary body welcomed the rest.

Brushing against the bush that hid him released the plant's strong scent and stirred a memory. Henry broke off a leaf and rubbed it between his fingers. Closing his eyes he drew in scent. The spicy aroma reminded him of long walks in the garden with Evangeline. A fresh reminder of his heavy burden of grief he'd carried since Evangeline's death.

The footsteps hesitated not far from the window as another person with a heavy tread walked into the room.

"Boss, the horses be saddled and ready to go." The voice of the croaking mocker was now subdued.

"Good. Go help Fisher look for the child, but, brat or no, we leave within the hour." The man cursed, his tone rising in anger. "That nun's gonna pay for the trouble she's caused. Kill her if you find her, but take care you don't harm the child. We won't collect a farthing if she is injured." The sound of the heavy tread of a big man scraped against the pine floor. Then the second man left.

Henry watched the big man exit the house, hesitate and glance from side to side as if deciding which direction to go. Torch light bobbed in the distance then disappeared into the forest.

Henry pressed back against the rough exterior of the house. He was well hidden unless the big man drew close enough to hear his labored breathing. The man lumbered away as if in no hurry. Another person hobbled up to the big man.

"Griswold, we leave now! Oui? Killing a nun? No good." He crossed himself. "I have supplies packed in the bags of the last two horses." He beckoned with a wave of his hand, and limped toward the closest horse. "Help me mount and let's go before the boss sees us."

With a grunt of disapproval Griswold boosted the Frenchman onto his horse and handed him the reins.

"Stop!" The one-eyed man ran toward the two men, a sword in his hand.

Griswold slapped the Frenchman's horse and sent him galloping away then turned to meet his boss with a raised left hand.

"Let the Frenchman go. He would only slow us down because of his wound. That means more money for the rest of us. Right?" Griswold stood his ground. His uninjured hand rested on his short sword in a silent reminder that he was also armed.

"I say who goes." One-eye took a step toward Griswold. With a growl of displeasure, he stopped and pointed in the direction the first man had gone. "Go help Fisher retrieve the brat so we can all escape before first light." He waved for him to leave. "I will make sure the nanny and the horses are ready to go when you return." The two parted ways when the one-eyed brigand stalked to the house.

With no one in sight, Henry stood, wobbled and grabbed the window's frame to steady himself. A prayer for protection and strength slipped from his lips, then another for wisdom to find his daughter and the nun who took her. Somehow he knew she would keep his child safe.

He winced as he stepped out of his hiding place. Staying here to wait for those cutthroats to capture little Sarah was not an option.

"Lord, please help me." Henry stumbled toward a horse saddled and ready for the brigand's escape. In his weakened condition, the animal would be his best way to find Sarah and the nun. There wasn't time to search for the King's guards.

He ran his hand down the horse's neck and spoke softly to soothe the animal then pulled a large wooden bucket beside it. The extra height of the upside down bucket helped him mount with minimal exertion. Still, his wounds throbbed in a constant pain-filled rhythm making them hard to ignore. The last time he'd been on a horse pursuing the kidnappers had not ended well. This time he had to succeed or risk losing his daughter forever.

He turned the horse toward the path the big man had gone. The brigand seemed to know how to track Fisher.

CHAPTER 13

*E*vangeline held the baby close and jogged through the trees until the foliage grew dense. She slowed to push through.

"A-r-a-a-g-h!" A man was not far behind her. She pressed through the thicket and hid behind a large oak.

"Who are you?" Fisher's challenge was ignored.

"Leave now and we may let you live." That voice was unmistakably Helen's imitation of her male persona as a member of Fox's gang.

Suddenly steel clanged against steel. Evangeline held the child close and remained hidden.

Relief was short lived as a hand reached out and touched Evangeline's shoulder.

"Shush. We're here to help you and the wee babe, sister." Wren stepped closer. "We need to hurry. There is another man coming who is very big." She tugged Evangeline away from the tree.

"How many are here to help?" Evangeline feared for her friends, knowing these brigands were trained killers.

"Others have been summoned, but only the Shepherdess and I have arrived, so far."

"Here, take the child and give me your sword. I will help H... the Shepherdess."

"Fox?" The woman's voice rose in alarm.

"No time to explain. Take the child and guard her with your life. We will meet at our usual place when we're done." None of the others had the skills or ability to help Helen like Evangeline. If Fisher escaped this conflict, then he would continue to pursue her child. He could not be allowed to leave this glen.

Reluctance warred with necessity as she delivered her child into the young woman's waiting arms. She gently touched Sarah's cheek before she took the sword and turned away.

The nun's habit was too cumbersome. She pulled off her wimple, the one-piece head covering would hinder her vision, followed by the heavy habit, dropping both on the ground near a big oak. The remaining rough-spun linen shift hung to her ankles, but did little to ward off the night's chill. If only she had the freedom of movement that breeches and tunic afforded. Grabbing the sword, she rushed forward to help her friend.

"Fight on!" Evangeline shouted their childhood motto. They used it when they trained against the castle guards to give them courage. Her yell gave Helen warning that it was Evangeline as she appeared at her friend's side. The intermittent clouds parted for a moment and allowed the moon to highlight the clearing and their opponent.

"I recognize your voice, nun. You have kept your beauty well hidden." Fisher swung his sword in an arc, bowed and grinned. "I shall enjoy this." His right arm bled from a fresh wound, though his actions didn't appear to be hindered. He lunged toward them then stepped back in an effort to intimidate them.

"You should be far from here." Helen scolded her friend before she circled to her right. Evangeline instinctively circled to the left.

They moved in a natural rhythm after years of sparing together as youths. Their training had taught them to put their much stronger opponents at a disadvantage until one of them could strike the immobilizing blow. Divide and conquer. A hunting technique learned from the way the wolf pack took down its prey.

The darkness was their friend with only the moonlight's spotty appearance. Fog swirled around their feet, muting the surrounding forest sounds and dulling the crude taunts of their enemy.

"Enough of this." Fisher swung his sword first at Helen then Evangeline, no longer amused at the blows they had landed that left him bleeding in many places. His sparring took on urgency as he rushed Helen.

She caught her foot on an exposed root and went down. Her head hit the trunk of a tree with a sickening thump. Her body lay limp and unmoving.

"No!" Evangeline rushed toward Fisher as he raised his sword to strike her defenseless friend.

Fisher turned and swung, knocking the sword from Evangeline's grip. He grabbed her clothing and jerked her toward him before she could recover.

"You are very beautiful. I shall have my way with you before you die." His breath was foul as he pressed his mouth against hers.

Anger surged at his touch. Evangeline pushed against him with one hand and searched for her cross and the blade that was hidden within, but it was trapped between their bodies. She relaxed her stance, taking him off guard. Jerking free, she slammed her fist into the wounded shoulder Fisher received taking Henry's carriage. He dropped his sword and bellow in rage.

"Now you will die a slow death!" Fisher grabbed her before she could escape. He fumbled to draw his knife.

"I don't think so." Griswold jerked the smaller man off his feet.

Fisher loosed his hold on Evangeline.

"Let me go." Fisher pulled his knife and jabbed at Griswold as Fisher dangled above the ground. "I shall kill you, too."

The attack only made Griswold angrier.

"You will be the one to die." Griswold growled and shook his captive like a dog shakes a rat.

Evangeline grabbed her fallen sword and turned to aid Griswold.

"Go to your friend, nun. I shall take care of this vermin." Griswold dropped Fisher and kicked him in the side. "It's time I teach you a lesson, little man."

Fisher jumped up and swung his blade at Griswold.

While the battle raged on between the brigands, Evangeline rushed to Helen's side. Dread stole her breath. Her friend lay crumbled at the foot of the tree, still as death.

"Helen." Evangeline brushed back the hood of her tunic, but the darkness made it hard to assess her friend's injuries. She could smell the coppery scent of blood and felt a sticky mass on her forehead where she must have struck the trunk of the ancient oak. Leaning closer, she placed her fingers below Helen's nose to feel for the slightest sign of breath. Her hand shook too much to be sure. Grief pooled in her gut at the thought of losing her best friend. She should have done something more to save her.

"Please, Lord, let her live." She clutched Helen's hand and patted it trying to awaken her.

"Oh-h, my head." Helen groaned, tugged her hand free and rubbed her forehead. "What happened?"

Relief swooshed out of Evangeline in a tear-filled gush of thanksgiving to God.

"You hit a tree." She helped Helen sit up.

The curses of the warring brigands grew more intense.

Fisher recovered his sword. Steel clanged against steel.

Griswold kept pushing Fisher away from the women's position, but by the intermittent moonlight she could tell Griswold was weakening. In spite of Griswold's superior size, strength, and prowess with the sword, Fisher remained in the fight. Concern quickened Evangeline. No matter who won the battle, she and Helen needed to leave now.

"Can you stand?"

"I think so." Helen groaned when Evangeline helped her up. She put a hand on the tree and took a deep breath. "I'm a bit wobbly." She started to sink back to the ground. "Maybe I should rest here. You go."

"I'm not going without you." Evangeline slipped an arm around her friend's waist to help support her.

The loud crash of a large animal charging through the brush startled the women. A man on horseback appeared on the far side of the clearing. The two brigands fell to the ground followed by an anguished cry then silence. It was too dark to see which of the fallen men had survived, for the gathering ground fog covered them like a shroud. The horseman stopped. Hopefully, his attention remained on the brigands, and he would not notice their escape.

"We need to go." Evangeline whispered. She practically carried her friend as they slipped into the forest and headed for their meeting place. Why none of their group had arrived worried her.

"Who did you send to summon the gang?" She slowed her pace to allow Helen to catch her breath.

"I sent Wren's little boy to tie the scarlet cord on the maple tree near the road as a sign to meet. Wren came with me. We met Mouse on the trail." She stumbled, and Evangeline caught her and kept her from falling. An urgency to keep going thumped against her chest, but she stopped at a downed tree and let her friend sit. They both needed a brief rest.

"I wanted to get back to help you and sent Mouse before evening to the meeting place with instructions to send the others to the farm when they arrived."

"Don't you find it strange that none of the others arrived?"

"It's possible that the cord came loose, or perhaps no one saw it before it grew dark." Helen's tone was less than confident.

"I sent Wren with my daughter to the mill to wait for us." Evangeline's voice lowered to a husky groan. A dark premonition chilled her spine. Fear sent her to her feet.

"I would tell you to go without me, but I know you won't. We must hurry." Helen stood and grabbed Evangeline's arm for support.

There was no time to waste.

CHAPTER 14

*H*enry urged his reluctant mount forward into the darkness, grateful for his years hunting and tracking game. The process of following the brigand through the unfamiliar forest had been excruciatingly slow, having to stop every few minutes to listen for his quarry's progress. Thankfully, the angry man's heavy tread and curses made it possible to keep on track even in the dark.

He arrived at a glen and glimpsed movement on the far side. Two shadowy figures disappeared into the forest.

Suddenly his horse snorted and reared, almost unseating him. Barely visible beneath the ground fog, bodies lay in a heap a few feet ahead. Was the nun among them? Before he could dismount to investigate, one person cursed, sat up, and shoved away from a larger body, stirring the fog around him.

"Get down. I need that horse." He recognized Fisher's voice. The man stood, staggered, then straightened. He stumbled toward Henry and raised his arm. The moonshine glinted off the knife in his fist.

"I think not." With a flick of his wrist and a heel to the animal's side, Henry reined the horse sharply so that its rear-end clipped the man, knocking him down. Turning the horse in the direction of the escaping figures, he left the angry Fisher cursing and sprawled on the ground.

Had one of those escaping figures been the nun? The horse shied when it reached the far side of the glen where Henry thought he'd seen movement. He calmed the horse with soothing words and stroked his neck. A dark heap lay near the base of the tree.

Anger rose like a flaming torch set to dry brush. If Fisher had harmed the nun, he would silence the brigand for good.

Dread swirled in his chest like the fog set in motion by the horse's impatient movement. He dismounted, keeping a hand on the horse's reins.

Kneeling down, he reached for the heap.

A knife whizzed past his head and stuck into the oak. He jerked around to see another figure rise from the fog and slam Fisher to the ground. Angry words and a scuffle stirred the fog like boiling porridge.

There was no time to intervene. Henry pulled the steel blade from the tree and turned his attention back to the bundle at his knee.

One touch of the cloth revealed no body beneath it. Drawing the coarse fabric closer to his face, he recognized the scent of lavender and honey. It was the nun's covering and veil. Relief warred with urgency. Where was his child?

He tucked the knife in his waistband. The more he moved the more strength grew within him, yet his bruised and aching body protested his actions. He gritted his teeth and mounted the horse then headed in the direction he'd seen the two figures escape.

〜

*E*vangeline helped Helen through the forest, their progress too slow to suit her impatience. She feared for the safety of her daughter, but she wouldn't leave her injured friend behind.

They were almost at the meeting place when she heard a commotion. Women's voices were raised in anger.

"I'm fine. Let's hurry." Helen's expression of weariness and pain did not match her words of assurance, but Evangeline nodded and they jogged the remaining distance.

"Thank the Lord you're here." The young mother they called Sparrow waved the torch she held and beckoned Evangeline toward a body on the ground. "Wren's been stabbed."

The injured woman was on the ground positioned on a stretcher made of two saplings connected by a large cape.

"Where's the child?" Panic edged Evangeline's gravelly voice to a familiar growl as she scanned each face.

The women stared at Evangeline with wide-eyed surprise.

"Yes, she is also the Fox." Helen settled down on the nearest stump, weariness filled her voice. "She gave Wren a toddler to bring here for safety. Has anyone seen the little girl?"

"No. We found Wren alone and bleeding when we arrived." Murmurs of agreement passed between Sparrow, Robin and Owl.

Evangeline knelt down to examine Wren and motioned to Sparrow to bring the torch closer. Wren had a serious shoulder wound by the amount of blood soaked through the linen covering it. "Bring me some moss. Quickly! There's plenty near the stream."

Owl rushed away to gather what was needed and returned within minutes. Evangeline packed the wound with the moss securing it with a strip of cloth she tore from the hem of her shift.

The bleeding had stopped but Wren's eyes were closed, her face pale as death.

"Wren, who did this to you?" Evangeline took a deep breath to gain control of her emotions and fought the urge to shake the unconscious woman for answers. Instead, she gently brushed dirt from the young woman's face. "Where's Sarah?"

"When we arrived, Wren kept mumbling something about a mouse. Do you think she meant Mouse did this?" Robin wrung her hands in despair. "She's the only one missing."

"I fear she is our traitor." Helen stood. Pain etched her brow. "I think I know where she's gone."

"Can you get Wren to the castle?" Evangeline glanced at the women and saw the nods. "Good. There is someone there who can help her. I'll come as soon as I can. If the wound should begin bleeding again, apply pressure until it stops." She put a hand on Sparrow's shoulder. "Please, Lord, give them strength, speed and safety for their task. And please save Wren's life. Amen." The women mumbled *amen* and crossed themselves. A solemn reverence filled the clearing, melting away fear and giving place to faith-filled determination.

Sparrow handed Evangeline the torch, then stooped to pick up one end of the stretcher, and the other two young women picked up the other end. Without further discussion they headed toward the road that led to the castle.

Evangeline turned toward Helen.

"Where do you think Mouse has gone?"

"I believe she's made a bargain with the devil." Helen's countenance turned to fury. The transformation stunned and alarmed Evangeline with her intensity. She had always admired her friend's ability to control her emotions and stay calm in spite of the circumstance. The Helen who stood before her now was anything but passive and calm. "Ox will pay with his life if he harms the child."

"Ox?" Evangeline followed Helen as she headed the short

distance to the abandoned mill where their disguises were hidden. She placed the torch in an iron bracket on the wall. The light brightened the dark room.

Each in their own thoughts, Evangeline donned her disguise as the Fox. She tugged on the leggings and tunic with muted tones of the forest but left the grotesque hood in its hiding place. The fear of being recognized was not as great as the need to be free of any hindrance that would keep her from seeing more clearly in the darkness any opponent who got in her way.

Helen dressed in a tunic and leggings and refastened her red hair within the leather strip, which had come loose in her battle. A large knot and dark bruise marred her forehead. She stumbled then righted, rubbed her neck then picked up a sword from their stash and swung it to limber her arm.

"Are you in much pain?" Evangeline asked her friend as they exited the mill. She took the torch and put it out by shoving it into the dirt. No sense leading an enemy to their camp.

"Not in as much pain as Mouse will be when I reach her." Helen led the way toward the trail that would take them to the Black Swan. "If she has harmed Sarah, she won't live long enough to feel anything but the cold steel of my sword."

Evangeline prayed that would not be necessary, that Sarah would be safe and waiting for her when they arrived at the tavern.

CHAPTER 15

*T*he rosy hue of early morning sun lit the dawn before Henry reached an old abandoned mill. A torch had been put out and left stuck in the ground. The tracks revealed many people had congregated here not long ago. His heart skipped a beat when he saw blood on the ground. There had been no blood on the trail along the way. There was no sign of the nun or his daughter. Perhaps he was on the wrong trail.

He dismounted and led the horse down a gentle slope to the water to drink. Sinking to his knees, he also quenched his thirst. His muscles protested every movement. He couldn't afford to rest long. Not if he wanted to catch up with his quarry. There had been two sets of prints he'd followed here. By their small size, he suspected both were women or youths.

Tugging the horse's head up from the tender grass where he grazed, Henry remounted and searched the clearing again for signs of the ones he'd been following.

"There!" His voice disturbed the silence and sent a flock of starlings fleeing the trees in mass, squawking in loud protest for being disturbed. Startled, Henry's mount danced sideways, tensed then bucked stiff-legged. Henry fought for control to calm the animal. His body protested the hard pounding, jerks and twists of the frightened horse's actions. The abuse to his injured torso beaded his forehead with sweat and loosed more aches and pains. His ribs burned and his head pounded with every heartbeat. He spewed a few choice words before he got his temper and the frightened animal under control. Anger at the stupid beast was pointless. He had to find the nun. Losing control now was not an option if he wanted to save his daughter.

In spite of his horse's hoof prints marring the area, he spotted several sets of footprints. One group of people had set off in one direction, but the shoe print with the slight indent on the heel was the one he sought. Its wearer went the opposite way, down a narrow trail. The worn path meant he could press the horse to go faster. He would catch up with who he hoped was the nun and her friend.

Providing he was actually following the nun. He ignored the doubt that had plagued him from the start of his quest and pressed his heels into the bay's side. His precious Evangeline had often told him when he wrestled with a hard decision to always follow his heart. Everything within him urged him onward.

Decision made.

~

*A*t the sound of a horse galloping on the trail behind them, Evangeline and Helen slipped through the foliage and hid. They couldn't see the rider from their location, but then he couldn't see them either. Had Fisher acquired a horse? The rider continued on without slowing.

Fear pressed Evangeline to increase her pace in spite of her exhaustion. It had been a long night without food or rest.

Remaining on alert for more travelers, they hurried toward

the inn. They reached the Black Swan but stayed hidden in the tree line as they drew closer. A large group of villagers stood outside the entrance murmuring amongst themselves.

Evangeline and Helen made their way around to the back and slipped inside. It took a few seconds for their eyes to adjust to the darkened interior of the back storage room.

"Have you seen a nun and child come this way?" A man demanded as if he were out of breath yet someone in authority.

"No nun." Several started talking at once.

Evangeline and Helen edged toward the doorway that led into the great room of the tavern and peeked inside.

"Henry!" Evangeline's gasp of alarm was lost in the roar of the crowd, as if each patron tried to have his voice heard. Helen grabbed her arm and frowned. She put a finger to her lips for silence. Evangeline nodded then turned her attention back to the scene before them.

"Enough! One at a time." Henry pointed to a younger man standing closest. "You. What happened here?" He pointed to a fat man and woman lying dead on the floor covered in blood. "Who are they?"

"That there's Ox, the tavern owner." The youth pointed to the dead man.

"Got his just reward, he did." A disgruntled man shouted from near the entrance. Others murmured agreement and disparaged the evil deeds of the dead person even as they crossed themselves.

Evangeline suspected by their actions, they were hoping to cancel any retribution from his accursed, departing spirit.

"I ain't sure who the dead woman is. It ain't his wife." The young man turned toward the crowd. "Anyone know this chicken-legged wench?"

"Nope. Not old Ox's pretty little wife." A white-haired man with one tooth grinned then wiped his mouth. Chuckles erupted through the crowd.

"This ol' crow and a couple of youngun's been livin' at widow Kutley's cabin helpin' her slop the hogs." A humped back old woman, bent over with age in a perpetual inspection of the ground, pointed a gnarled finger at the corpse.

"And helpin' herself to anythin' what's not nailed down." Another voice yelled from the back of the room. Others chimed in with accusations against the woman.

"But what happened to these two?" Henry raised his hand to restore order.

"The king's guards had just left the inn headed toward the castle, when a man with an eye patch rode up." The young man who'd first offered his help stood straighter as all eyes turned to him. "He looked angry and mean." He tried to demonstrate with snarled lips and clenched fists.

"Maybe he be the Fox." Others chimed in with speculation and questions.

"I be thinkin' the same." He raised his hand for silence as he'd seen Henry do. "I was outside ready to leave, but the way he stomped into the door made me turn around and go back inside. I figured iffen it was the Fox then there was goin' to be some excitement." After more murmurs settled down he continued. "I sat right over there and saw it all." Everyone turned to look at an overturned table in the corner. His voice grew more confident. "The man yelled, 'I want to talk to the innkeeper.' Old Ox wasn't happy with the man's tone and told 'em so. The stranger shoved old Ox down onto a chair. He drew a knife and poked it against Ox's chest." Gasps of the crowd made the youth smile.

"Aye, I saw that, too." An ancient seaman with a peg leg leaned on his crutch and pushed through the crowd. His stench was bad and the crowd retreated a few steps and let him pass.

Evangeline got a whiff and grimaced. She knew the man from his many ailments which had brought him to the abbey often to be treated. He did odd jobs from grave digging to skinning and tanning hides, which accounted for the smell of death that clung to him.

"The stranger demanded Ox give 'em all his money." The crowd mumbled in excitement and pressed in again lest they miss something. "Ox jumped up and bellowed like a crazed bull ready to charge. His face turned redder than that there blood on the floor." Clyde paused for emphasis. "Then Ox grabs his chest and keeled over where you sees him now."

"But did you see this here woman come in with a baby?" The young man raised his voice to be heard over the crowd. He wasn't happy about sharing the limelight. Once he had their attention again, he continued. "The stranger was huntin' for Ox's coins when that woman came running inside carrying a squawlin' babe in a leather bag slung over her shoulder like a sack of corn. The wench screamed when she saw ole Ox dead on the floor." The young man turned to face the crowd and vaulted upon a nearby table then back to the floor. "The robber leaped over the bar and stood in her path. He says, 'give me that brat', but the woman didn't budge." The youth's voice lowered in a dramatic way and spoke to the crowd, ignoring Henry.

"Frozen with fear, me thinks." Clyde interrupted again. "The stranger grabbed for the bag containing the child and the woman went wild, swinging her arms at the man." Everyone backed up as he demonstrated the woman's actions. "He drew his knife and stabbed her in the chest twice before she turned loose the bag." The old seaman waved his crutch in the air then slammed the end against the wood floor with a loud thump to indicate the battle. "The babe's howlin' got loud enough a deaf man could hear it. Before the woman hit the floor, the murderer jerked the bag away from the woman and ran out." Clyde pointed to the doorway and the crowd, caught up in the story, turned to look at the open doorway, as if they might see the brigand escaping. "He got on his horse and rode away like the king's army was after him."

"What did the child look like?" Henry's tone had risen to near panic as he grabbed the old seaman's filthy tunic, ripping the ancient fabric.

Evangeline could barely draw a breath. She was too late? Sarah was gone? The brigand had taken her?

"Only its head stuck out of the bag. It had light brown hair and a squall that could raise the dead." His voice rose in desperation as he pointed to the floor next to the bodies. "That fell from the bag when the killer grabbed it from the dead woman." The nearest person stooped and picked up the bit of cloth and held it up.

"Aye, that there came from the bag."

"Sarah!" Henry loosed the man and grabbed the cloth. His eyes were wide with fear, the same fear that clawed at Evangeline when she recognize Sarah's blanket. "Which way did he go?"

The seaman and the boy pointed out the direction at the same time. Henry turned for the exit pressing through the crowd of onlookers. Evangeline left out the back door with fewer obstacles in her escape and managed to beat him outside. She headed toward the front of the inn with the intent of taking the nearest mount. As she turned the corner, Helen was out back with a horse saddled and ready.

"Go. I filled a bag for you with milk and supplies for the bairn when you find her. I'll stay here and deal with this mess." She handed Evangeline the reins. "I'll send someone to fetch the king's guards to follow you."

Helen must have slipped away to the stable while Evangeline had stayed to listen.

Evangeline gave her friend a quick hug and leapt onto the horse sending it into a gallop in the direction the men had pointed.

The crowd outside the inn jumped out of the way to let her pass.

"Wait." Henry shouted.

Dread soured her empty stomach with the thought of what would happen once he caught up with her. She shoved the thought away. First, they must save their daughter from being sold. In her heart she knew, for as sure as the sun rose, Henry would not be far behind.

Why did that thought comfort her?

~

*T*he crowd had cheered the rider on. But Henry knew only one person who rode with such reckless abandon. Evangeline. His Evangeline. But how could that be?

He mounted the bay and charged after the unknown rider. His thoughts ran through his mind at equal speed.

After the fire, only four bodies were recovered, those of the servants and guards. Evangeline's body could not be found and was thought to have been burned to ashes. His grief, as well as his need to protect little Sarah, had stopped him from searching further. Another stupid mistake, one of many his pride had suffered him to make.

Every jolt of his mount's pounding hooves upon the hard trail loosed more painful memories.

The nanny's confession had revealed who had hired the brigands.

Millicent.

She had pursued him long before he met Evangeline. Millicent had been one of three young women his father had considered as a prudent union. He had pressured Henry to pick a bride at the king's ball, then Henry saw Evangeline and no other would do.

That he had even for one moment considered Millicent as a potential wife sent a stab of repulsion at his gut.

Every murmur hinted of Evangeline's infidelity had come directly from Millicent or one of her maidservants.

His grief over his brother's death had kept him from seeing the truth.

Evangeline had tried to tell me.

Everything they'd suffered was his fault. He'd been so stupid.

His horse stumbled, almost going down bringing his attention back to the present. Caution warred against his urgency to reach the rider ahead of him and little Sarah. He pulled back on the reins to slow the tired animal to a walk. If the horse fell, Henry's already injured body would not fare well. There would be no second chance to find the truth or make things right.

CHAPTER 16

*E*vangeline urged the horse faster, though she knew the gelding was giving his all. She would have to slow their pace soon or risk both her and the horse collapsing from exhaustion.

Only prayer and a stubborn determination to reach her daughter kept her in the saddle. After battling brigands, then helping an injured Helen make it to the inn, with no time to rest, she was near the end of her endurance.

"Please, God, give me strength." She swiped away the tears that blurred her vision.

Searching the trail ahead revealed only an oxen cart and a lone farmer. She slowed her mount to a walk when she reached them.

"Have you seen a rider with a child go by?" Weariness reduced her voice to a gravely whisper.

"What say?" The elderly man squinted up at Evangeline and cupped his left hand against his ear as if trying to catch her words.

She took a deep breath and tried again, praying her raspy words spoken slowly could penetrate his lack of hearing.

"Yep. A mean lookin' bloke with a bag full of squallin' babe passed me not long ago." He nodded and pointed to the right fork in the road. "Went that way, toward the coast."

"Thank you." A flash of renewed energy filled her with hope knowing she was close to catching the brigand. She turned her mount toward the trail indicated and nudged the horse into a trot, then pulled back the reins to stop.

If Henry took the wrong path, she would have to deal with the brigand on her own. Not that she couldn't take on any brigand if her body was rested, but truth be known, she needed Henry's help until the king's soldiers caught up.

Decision made, she rode to an ancient oak growing nearest the right path and pulled her knife. She made quick work of hacking an arrow into the trunk pointing to the direction with her initials ES below it. Her hand stilled in hesitation before she continued to carve and encircled the letters in a heart. Only Henry would understand the significance of their private code. Her chest heaved with a sudden fear of revealing her secret. Too late. The deed was done. She kicked the horse into a gallop.

Every horrible thought of what her precious daughter was suffering at the brigand's hands filled her with fear and fury. Had he injured her by his rough handling? She was only a baby. Anguish loosed a sob deep from her soul.

No, he would want her to be safe if he was to collect his reward.

Her anger flared as hot as the fire One-eye had set to kill her. He would pay with his life.

❧

*H*enry allowed the bay to walk until the animal cooled down and its breathing slowed to normal. After the brief rest, he kicked the horse once again into a gallop hoping that alternating rest then speed would keep the animal on its feet.

He approached a fork in the road. With no sign pointing the way to the coast and no one in sight to ask directions, he pulled his mount to a halt while he studied the tracks in the dust. A wagon pulled by oxen had gone left. A flock of sheep had been driven to the right trail, obscuring any other prints. Frustration and indecision plagued him.

"Please, God, show me which way to go. I can't find them on my own." He closed his eyes hoping for divine intervention.

The tired bay took the opportunity of the relaxed hold of the reins to wander into the taller grass beside the road.

Henry opened his eyes, disappointed that he hadn't heard a voice from heaven. But with the sin of pride in his life, why would God speak to someone such as he?

He pulled the bay's head up from grazing. A decision had to be made. With a tug on the reins he turned the gelding toward the left trail when something caught his attention. The midafternoon sunlight highlighted a freshly carved arrow pointing to the right fork, but there was something more carved below it. He rode closer for a better look.

His breath caught in his chest when he saw the heart carved beneath the arrow and the initials etched within.

E.S.

Evangeline Stanton. Initials drawn within a heart was their secret code to authenticate notes sent to the other. It was also used to mark the way in their newlywed games of hide and seek. Warmth heated his torso with those intimate memories then a chill of suspicion slammed the door on the past. Was this a trick to throw him off the trail? His heart said no.

Evangeline was alive? Could it be? Only one way to find out. He kicked the horse into a gallop down the right fork in the road. Within the hour his horse had stumbled twice. Urgency demanded he hurry but reason won out. Killing the exhausted animal by continuing this pace was not an option. Henry pulled the gelding back to a walk. The bay tensed and alerted Henry to the scene ahead.

A horse stood beside the trail, head down munching grass.

His horse whinnied. An answering whinny responded. Where was its rider? Could it be a trap? Bandits?

He drew from his shirt the knife that Fisher had thrown at him—Henry's knife as it turned out.

Glad for the weapon, he wasn't sure he was up to winning a battle in his present condition.

"Who goes there?" He hoped the authority in his voice would make any robber think twice. Holding back a groan of pain, he straightened his posture in the saddle so as not to reveal his weakness.

"Tis only me." The gravelly voice of the nun sent joy leaping in his chest until worry halted his exaltation. Where had she come from? Had she been chasing the brigand, too?

"Are you hurt?" He dismounted and rushed toward the woman.

"No. But my horse has thrown a shoe and is lame." She stepped out of the shadow of the horse allowing the sunlight to highlight her features.

Shock surged through him with the force of a hurricane slamming into the shore. He staggered back two steps. Clothed in men's pants and a tunic, the raspy voice was that of the nun's, but the face...

"Wha-a-t?" His legs threatened to buckle. His breath escaped him and his heart pounded hard as if trying to escape his chest. "Evangeline?" He whispered her name again and again. As if in a trance, he stepped toward her until he was within reach and pulled her into his arms. Shock loosed deep gut-wrenching sobs, which racked his body. He tightened his hold and drew in her fragrance. Could it truly be his beloved?

"Please, you're crushing me." She clung to him a moment before she pushed against his chest.

Reluctantly he loosened his hold but refused to release her.

"Evangeline?" He touched her face and traced every feature. "Please, God, let this not be another torturous dream." He touched her hair. The shorter locks barely brushed her shoulder. Her height was right, she fit right under his chin, but instead of creamy white skin, soft curves, and gentle countenance, this woman had the darkened skin and toned muscles of a common laborer. Was this truly his Evangeline? She must have recognized his doubt, for she tensed and squirmed out of his grasp.

"It is not a dream, Henry." She raised her chin. Defiance sparked from her eyes. "I am alive."

It was as if she'd slapped him. Pent up fury replaced his relief.

"Where have you been?" He grabbed and shook her. "I thought you were dead." At first she offered no resistance, then she stiffened.

With a growl of protest she broke his hold with sudden upward thrust of her arms against his.

His anger was not as easily thwarted. Fists tight, he fought for control of the betrayal that raged within him.

"To the world, Lady Evangeline is dead." Her expression of grief was real, but the gravelly voice was not the sweet teasing tone that still taunted his dreams.

He threw his hands up in disgust, stepped back then folded his arms to keep from grabbing her again and shaking the truth out. He had died a thousand deaths since that fire.

"Why?" The anguish he'd lived with so long quickly turned again to anger. "I demand you explain." His voice rose to a shout.

Her expression hardened into a familiar defiance with an air of regal dismissal before she turned away. "Explanations can wait. Sarah is my first priority." She left him fuming while she led her limping horse down the road.

"Do you know where the brigand is taking Sarah?" He hated to wait to satisfy his need to know the truth of why she would abandon their child and their marriage, but she was right. Sarah was their first priority. There was no time for a long discussion at the moment, but he vowed there would come a time, even if it took locking her in a room until she told all. It couldn't come soon enough.

"I overheard the leader say that a Spanish merchant waited for him." She turned her focus on the road beyond. "I caught sight of him just before my horse went lame. He's not far ahead, and his horse will also need to rest."

"Did you see Sarah?" He was not about to let Evangeline out of his sight and hurried to her side, tugging his tired mount behind him. Their only option, unless they came across an inn or a farm with fresh mounts, was to allow his bay to rest. The gelding was too tired to carry one rider and certainly not two. Walking only exacerbated Henry's aches and pains, also proving he was not caught in the middle of one of his many nightmares concerning his wife.

"I heard her crying." Her voice caught with emotions. She paused and took a deep breath. "I tried to reach him, but he heard me and whipped his mount to go faster." Her shoulders shook with silent sorrow. "I couldn't follow."

He started to reach for her but stopped himself. She didn't deserve his comfort.

"Why, Evangeline?" Grief kept his tone soft but the question was filled with anguish.

"I thought you had abandoned me after my baby died. I was inconsolable." Her voice was strained and barely above a whisper.

Henry stepped closer. Misery pooled tears in her eyes, and it took effort for her to speak.

He wished he had been more forceful with his demands to speak to her after Sarah's birth. One person stood in his way every time.

"Millicent." He loosed a few choice curses. "She convinced everyone that you had rejected the baby and refused to see the child." He rubbed his pounding temple. "I was a fool to listen to that wicked woman."

"You believe now that she had come to spread lies and rumors to separate us?" Surprise highlighted her tone. She stopped and turned toward Henry as if to search for truth.

Guilt burned his conscience. He nodded. There was nothing he could do to fix the past. Regret was a heavy burden. Millicent had caused so much damage and would pay for her lies. "I'm sorry for ever doubting you."

They led the two horses and walked in silence.

"Can you tell me where you've been?" Henry kept his tone low to hide the anger that still simmered beneath his chest and threatened to burst through, demanding an accounting for every day she'd been missing.

"I—"

"Stop them!"

The shout had Evangeline and Henry drawing their weapons. A team of runaway horses sped toward them. The driverless wagon they pulled lost a barrel then another with every bump in the road. The loud crashes of splintering oak and pungent odor of the ale spilling out spurred the frightened animals into a frenzied need of escape.

As if with one thought, Henry and Evangeline stepped into their path, shouting and waving their hands. The frightened team veered off the road onto a freshly plowed field stopping the rampage as the heavy wagon sunk into the soft earth.

Two men on horseback raced up. One stopped before them and the other veered off toward the field.

"Thank you. I feared they would run over some poor souls." The older man dismounted and reached out his hand toward Henry. "Your bravery and quick action were the answer to prayer." He gave a polite nod to Evangeline, though his brows shot up when he realized she was a woman dressed in manly attire. The younger man dismounted when he reached the team and worked to calm them.

"Sir, as a reward for saving your wagon may I ask a favor?" Henry knew his ragged appearance hardly called for such as he was about to ask. He drew what energy he had to stiffen his posture and hopefully reflect his high-born heritage.

"Depends." The man was now suspicious, his hand rested on his weapon. "What 'tis it you want?"

"Your mounts." Henry raised his hands at the man's obvious suspicion. "We only need to borrow them to get to the port and will leave them at the nearest livery." He offered the reins of his mount. "We will leave our horses in exchange."

"I don't think..." The man glanced at their sheathed weapons, clutched his horse's reins and backed away.

"Please, sir. Our daughter has been kidnapped, and we must reach the port before the kidnapper sells her." Evangeline's voice cracked with emotion, and tears streamed from her eyes. "Our horses are exhausted from the chase."

The older man could no more resist Evangeline's plea than Henry had been able to deny her anything she asked of him. His conscience burned at the one time he refused to give her what she wanted. He hadn't sent Millicent away, and it had cost him everything.

"We rode by a mean-lookin' blighter with an eye patch walkin' into town with a bawlin' baby in a bag. That your child?"

"Yes! Please. He has our daughter, Sarah." Evangeline grabbed the man's hand, which caused him to harrumph and clear his throat, fighting the emotion that clouded his features at her plea.

"Here, take Brownie. He's a strong mount and can easily carry the both of you. Town's just a few minutes away." He dismounted and handed Evangeline the reins but continued to eye Henry with distrust. "I'll see to it your horses are cared for at the livery. Just leave Brownie tied to the post outside the pub. It's just across the road from the docks."

"May the Lord bless you for your kindness." She gave him a peck on the cheek that caused the man to turn crimson.

A flash of jealousy caused Henry's thank-you to sound more like a grumbled curse.

Henry mounted the horse first then reached down to assist Evangeline.

"Wait." She grabbed the bag off her mount, returned and handed it and her sword up to him.

They linked forearms, and he swung her up behind him. Henry handed her the sword first, which she sheathed at her waist, then gave her the bag. He waited while she settled the long strap at an angle to rest behind her back and placed her hands on Henry's waist.

"I'm ready." She snuggled close enough he could feel the heat from her body pressed against him.

Eighteen months apart and all the anguish she had caused him, yet she still stirred him like no other woman. Already he felt the heat of need for her course through him.

He kicked the horse with more vigor than he had intended. The big gelding leapt forward into a bone jarring gallop.

Evangeline tightened her grip, elevating his torture. He flexed his injured muscles allowing the searing pain to clear his thoughts.

The man was right. Brownie turned out to be a sturdy steed with a stride that ate up the distance. Henry tried to concentrate on the ride but Evangeline's nearness caused his thoughts to wander to areas best not explored.

They rode past the body of a horse lying beside the road. The brigand had ridden the poor beast to death.

Prayers for Sarah's safety pushed all other thoughts from his mind.

Soon they were close enough to the port to smell the salt air. The high-pitched screech of sea birds might have easily been mistaken for a child's cry. Henry pressed his heels into Brownie's side for more speed.

CHAPTER 17

*E*vangeline clung to Henry to keep from slipping from Brownie's broad back, but also because of a sudden overwhelming need to be close to him. Tears stung her eyes as the memories of their courtship and marriage flooded her thoughts. They'd once had such a close bond of love and mutual respect, which few high-born couples of the realm would ever experience.

She knew by the way he leaned slightly to the right that the pain from his injuries was dictating his posture. Just as she knew no matter how bad that pain, nothing would stop him from saving Sarah. A sense of pride swelled within her for her husband.

The shouts of people bargaining for fish meant they had arrived at their destination. Henry slowed Brownie to a walk and stopped him in front of the tavern as the horse's owner had requested.

Evangeline slid down. The extra weight of the sword and bag of supplies almost toppled her over in her exhaustion.

Henry grimaced as he dismounted, his lips pale and pinched,

his brow furrowed by pain. He paused for a moment, steadied by a hand on the horse, and straightened to his full height.

She adjusted the bag so she could reach inside and pulled out two strips of dried beef, handing him one.

Hearty aromas of roasting meat and ale from the pub enticed the passersby from the opened doors and tortured her with much needed nourishment.

Her stomach rumbled loudly followed by an equally demanding growl from Henry's mid-section.

"Here. We need to eat. There's no time to stop for a proper meal, but we'll need our strength for when we find Sarah."

"Thank you." He nodded without making eye contact then took a big bite of the jerky and chewed. "Let me have the sword."

She stepped back to refuse but saw only concern in his eyes, not doubt that she could use it. The relief she felt at releasing it to him surprised her. It felt good to let him take charge. Then she knew. God was really in charge, and she could trust Him, too.

The noise of the crowd that bustled about the busy port on market day made it easy for Evangeline to remain silent. She and Henry walked side by side toward the wharf, where two ships were being loaded with supplies. Weariness kept their pace slow, but the dried beef was already giving her some much needed energy.

"There!" Henry hurried toward a ship with Spanish markings.

Evangeline couldn't see what alarmed him, but she shifted the bag of supplies behind her to free both of her hands, drew her knife, and sprinted after him, afraid she'd lose sight in the throng of people.

"Sarah!" Henry's cry sent a rush of fear through Evangeline. There on the gang plank was the brigand handing over their child to an older man in captain's attire. At Henry's cry, the brigand turned toward them and drew a knife from his belt.

As she caught up with Henry, he pointed to the man disappearing down the gangway and handed her the sword.

"Go. Save our daughter. I'll take care of this vermin." He glanced around him and grabbed a long pike with a hook at the end used to snag the ropes of docking ships. It would make a lethal weapon in the hands of a warrior. Henry swept it in front of him to clear the spectators.

"Cast off!" The captain held the child tightly against his chest, and raced up the gangway toward the deck of the ship yelling orders at his crew. "Repel all boarders!"

Evangeline swung her sword with precision disabling all in her path and made it aboard. A sailor with arms the size of Christmas hams stepped into her path. He grabbed for her. She sidestepped and smacked him up along the side of his head with the flat of her blade. The strength of the impact staggered her back, and the sailor dropped to the deck unconscious at her feet.

A growl turned her toward another deckhand charging toward her waving a knife with deadly intent. She barely had time to raise her sword when he ran into it. The look of surprise lit his features before he fell, his life's blood spilling onto the deck. Using her skill with the sword, she had managed to only wound or disable her opponents up to now. She had not intended to kill anyone, but a flash of regret for his death was all she allowed. She had to save her daughter and would allow no one to stand in her way. A wave of panic washed over her when she swept the deck with her gaze. Where was the captain? She spotted a doorway and two men guarding it.

"That child is my daughter," she shouted. "Move out of my way or die." The fierce tone of a mother's determination must have shown on her face, for the men stepped aside offering no further resistance and let her pass.

With a quick glance behind to make sure none pursued, she opened the door and slipped through. She went down a set of stairs into a long mahogany-paneled passageway lined with many doors. Ignoring the overstated opulence of the exotic wood carvings and fine craftsmanship, she paused to listen. A baby's cry led her to the third door on the right. Locked. She jammed the blade of her sword into the space between the door and the frame and pried. The wood splintered. The door swung open.

Inside, Sarah lay on a narrow bunk, tightly wrapped in bunting, which pinned her arms to her side and kept her from flailing. Her daughter's tears tore at Evangeline's heart. She rushed toward the baby, dropped the sword and drew her knife to free her child from the soiled cloth binding her.

Slam!

The door to the room shut and nails pounded into the frame. She was trapped.

"Senora, you have done enough damage. You will be my guest as long as you care for the child." His English was tainted by a thick Spanish accent, but his intent was clear enough. She would live as long as he needed her, not a minute more.

"You have stolen my child and will pay with your life, Senor." Evangeline spoke to him in Spanish. "I am Lady Evangeline Stanton. My husband, Lord Henry Stanton, is the king's cousin. Kidnapping me and my child is an act of war."

"You lie!" The guttural cursing that followed was that of an uneducated commoner. That the captain of this ship had wealth meant he was most likely a pirate and not above killing or stealing to get what he wanted. "You do not fight or dress as a lady of the realm. Why should I believe you?"

Shouts of the crew sounded, then heavy footsteps hurried away from her door. With a loud creak, the ship lurched to one side then righted as the sails unfurled and gathered wind. They were underway.

God help us.

~

*H*enry pushed through the crowd until he found the murdering thief that stole his daughter. "Stop. You cannot escape."

The brigand swung his knife at Henry and tried to back away into the crowd, but they pushed him toward Henry. Once within reach, Henry knocked the brigand to the ground unconscious. He stood over him with enough hatred to run the man through for what he'd done. The crowd that stood apart during the fight now closed in.

"Get me some rope to tie up this murdering kidnapper." He straightened and drew a calming breath. Revenge was within his grasp, and yet he had hesitated. The man was guilty as sin. No judge would fault him. Then he knew. The Judge of all mankind was the one he needed to please. He had warned him that vengeance was His.

"Hey, *Your Lordship*, the Spanish ship has sailed." Laughter rang out around him. The man pointed to the escaping ship.

"I am Lord Henry Stanton. I need a fast sailing ship to go after that vessel."

"And what you got for coin, *your Lordship*?" A weathered-skinned salty smirked from the crowd.

"I am the king's cousin and he'll see that your fee is doubled." Henry knew his shabby appearance was a hindrance to his claim. "My wife and child have been kidnapped. I need your help...please." His voice wavered with emotion.

"No royal says please. You're a fake." Many voices rose in agreement.

"I'll take ye." A small man with white hair stepped forward. His face wrinkled and weathered into burnished leather. His eyes were a piercing blue that narrowed as they pinned Henry with a stare, as if he could see past his ragged appearance to the truth. "Come along, laddie, or we'll miss the tide."

A Scotsman. The Scots were sworn enemies to the English realm. Could he trust him? Did he have a choice? No. If he wanted a chance to catch the Spaniard, he needed to pursue now.

Henry jerked the bound brigand to his feet and shoved him before him, trailing after the captain and wishing he had soldiers to assist him in battle once they reached the Spaniard's ship.

"My ship's the Sea Hawk. As fine a vessel as ever sailed. We'll catch 'em." The captain's pride in his ship was evident in its well-maintained condition.

The crowd parted so they could move to the docked ship. The captain issued orders that sent his crew scurrying into action. Leaving two men behind to protect the abandoned cargo that waited to be loaded on the dock, the rest of the crew made ready to sail.

A glimpse toward the full sails of the fast retreating ship suddenly overwhelmed Henry. Where were they headed on this endless ocean? It could be anywhere. He couldn't get his breath for the panic that threatened him with the thought that he might never see his family again.

"Please, God, help us all." Henry's plea came from deep within him.

He gave the captive brigand an angry shove up the gang-plank, but halted midway as a commotion drew his attention to the street. A miracle.

A half dozen of the king's guards galloped into the village and stopped at the dock.

Energized by the quick answer to prayer, Henry handed his captive over to the nearest sailor with orders to watch him before he hurried down to greet the men on shore.

"Lord Henry." The commander of the guards saluted.

"Commander Garrett." He slapped his friend on the shoulder. "I'm very glad you're here."

"All aboard!" A crew member shouted down at Henry.

"Come, my daughter has been kidnapped by a Spanish captain. We must leave posthaste." Commander Garrett motioned to a man who stood gawking from the doorway of the stable across the street. The stable hand dropped the rake in his hand and hurried over to them.

"These animals are the property of the King of England. I'm placing them in your care and protection until we return." Commander Garrett handed the man some coins and promised more when they retrieved the horses.

As the guards gathered their gear off their mounts, a commotion broke out in the street. Amidst loud cursing, a sailor staggered out of the pub and shoved through the crowd.

"Wait. What have you done with my ship?" His slurred words were in Spanish. "I'm first mate. They can't sail without me." His alarm and drunken condition had him stumbling into the guards before he fell at their feet.

"It appears as if we have a crew member left behind from the fleeing ship. Bring him." The commander ordered then turned to Henry. "The man may know where his ship is headed."

"Good thinking." Henry nodded his approval then preceded the men aboard the Sea Hawk. Two of the guards gathered up the wailing seaman and took him aboard.

Angry crewmembers blocked the Englishmen's entrance until the ship's captain issued a harsh command in Gallic that sent them grumbling back to their jobs. Scotsmen and Englishmen confined on the same ship... *God, save them all.*

Once the ship was in full sail, Henry explained to the captain and the commander about the events leading up to and including taking the one-eyed brigand prisoner. His brief mention of Evangeline also being aboard the Spaniard's ship raised the commander's brow, but he remained silent. Henry would explain to his friend later.

He made his way to the bow and watched for even a speck of the Spanish ship. With the information from the drunken sailor on the direction the ship was headed, the captain was convinced they could catch them within a few hours if the winds were favorable.

If not, well, then Henry would follow the Spaniard to the ends of the earth to save his family.

CHAPTER 18

*E*vangeline found a bucket of water and was able to get little Sarah cleaned with none of the fussing she usually made when her face was wiped. She had examined her daughter from head to toes and found only minor bruises from the rough handling. A prayer of thanksgiving came out with a sob of relief releasing the knot of anger and fear she'd refused to give leave before now.

Little Sarah rubbed her eyes with chubby fists but managed to drink a cup of the goat milk before she fell fast asleep. Curious. The poor dear must have been exhausted from her mistreatment. She cuddled Sarah until she was satisfied her daughter was fine then laid the sleeping child on the narrow bunk. Placing the babe against the wall, she protected her from rolling off with a folded blanket. Her daughter's sweet face was puffy and red from all of her crying, but sleep smoothed her features with peace. How could anyone mistreat such a precious child?

Anger again flamed within her. Though she'd hope to fulfill her vow of revenge, she would be satisfied if Henry had made the brigand pay with his life.

A shiver of apprehension chilled her body, and she rubbed her arms. She never expected to see Henry again, and certainly never expected to feel the attraction as strong as ever when she wrapped her arms around him during the ride to town.

She still loved her husband in spite of it all. How could that be?

God forgives us as we forgive those who trespass against us.

Husbands, maybe, but did that include brigands and pirates?

She stopped her pacing and glanced out of the small glass-and-brass porthole. No pursuing sails. Only a vast ocean which met a billowing bank of darkening clouds low on the horizon.

The motion of the ship in full sails made it hard to stand. The hull crashed against the waves taking them farther and farther away.

Where was Henry? She knew he would find them. Peace warmed her like a hug. The weariness she'd ignored until now refused to be denied.

Evangeline slipped off her shoes and joined her sleeping daughter. She traced Sarah's soft features with her fingertips. Intense, fierce love of a mother for her child rose from deep within her.

"God, please keep us safe and bring Henry to us." She closed her eyes and whispered every prayer she could remember for protection until sleep overtook her.

Pounding on the door startled her awake. The room was dark. A moment of worry had her examine Sarah, but she could tell by her steady breathing, the babe remained asleep. Strange. The racket should have awakened her. Evangeline slipped from the bunk, then made sure the blanket remained wedged against her child. It should keep her from rolling out onto the hard floor as the ship rose and fell with every ocean swell.

Groggy from sleep, she padded barefoot toward the door.

"Shush. The baby is asleep," she admonished the noise maker.

"Capitan Fernando wants to speak with you, Senora."

"You can tell the captain that *I want* to return to England immediately." She made certain her voice held authority.

"No, Senora. He will not turn around. His wife, Isadora, is very sad after the still birth of her child. Capitan hopes a child will make her happy and she will get well." The man sighed. "Please, Senora, speak with him."

Her stomach growled loudly.

"He will give you food."

"I will speak with him, but I will not leave my sleeping daughter."

"I will tell him." Retreating footsteps echoed down the hall.

The thought of food made her lightheaded. The last pieces of dried beef had sustained her for a while, but her stomach ached for more. She needed to keep up her strength for Sarah's sake.

Heavy treads stopped outside her cabin. The sound of nails being pulled out of the frame followed with the door swinging open. Three men lined the narrow hall. The large man holding a heavy iron crowbar stood closest. With an anxious glance at Evangeline, he stepped aside, and the captain filled the doorway.

"You dare defy me?" He took one step inside, his voice deep and intense. "Because you are distraught, I will let that pass... this time only." A frown furrowed his brow, and his dark eyes flashed with anger. He waved another man inside. This one held a tray covered with a linen cloth. With a nervous glance, the servant sidestepped Evangeline and placed the tray on a small table with ornate edges, which was bolted to the floor to keep it from shifting on a moving ship. The servant then lit the two hanging lanterns in the small room before escaping into the hall.

"Sit. Eat. Then we talk." The captain leaned against the doorway and motioned toward the table.

Evangeline was too hungry to argue. Facing the Spaniard, she lifted the cloth. Crusty bread that had been seasoned and brushed with olive oil teased her senses. After a tentative smell, she took a bite. It tasted surprisingly good. She glanced up at the captain and saw a smile touch the corners of his mouth. He had won this battle. Let him. She needed strength and he had foolishly supplied what she needed to defeat him.

The wine he supplied was good, but not supreme. She could live with good, although it had a bitter aftertaste. Another sip to wash down the bread made her smile with appreciation.

"I see you like our Spanish wine, yes?" His tone was full of pride. "My wife's family owns a vineyard where this was made."

"It's not as good as French wines, but it's palatable." She dabbed her lips with the linen napkin that accompanied her meal.

"The French, ha." He spit on the ground and wiped his mouth on the sleeve of his blouse. "They do not hold a candle to our wine, women, or warriors."

At the mention of warriors, Evangeline swung her gaze to her sword wedged against the bunk just out of arm's reach. The captain had edged forward during their conversation and now lunged for her weapon. Evangeline reached it first and pointed it at the captain's chest.

"I shall retain this." She watched the captain hesitate. By his expression of alarm there was no doubt he had been told of her expertise with the weapon.

"Senora, you do not need this." He gave a dismissive wave at the deadly blade but backed toward the open door. "You are safe under my protection. I have given orders. No one on this ship will dare harm you or the child."

"*My* child." She took a battle stance with the sword raised and stepped toward him, all thought of food gone. "My husband, Lord Henry Stanton, favored cousin of the King of England, will come for us as surely as the sun rises. God and England will avenge any who stand in our way to protect our daughter."

"We will speak later, after you have rested." The door slammed followed by mumbled voices too low to understand. Footsteps receded, but the shadow under the door revealed the presence of a guard.

Fine. She had no place to go at the moment. She checked on her still sleeping daughter. Assured that Sarah was safe and comfortable, she went back to finish her interrupted meal, but kept the sword close by her side. Stomach satisfied for now, she took one last sip of wine. The bitter aftertaste kept her from enjoying it.

Rolling her shoulders, she fought a sudden heaviness in her limbs. She must remain alert, rested, and fed to be ready to fight when the time came.

She stretched and paced a few steps, but the effort became too much. The sword slipped from her fingers. She couldn't keep her eyes open. Anger burned in her gut with the realization that the tainted wine must had been drugged. Sarah's undisturbed sleep was no doubt also a product of that sleeping draught. With determined effort, she made it to the bunk to lie beside her daughter then fell into a deep and dreamless sleep.

～

*H*enry paced the deck when not searching the horizon for the Spanish ship.

"Lord Stanton, please. Ye must eat and rest. I have men who will alert us when they spot our adversary." The ship's captain motioned him inside the cabin.

A quick glance up at the crow's nest then down at the bow of the ship, where men scanned the vast ocean, even one with a spy glass, confirmed the captain's claim. A wave of hunger pushed Henry to precede the captain to his quarters, where a table was set with crusty bread, dried meat and ale to drink. He collapsed onto a chair, weak in the knees. His body needed nourishment if he wanted to be fit for the fight that was surely coming when they caught up to the man who kidnapped his wife and child.

Commander Garrett joined the captain and Henry moments later.

"The man we captured is the Spanish ship's first mate. He'd been in the tavern when his captain sailed without him. After a bit of persuading, he told us the captain's destination." Commander Garrett pressed his finger on a spot on the map which was laid out on a long shelf against the wall. He found his place at the table, filled his plate and dug into his meal with the zeal of a hungry man. "I also questioned the one-eyed man with the information you gave us."

"And learned what?" Henry asked.

"He confirmed that Lady Millicent had hired him to kill Lady Evangeline and the child." He paused to take a sip of ale. "She will hang for what she's done."

Confirmation was a harsh reality. Millicent believed she had gotten away with Evangeline's murder and the deaths of her servants and guards. Then, when she failed to get him to bed her or take her as his wife in Evangeline's place, she'd hired the brigand again, this time to kill little Sarah.

Henry fumed silently as the commander continued.

"Apparently the brigand's not ashamed of his profession, for there was no remorse as he told of his evil deeds. He bragged how he had gotten away with murder and how he would yet escape the executioner's ax."

"That is not possible." Henry stood and paced the small room.

"If he believes he will escape, he is a fool." The commander turned to the captain. "How long before we overtake the Spaniard?"

. . .

"We left the bulk of our cargo on the dock, which has lightened our load. That should make us faster than the more heavily burdened Spanish ship. Even though they have a head start, with a steady wind at our back, we should catch up by early morn." The captain smiled with assurance. "They will not escape."

Henry took his seat and resumed eating. The food he forced himself to consume could have been sawdust, though the other men at the table appeared to appreciate it. Worry kept him from tasting even the hearty ale he used to wash down his meal, but he could feel strength return to his limbs.

"Sorry, we did not arrive in time, Lord Stanton. We followed as soon as we heard of your mission to save your daughter." The commander wiped his mouth and leaned back. "I left behind my second in command, Captain Armand Degraff, who is familiar with the area, and several good men who will report to Lord Brighton and aid him as needed to deal with the imposter who kept him hostage."

"Good." Henry took a breath, relieved that he would have some good news to share with Evangeline when he saw her.

A frantic knock came on the door. The servant frowned and stepped out. Anxious whispers from outside caused the captain to rise, excuse himself, and also exit the room. Moments later he returned, his brow furrowed.

"We have a storm squall gathering to the north and headed our way." He glanced at the half-eaten meal and his guests. "I suggest you stay here, Lord Stanton, and get some rest." The captain motioned for the king's guard to come with him. "Commander, you and your men will be safer below, strapped to your bunks. It will be rough seas until it passes." He motioned for the guard to follow the sailor waiting in the hall. The captain turned and faced Henry. "The Spaniard is a ruthless man. Some say he was once a black-hearted pirate who captured a merchant's ship. The story goes that he fell in love with the captain's lovely daughter, who was on board the vessel. The short of it, they married, and she made an honest man of him. Now he be the captain of the very same merchant ship he once captured. As a pirate, he's experienced sailing rough seas. Yur family should be safe with him. Try naught to worry. We will catch him when this storm blows o'er." With that he shut the door and left.

A servant came in to secure the cabin by clearing away the food and drink and gathering the dirty dishes. His anxiousness was evident in his worried features and hurried actions. His refusal to make eye contact with Henry and the man's mumbled prayers to the saints meant the young sailor was expecting the worst.

When the servant left, Henry prayed also.

"God, please keep my family safe." His selfish request burned his conscience. "And protect these brave men and the ship as they fight the storm. Use the wind to speed us toward Evangeline and Sarah." He stretched out on the captain's bunk and secured the three straps at his foot, chest and middle to keep him from rolling out.

Would life ever be peaceful again? His last thought before sleep claimed him.

CHAPTER 19

*E*vangeline awoke to the cabin door closing and a vague
memory or dream of a violent storm. A quick glance at
Sarah found her awake and staring back, a watery fist stuck in
her mouth. The toddler flung out her wet hand and touched
Evangeline's face, smiled and cooed, "Mum, Mum, Mum."

She gathered her daughter into a tight hug, tears of joy
running down Evangeline's cheeks. "Yes. I am your mum, sweet
baby."

Loud voices erupted outside the cabin door. Instantly, the
chill of danger pricked her neck. She pushed Sarah behind her,
sat up, and swung her legs over the side. The room swam, and
she braced her hands on either side to keep from tumbling to
the deck. The grogginess and pounding head were the afteref-
fects of the drug put in the wine to put her and Sarah to sleep.

Panic thrummed against her chest as men conversed outside
the cabin door. The cabin was disheveled. The few items that
had not been secured were strung about the small space. Besides
a violent squall in the night, one sweeping glance confirmed
she'd had a visitor while she was sleeping. The dishes from her
meal were missing, as was her sword which, she had tucked

next to her side. Patting the bulge in her waist band confirmed the intruder had not found the knife she kept hidden in her sash or the one in the heavy cross she wore.

"God will provide and help us when the time comes." She smiled and patted her daughter's cheek. No point in worrying about something she could not change. She took a deep breath and blew it out slowly, allowing the frustration to depart. Her focus needed to be on Sarah. The movement of the ship was minimal. Perhaps the sails were down. The sounds of pounding and saws above deck probably meant the crew was making repairs from the storm. Hopefully nothing serious had broken. All they had to do is keep the boat afloat until Henry arrived to get her and Sarah.

The dizziness almost gone, she drew another cleansing breath and stretched to release the kink in her back. A quick scan of the small room drew her attention to a fancy gown which had been left draped across one of the chairs.

Gathering Sarah and resting the babe on her hip, she walked to the garment. A bit flashy for her simple taste, yet it was crafted of fine silk. The blue shade was the color of delphiniums like her mother had loved and planted in her flower garden.

Evangeline stroked the soft material and sighed. It had been a very long time since she'd worn silk against her skin. After setting Sarah on the floor, she picked up the dress and pressed it against her body. It should fit. The style was high-waisted, but the bodice was cut too low for her comfort. She swirled the cloud of silk in a swishing motion that sent the little girl into a fit of giggles.

"You like this, too?" She knelt down when Sarah pulled up using the dress, fisted the material, and tugged. With gentle patience, Evangeline untangled Sarah's fingers from the delicate fabric, then cuddled the toddler.

"Your father will make sure you have many such fine dresses as you grow up." With a quick prayer for Henry's safety, she stood and placed the garment out of Sarah's reach. Smoothing the few wrinkles, her hand dislodged a piece of paper. Evangeline stooped and pick it up from the floor.

Capitan demands you discard the rags you have on and wear this to join him. He has food for you and the child. If you refuse, you will both go hungry.

The note had been carefully penned in English.

Fury burned within Evangeline at the very thought of the pirate giving her orders. She would rather starve than comply. Fuming, she paced the small space disparaging the note and the man who sent it.

A demanding squawk came from Sarah, who stood on wobbly legs hugging the bunk, trying to maintain her balance with the moving ship. She was done playing and wanted to eat again.

The goat's milk was nearly gone. There was not enough to satisfy her little tummy. For that reason alone, Evangeline would submit to the captain's threat.

As little Sarah's fussing built to a demanding wail, Evangeline removed her tunic and pants, then tugged on the undergarments left on the other chair and finally the dress. They did fit, though the dress was cut too low and fit snug across the top, revealing way too much cleavage. Tugging the garment higher didn't help.

At a tap at the door, she hastily tore a strip of lace from the hem of the petticoat and stuffed it in the offending gap. Hopefully it would remain in place long enough to get through the meal.

"Senora, Capitan awaits. Are you...? Stop! You cannot be down here." The man's voice raised in alarm.

Angry shouts erupted into a loud altercation of men fighting with the distinct sounds of flesh pounding against flesh and bodies hitting against the walls.

She gathered Sarah, quickly wrapped her in a blanket, and shoved her in the small closet at the end of the bunk. The child howled when Evangeline closed the door, which broke her heart, but she needed Sarah to be safe while she dealt with whoever fought to get inside her cabin. She grabbed her knife from the table where she had laid it while she dressed and hid it in the folds of the dress at her side as the cabin door slammed open hitting the wall.

"You killed my brother!" The man with the Christmas ham-sized arms filled the doorway. The guard lay bleeding on the deck behind him. Fury lit the standing man's features, and in his fist he held a knife with curved blade crimson with blood. He advanced toward Evangeline. Bloodshot eyes narrowed with intent, and the strong smell of ale carried on his breath.

"Mum, mum, mum." Sarah sorrowful plea was like a splash of cold water.

Fierceness born of a mother's love strengthened her limbs. Her thoughts cleared.

"Your brother fell upon my sword and killed himself." Evangeline's voice came out a husky growl. She stood her ground, her mind filled with lessons learned as a teen for such a time as this. Her dress would restrict her movements. If only he had appeared while she still wore the tunic and pants she would be more agile and less encumbered. She gripped the hilt of the knife, freed it from its hiding place and tensed, readied for her moment.

Loud voices and heavy footsteps echoed from the hallway.

"Stop, Raoul! You harm this woman or child, and I will personally hang you upside down from the yardarm and strip the flesh off your miserable body, inch by agonizing inch."

Raoul hesitated, the fury in his eyes changing to doubt. "She killed my brother."

"Miguel killed himself when he charged her. She turned and raised her sword, and he ran into it." The captain stepped inside the already cramped space. "Drop your weapon and live."

Evangeline eyed the madman and pressed back to the end of the bunk, prepared to defend the closet where her daughter wailed.

The captain lunged forward, knocking the knife from Raoul's hand with a loud crack of breaking bones. Two sailors pressed inside and wrestled the crazed man. Even with a broken arm, the man fought against his captors, breaking the table and chairs in their battle. Evangeline kept out of the fray by pressing back against the closet.

More well-placed blows by the captain as the sailors cornered the vengeful brother rendered him bleeding about the face and neck and nearly unconscious.

"I will kill you all," he bellowed as he was dragged up the stairs and out on deck. His angry screams turned to pleas, each word echoed through the corridor. "No! No!"

A loud splash, then silence.

"There. No worry. He will no harm you or the child." He shrugged as if that was the only just punishment for such a crime. "No one defies my orders and lives." The tone of the warning was directed at Evangeline. The captain smiled showing one gold tooth. He pushed aside the broken furniture to allow Evangeline a path through the debris and reached out to her.

Evangeline ignored his hand and retrieved her crying daughter, rocking her in her arms.

"Good. You please me by wearing the dress." He smiled and gestured to the open door. "We shall eat now."

"Capitan! We are being pursued." A sailor skidded to a halt before them, his face flushed and his breath coming in short gasps. "It is the Sea Hawk. She is gaining and will be within grappling range within the hour."

"I know the captain of the Sea Hawk. He is a good man. Why would he be pursuing me?" He turned and stared at Evangeline. "Tell me the truth. Was that man fighting on the docks your husband?"

"Yes. Lord Henry Stanton." She cradled her daughter on her hip while hiding her knife behind her. "I told you. That brigand stole my daughter. Would you allow someone to kidnap your only child and get away?"

"He assured me the child was an orphan of royal blood without mother or father to care for her upbringing. He warned me to leave immediately, for those pursuing him meant to harm the child." The captain searched her face then rubbed his chin. Even the slightest hesitation in the stern pirate's countenance gave Evangeline hope for a peaceful end.

"We are her parents. Henry will not hinder you from your journey home *if* you let Sarah and me go." She straightened to a more regal posture. "I give you my word."

"I will think on it." The Spanish captain glanced down at Sarah then stepped out of the cabin and gave the sailor a quick order before striding off.

The crewman gave her an anxious glance and slammed the door closed.

CHAPTER 20

*H*enry splashed water in his face to banish the weariness from his eyes and readied to go above deck. The few times he'd fallen asleep, his dreams had been as turbulent as the storm that tossed the ship on giant waves all through the night.

A clipped knock at the door sounded before it opened.

"Good to see ye be awake, laddie." The captain smiled, though his tired features exposed his weariness. A servant pressed by the captain and put down a tray of the same food of dried meat and bread. Their limited stores were due to the supplies left on the shore.

"It looks as though you could use this fine bunk about now." Henry waited for the captain to sit.

"Aye, 'tis true. Sleep would be nice, but I have good news that canna wait." He motioned to the food. "Sit, eat. There is much to discuss." The captain sunk into a chair and dug into his food then motioned for Henry to do the same.

"Tell me your news, then I'll eat." Henry sat directly across from the captain.

"We've spotted the Spanish ship ahead." The captain shoved another bite of bread into his mouth and chewed.

"How long before we board her?" Henry stood unable to keep from pacing.

"An hour, more or less." He took a swig of strong tea, to which, by the smell, he had added a small measure of whisky. "Plenty of time for you to eat. Ye'll need yur strength when we catch 'em." He paused and gave Henry a stern look. "Unless you'd prefer to let yur guards rescue yur family while ye wait in safety aboard my ship."

"What? No. I demand to be the first aboard to rescue my family." Henry said, fists clenched at his side.

"Then eat." The captain smiled.

"You're right." With a sigh of resignation, Henry took a portion of dried lamb, stale bread and poured himself some hot tea. With every bite his body grew stronger. His ribs still ached but not enough to keep him from doing what he must to fight off the Spaniards and save Sarah and Evangeline. He drained his cup of the strong tea.

"Thank you, Captain, for the food." A nudge of conscience made him continue. "And for all you've done."

Captain Fritz stood and walked over to a small wardrobe at the end of the room. "I think ye'll have need of this shortly." He handed Henry a sword with a royal crest emblazoned on the front of the hilt.

"The house of Cornwall?" He rubbed his thumb across the crest of an eagle's outstretched claws. He had never heard of this clan.

"'Tis something I acquired in my travels." A sharp knock sounded, then a sailor opened the cabin door. The captain walked to the doorway to converse with him, his words too low to hear, but the sailor's expression was that of a serious matter. Without a word to Henry, Captain Fritz and the servant stepped out of the cabin leaving Henry alone.

He rolled his shoulders to loosen his stiff muscles then swung the newly acquired sword to limber his arm. Shifting into a fighting stance, he thrust the borrowed weapon out with force as if to impale a certain Spanish captain. A sharp pain in his side sucked the breath out of him. Weakness in front of his enemy was not an option. Determination and a few more jabs helped assure him he could endure. Using a few more maneuvers to get familiar with the weight and hilt, he was satisfied that the sword would do well in a fight. It was finely crafted and exceptionally well balanced.

The loud slap of bare feet pounding against the oak passageway stopped at the cabin. The door was thrust open without a cursory knock.

"Cap'n says come now. We're closing fast on the Spaniard's ship." With that, the young man turned and rushed up the stairs to the deck.

Henry followed on the sailor's heels. When he reached the open air, he was met with a vision of organized chaos as crew members rushed to do their duties at the bark of the first mate's orders.

The anticipation of the eminent battle had the commander and his men armed and ready. They stood at the railing, out of the way of crew. Henry joined them there, his focus on the ship growing larger with each passing swell.

"Dead ahead, Cap'n." A sailor shouted down from his perch in the crow's nest.

"Aye. I see 'er, Davy." Captain Fritz walked toward Henry and the king's guards.

Henry pressed against the ship's railing, hoping to catch sight of Evangeline. He watched the sailors on the Spanish ship running for their posts. The salty mist hit his face with every dip of the hull, cutting through the waves. They were speeding toward his family and his future. "Please, God, keep them safe."

"Aye. With God's help there'll be no blood shed today." The

captain patted Henry on the shoulder. "However, we must be prepared." He motioned to the commander and gathered in the center near the main mast. "Commander, we're not warriors with yur battle experience, but we can fight. You don't live on the sea without knowing a thing or two about how to protect yur ship, crew, and cargo." He spread his feet with the ease of a man used to the movement of the deck beneath him. "I yield to yur leadership in battle. How can we help?"

"I am more used to fighting on solid ground." Commander Garrett grinned. "Therefore, while on board, my men and I are at your command, Captain." He snapped to attention.

The captain of the Sea Hawk nodded his approval. "I suggest you leave yur armor behind and take only yur weapons."

The guards interrupted with mumbled displeasure.

"Laddies, if you be knocked overboard, you'll sink like a rock." As the English guards removed their armor without further comment, the captain gave simple instructions detailing the process of sailing the Sea Hawk alongside the Spaniard's ship and throwing grappling hooks to secure their vessel to the enemy's ship. With that accomplished, the crew would make ready the gangplank for the commander's men to board. He assured them his crew would assist in the taking of the enemy's ship.

"I will board first." Henry's words were addressed to the commander but his eyes never left their destination.

"But..." The commander's protest died in his mouth when Henry turned and scowled at him. "We will be right behind you."

"Our sole objective is to find my wife and child and get them safely back aboard this ship. After that, do whatever necessary to take the Spanish captain captive to answer for his crime of kidnapping." Henry glanced back at the commander, who nodded his agreement, contrary to his pinched lips and scowl of disapproval.

Boom!

The unmistakable explosion of a cannon followed by the swoosh of the projectile arching toward them. The sea exploded in a geyser, rocking the Sea Hawk but not touching it. The cannonball had landed in the ocean directly in front of their ship's bow.

Captain Fritz expression of calm control never wavered as he encouraged all aboard to stand fast.

Another warning shot, this time close to the starboard side, rained sea water across their deck. The crew of the Sea Hawk continued in their duties. No sign of fear shown in their eyes, only determination to follow their captain's orders to the letter.

Admiration swelled in Henry's chest at such dedication of the crew to the man who led them. It said something about the captain's character, which Henry had already concluded was trustworthy and honorable. He would see that the king rewarded this man for his bravery when this was over.

"Bring me the prisoners, Mister Shamish." The captain shouted at his first mate. The man disappeared below deck. Within minutes, he and two other crew members shoved the combatant brigand and the loudly complaining first mate of the Spanish ship toward the waiting captain. "Fasten them to the railing at the bow."

Another cannon ball rocked the ship in a narrow miss. The Sea Hawk was shoved to the right by the large wave, but the helmsman quickly corrected its course.

The prisoners were now chained to the bow, each of the men had a hand left free to show they were uninjured. They waved wildly at the Spanish ship, screaming at them to stop firing.

It worked. No further cannonballs came at them as the Sea Hawk drew near enough to board.

Captain Fritz stood at the railing and nodded to his first mate.

"Give us the woman and child and in exchange we will give you our prisoners." He shouted in Spanish. The first mate's words evoked cursing from the Spanish crew and taunts intended to provoke the sailors of the Sea Hawk, but Captain Fritz's crew restrained themselves from trading insults.

"Give me my first mate, and I will let you live." The man Henry had watched taking Sarah up the gangplank now stood with his hands on his hips and an angry curl of his lips. "If you do not comply, I'll sink you all."

"No, brother!" The first mate's whine had been all in Spanish, but Henry, and apparently Captain Fritz by his grin, understood the language and the leverage they had been given with the man's revelation. "Free me, Juan. What would Isadora say?"

"Shut up, you fool!" The captain cursed the man and glared at Henry and Captain Fritz. He must have recognized their understanding of the new information for he spun on his heel and disappeared from view.

"What now?" Henry turned to Captain Fritz.

"We wait." The Sea Hawk's captain kept his gaze trained on the other ship. His crew waited his orders.

A man's scream of pain was followed by a woman's angry protest in Spanish, then English and Latin. Her appearance on deck was followed closely by a sailor with blood on his tunic.

"Evangeline!" Henry shouted. She held Sarah in her arms.

A hand restrained him from climbing the railing and leaping aboard the other ship. A second glance proved they were not yet close enough for him to have survived that leap. His heart thudded in anticipation for the moment the ships shifted closer. Ropes were being thrown across and secured by each of the crews. Tension was high, every man prepared for battle at the first call to board by either captain.

Evangeline wore a silk gown of blue marred by the coarse material of that ratty bag of hers that she'd strapped across her chest. She gave the long dress an impatient kick with her foot as it impeded her movement. She held fast to Sarah on one hip and wielded a dagger with her free hand.

The Spanish captain motioned for a nearby sailor to restrain her, but the man backed up instead when she pointed the blade at him.

Two more of the crew stepped closer with intent to capture her.

"Don't touch her, or he dies!" Henry's tone was heavy with intent. He held a blade against the Spanish prisoner's throat.

"Go ahead. He is more trouble than he is worth." The Spanish captain spoke in heavily accented English, perhaps to keep his crew from understanding his words.

"No! Please, Juan! Mother of God, save me!" The prisoner sobbed in unrestrained anguish.

All activity halted on both ships. The crew's attention was trained on the scene before them.

The rustle of blue silk caught Henry's eye as Evangeline edged toward the gangplank now connecting the two ships. His heart thumping with fear for his wife and daughter barely allowed enough air to breathe. With determination controlled by experience, he returned his focus to the Spanish captain, who eyed him as if trying to discern if Henry would follow through with his threat. Henry tightened his hold on the prisoner, his eyes narrowed with intent.

"I will let the woman and child go." Capitan Fernando motioned the Sea Hawk crew forward to help Evangeline cross over with the child. "Send my idiot brother-in-law to me." He hesitated then added. "And the one-eyed man."

"Only if you give me your word that you will not fire on us as we leave." Captain Fritz stood, arms crossed, to confront the Spanish captain.

"I swear on my mother's grave that you will not come to harm by me or my crew. You may depart in peace...this time." Captain Fernando's anger at his defeat did not set well by the glint of fury in his dark eyes. "Until next we meet, Captain Fritz." He gave a nearby crewman a hushed order, then turned on his heel and disappeared below deck. The incident was finished as far as he was concerned, but his threat hung in the air like a snake coiled ready to strike when least expected.

With a nod from the Sea Hawk's Captain, Henry dropped his hand and let the crew deal with loosing the prisoners. He rushed to the gangplank and met Evangeline as she stepped aboard.

"Here, let me take the wee lass below. I'll tend to her needs and guard her with my life." An older crewmember with a wrinkled face and kind eyes stepped forward. He reached out toward the child.

~

*E*vangeline felt the tension on deck. Was it possible the Spaniard was waiting for the prisoners to reach his ship then try and take their ship? She wanted Sarah safe and looked to Henry, who nodded his approval before she handed her daughter to the man. He hugged Sarah to his chest, turned and escaped below deck.

The crew pushed the Spaniard's brother-in-law forward, leaving his hands bound in front, and shoved him onto the gangplank. The man scrambled across the narrow plank cursing the whole time. Halfway across, he stumbled and nearly fell into the ocean, but a quick-thinking crewmember aboard the Spanish ship jumped onto the shifting gangplank to grab the ropes binding the Spaniard's hands and jerked him onboard, both landing on the deck in a heap. The crewmember's reward for risking his life was a curse from the ungrateful man and a threat to have the rescuer flogged, as the man disentangled himself and stood. The crew grumbled their disapproval and helped their shipmate up with a pat on the back.

The Sea Hawk's crew adjusted the gangplank then brought the brigand up ready to send him across next. He blanched white when he saw Evangeline face to face.

"You're dead." He gasped. "I killed you." The brigand touched his eye patch and cursed her.

"Yet I live." Evangeline held her dagger high ready to strike.

The brigand screeched in alarm and tried to back away, but one of the king's guards grabbed him by the shoulder.

"Why should your blood be on my hands?" She lowered the knife. "I refuse to be shackled to you or your deed another day. I choose to forgive you." The words of forgiveness tasted like bile, but as soon as they were out, it was as if a huge burden had lifted.

"Well, I don't forgive you." The brigand touched his eye patch with his tied hands then spit on the deck. The guard gave him an angry shove onto the gangplank and waited with raised weapons until he crossed.

The gangplank and ropes were loosed, and the ships drifted apart. The distance between the vessels grew wider with each rise and dip of the swells beneath them.

"Someday God will make him pay for what he's done." Henry drew Evangeline against his side.

As the ships drifted apart and the Sea Hawk's crew made ready to sail, One-eye leaned against the railing and smirked.

"I told you I'd live to seek my revenge another day, unless Lady Millicent gets to you first. She will be very angry that you and that brat still live." He threw Evangeline a kiss. "Until then—"

His words were cut off, when in a scurry of movement, three sailors grabbed him, tied a skiff anchor around his neck, and threw him overboard. He sunk beneath the water instantly. No last defiant words or pleas for mercy.

Evangeline hid her face against Henry's shoulder. "As much as I wanted him punished…"

"I know." Henry turned her away from the departing ship. "He was right when he bragged that he wouldn't see the executioner's blade."

"The confession from the man she hired is your proof. Millicent was behind it all." Her tone was low with barely restrained anger and laced with accusation as she stepped out of his embrace.

"She will not get away with more treachery." He touched her shoulder. "We will need more proof than the last confession of a dead brigand. She is from a powerful family with blood ties to important people in high places."

"That I live is proof enough." She stopped and turned to face him. "If that is not enough, his testimony was heard by the king's men. That witch will not escape the hangman's noose for her crimes." She continued toward the heavy oak door through which her daughter was taken. Determination stiffened her once graceful stride, and the hardened expression of a warrior readied for battle caused the crewmembers in her path to step quickly aside.

Her thoughts were jumbled with anger and worry. How would she explain why she told no one she had survived? Her disappearance and secret life would require an explanation that caused her gut to burn with dread.

CHAPTER 21

*H*enry came up behind Evangeline and put a comforting hand on her shoulder. They entered the galley. Large wood tables lined the room, where the smell of something cooking on an ancient cast iron contraption filled the space. They found Sarah hugged to the cook's side as he paced about, singing to their daughter a happy Scottish tune and laughing at her attempt to sing along.

"She be a bonny lass." The cook saw them and handed over his charge to Evangeline.

After thanking the older man for watching Sarah, the three were escorted to a cabin. The long gown hindered Evangeline's every step until she bunched it in her hand to keep it out of her way. As lovely as the butter-soft material felt against her skin, she missed the freedom of her crudely woven tunic and pants. She had tucked those items inside her bag, but she doubted Henry would approve of her donning them again.

"Here." A crewmember opened the door and stepped aside. "The capt'n hopes ye'll be comfortable in 'ere. He'll speak with ye later."

Henry pressed his hand against her spine to guide her inside. His touch loosed a flash of emotions.

"Since it could take a couple of days to return to England," Henry said, "Captain Fritz insisted we use his cabin during the journey. It's the largest on the ship."

"Where will you be staying?" Heat burned her cheeks, and she couldn't look him in the eye.

"Here with my wife and daughter." His voice was firm, but, with a gentle touch, he raised her chin. Humor and challenge glinted in his eyes. She knew him too well.

Turning out of his grasp, she took Sarah to the only bed in the cabin.

The lock on the door clicked.

"There. We won't be disturbed until I have the answers to all of my questions." The humor was gone from his tone.

"That talk will have to wait. I need to change Sarah." Evangeline cuddled her daughter, who seemed content to watch her parents' discomfort.

A sharp rap caused Henry to mumble a curse, but he unlocked the bolt and opened the door.

"The cap'n wanted to know if I could take the wee bairn back to the galley to feed her some porridge I've made." The older man shifted from foot to foot. "Sorry, I haven't any milk because our stores, including a couple of milk goats, were left behind when we sailed in such a hurry." He glanced up from the deck. "But my five bairn have all grown healthy on this hearty fare." His eyes twinkled with the pride of a father who loved his children.

Scotsman or not, Evangeline trusted him immediately. She snuggled her freshly changed daughter in her arms and walked over to him.

"They call me Capt'n Cook 'cus I rules the galley, but you can call me Billy." He reached for Sarah, who held her arms out to the smiling man.

"This is Sarah." Evangeline handed her over to him once again and brushed a soft curl away from her precious little face.

"I'll bring this sweet lass back to you in a wee while when she grows weary of the company." He cradled the baby with the ease of a man having done it many times, and left singing an off-tune song about flying fish and wild ponies. Sarah giggled. The happy sound stirred joy within Evangeline, who drew a relieved breath. Her family was all together, safe, and headed back to England...and home. Where they called home would certainly be part of their imminent discussion.

Satisfied that her daughter was in good hands, she closed the door and fastened the lock. She turned and saw the surprise in Henry's expression.

"I want answers, too." She slipped passed him and took a chair at the table. He followed and sat directly across from her.

❦

Their sometime heated discussion about why they'd been separated eighteen months lasted for over two hours. Besides the long chain of events leading up to this moment, speaking her mind and Henry doing the same had taken a toll on her, both physically and emotionally. In all that they discussed, she had purposely neglected to mention anything about her part in using the persona of the Fox to rob from the rich and give to the poor. That discussion, if it ever happened, would need to wait for another time and place.

A knock brought Henry to his feet. He stretched, walked to the door and opened it.

"The cap'n said I was to bring this." The sailor brought in a tray of food and drink.

"Where's Sarah?" Evangeline stood and braced herself against the table as exhaustion weakened her limbs.

"The little tike's happy as a princess holding court, with all of the men waitin' on her 'and and foot. The crew has been away from their families for several months and the lil' miss has been a tonic for their lonely hearts." The servant grinned. "I have to hurry back. It's time to feed her again. Cook said I could help this time." He turned at the door. "If it's all right with you, I'll bring her to you afterward." His hopeful expression soothed her doubts.

"As soon as she's fed?" Her voice was low and gravelly from so much talking.

"Aye." He whistled a happy tune, closed the door and walked away. She missed her daughter but the time spent alone with Henry had been fruitful...mostly. Having held on to the bitterness for so long, it was strange to let it go. He had openly answered every question about his involvement or lack thereof with Millicent, and she recognized the truth in his eyes. He regretted having been an unwilling believer of Millicent's lies, but he had never bedded the wicked wench and truly wanted to see her pay for her crimes.

Could they put aside their grief over the past and live as husband and wife again? Did she want to? The physical attraction was still there. She could feel it in Henry, too. But was it enough?

"I love you, Evangeline." Henry encircled her waist from behind. "I always have, from the moment I first laid eyes on you there's been no other woman for me." He turned her around to face him. "You must know deep in your heart that I would never betray you." His lips touched hers with tenderness that lit the fire of passion in both of them. A look. A touch. That was all it had ever taken to ignite the fire between them.

The cabin door opened.

"Oh, sorry, your lordship. I knocked." The cook smiled and dropped his gaze to the deck. "Our wee miss is ready for a cuddle with her mum before she goes to sleep."

Evangeline stepped out of Henry's arms gaining control of her wits in the process and went to Sarah. The baby whimpered and reached past Evangeline to Henry.

"Da, da, da." She leaned out with her arms toward her father, who edged past Evangeline to gather his daughter into his arms.

Guilt and regret rushed over Evangeline at the rejection. She should have been there for Sarah from birth. Tears burned her eyes. She turned away to keep Henry from seeing her hurt and busied herself preparing the bed for her child. There was no way to undo the past or get the time back with her daughter, but they could have a future together. *Please, God help us become a real family.* She swiped away the tears before she glanced up to make sure Henry hadn't noticed.

"Thank you for taking such good care of my...our daughter." Henry cradled Sarah against his chest. Sarah's fist went into her mouth, and she settled into his arms.

"Aye. She's a bonny lass." Billy stepped out of the cabin and closed the door behind him.

"I've kept her near me since her birth. When she's overly tired she wants only me to comfort her." Henry paced around the small space, rocking her in his arms and humming the old lullaby Evangeline had hummed while she was pregnant. It had been the one her mother had sung to her when she was little.

"You remembered." Healing warmth spread through her as she watched him hum and pace until Sarah fell asleep.

"I wanted Sarah to have a connection to you even if you weren't there to sing to her." Was that a hint of chastisement in his tone? He laid her gently on the bunk and tucked a blanket around her.

"I thought my baby had died and you had conspired with Millicent to have me killed. I had no reason to go back to a life with you." Her voice raspy with grief.

"I'm sorry." His tone contrite, he rubbed his face. "I don't blame you." She saw the dark shadows under his eyes and the weariness that lined his features. The long day filled with turmoil, along with his injuries, had worn him down. "I died, too, when I saw the hunting lodge burned to the ground and the bodies of your murdered servants and guards." He turned to face her. "I'd begged God to find you alive after no sign of your body was found within the wreckage. But after weeks of searching produced nothing, you were assumed dead. I poured my grief into raising Sarah. I took her everywhere with me." He sunk down to a chair and pulled Evangeline onto his lap. "God has answered my prayers." Emotion muffled his voice. He cleared his throat, took a deep breath, and released it. "I know what happened to us is going to take some time to get over, but I do not intend to lose you or Sarah ever again. Understand?" His lips lowered to hers. The kiss lingered until both were shaken by the intensity.

"Since the bed will not accommodate all three of us," she said, "I'll make you a pallet on the floor." She longed to believe him, but her suffering had etched deep wounds of suspicion that would take time to heal. If she could forgive a murderous brigand then she should be able to forgive her husband. She pushed out of his arms and braced herself against the table until her legs would hold her. Keeping her focus on her task, she spread out a blanket on the floor and one to cover him. She tried to ignore the sound of him pulling off his tunic. She straightened and noticed the dark purple bruising around his upper torso hadn't faded much since she'd last seen it. His pain must still be intense.

"Let me tend to your wound before you lie down." She took a small bottle of witch hazel out of her bag, dabbed it on a cloth. He caught her hand to stay her.

"I'm fine. It's not as bad as it looks." He smiled when he caught her staring at him then loosed her. "I have missed your touch, but perhaps it would be best if I tend to my wounds this time."

"At least put this against your skin while you sleep. It will help with the pain and swelling." She blushed and handed him the cloth. He accepted the offering and smiled.

"Get undressed and I'll blow out the lanterns. We'll need our rest for once we arrive. The journey back to Brighton Castle will be much more demanding. I fear there may be more battles to wage to set everything aright."

She felt the heat burning her cheeks, her mouth too dry to speak. After only a short time married, she had experienced no embarrassment disrobing in her husband's presence. But now, panic raced up her spine. He would see the scars on her back and be repulsed.

"I'll sleep in this gown." The front was cut low but it had a high back with a starched collar that hid her back.

There had been no mirrors in the convent but she had found two at the abbey hidden behind an old cabinet. The old priest was bald and pious with no need of them. Gilded and very ornate, the platter-sized mirrors had most likely been a gift from a rich parishioner or perhaps penance from a guilt-ridden thief.

After hanging one on the wall, curiosity caused her to use the other to view her back. She had cried for days at what she'd seen. The grotesque puckering of her skin from her burns marred most of her back. The thought brought fresh tears, and a knot of grief settled in her mid-section at her disfigurement.

"Evangeline, we are still married, and you know well that I've memorized every smooth and perfect inch of you." Heat flushed her skin when she met his knowing gaze. He was remembering their days of exploring each other. "However…" He brushed a tear from her eye. "I will turn away so you may get undressed in private." He sat on the pallet with his back toward her.

Ignoring him, she remained clothed but unlaced and kicked off her shoes then slipped onto the bed next to her daughter and covered up. Her back was to him, but she heard him turn down the lantern and settle down. After his breathing grew heavy with sleep, she relaxed. How could she ever resume married life if she remained afraid for him to see her scars?

CHAPTER 22

*A*t the bow of the ship, Henry leaned against the railing, closed his eyes, and lifted his face toward the heavens in prayerful gratitude to God. Contentment filled his heart. Evangeline lived. He had awakened early, fearful it had all been a dream, and relaxed as he watched his wife and daughter sleep. No words could describe his love and joy knowing his family was whole again.

He drew a deep breath and exhaled. His ribs still ached, especially when he stretched, but his body was mending. For the present, he had no pressing responsibilities except to watch over his family.

Movement in the water below him drew his attention. A pod of dolphins sped alongside the ship, leaping and flipping in a watery ballet, then disappeared under the sea. The spectacle made him smile.

They could roam the ocean's depths and tease those who were restricted to the surface. The sight made him long for such freedom. To live a simple life, without the heavy burdens of responsibilities due his birthright, would be foreign to him.

Heaviness tried to blanket him with regret and dread. Once

they reached shore, his life would again be filled with decisions to be made, following the king's dictates, keeping peace, and righting wrongs.

With another deep breath, he shoved away the melancholy that tried to settle on him. There was no place in his life for complaining when his prayers had been answered and his wife and child were safe again. Those blessings were worth the long hours and responsibilities of being titled.

"I thought I'd find you here." Commander Garrett stepped up beside him. "The winds have been extremely favorable. According to the first mate, we should be in sight of English soil by tomorrow's first light." He turned his back on the ocean and faced Henry. "I suggest we start out for Castle Brighton immediately upon arrival. What say you?"

"I agree." Henry had been glad for the brief reprieve, but once docked, he could not postpone the journey back to Brighton to deal with the trouble there. Though with Evangeline again at his side, life would never again be dull or mundane. He smiled. "It would be good to have a carriage or, at the very least, a wagon for Lady Evangeline and Lady Sarah to ride in for the return journey." Keeping her confined to a carriage would keep their pace reasonable...and safe. The thought of trying to keep up with his wife as she raced toward Castle Brighton at breakneck speed, made him cringe with fear. She wouldn't like it, but he would insist she ride in the conveyance for their daughter's sake.

"I will attend to acquiring a carriage the moment we disembark." Commander Garrett returned his gaze to the sea. "It will take longer traveling with a carriage, but if we leave without delay, travel all through the day with only short breaks, we should still be able to make the castle near nightfall."

"Is something bothering you?" Henry asked his old friend.

"I have been tasked with taking Lord Brighton back to

England to be held responsible for the crimes against the crown."

"What?" Evangeline stood behind them, eyes flashing in anger, hands fisted at her side. She took his breath away. Even in her wrinkled gown and windblown hair, she was the image of a warrior princess fit to hold court or wage war. "My father has been held hostage in his own castle. His failing health…"

"No one will take your father anywhere." Henry stepped to her side and faced the commander.

"I have my orders." A sudden flash of concern lit the commander's eyes. He stepped away from the railing, and his hand closed over the hilt of his short sword. "However, I will send a courier to England with the details of what I find. I'm sure once the king knows the truth, he will amend my orders." He planted his feet and straightened his posture, every inch a man used to following orders and commanding his men to do the same. "Until then, I will remain in charge of the castle and sort out the truth. Be assured that I will not act without further orders from the king." He glanced from Henry to Evangeline. "Agreed?"

"Agreed." Henry and Evangeline spoke as one.

"Splendid." The commander slapped his hands together. "I'll leave you now to see what Cook's prepared for us to eat." He turned and left.

"I will not let them accuse my father of crimes he did not commit." She watched the commander's retreat.

"Commander Garrett is a good and reasonable man. I've known him all of my life. He will not cause harm to Lord Brighton." Henry encircled her shoulders with his arm and guided her across the deck toward the galley. "You must know that I will defend your father with my life."

"I know." She relaxed within his embrace. "I'm worried about what has happened since we've been gone."

"I've learned some very hard lessons recently." He stopped

and turned her toward him. "Most important is that I must rely on God to take care of those I love. Second, I am helpless to fix my troubles without Him." He leaned in and kissed her on the top of her head. She lifted her face, and he dropped a kiss on her lips but refrained from deepening it when the crew hooted and whistled.

"We must keep my father safe." She whispered.

He hugged her close. In his heart he vowed, with God's help, he would not let her down this time.

~

*E*vangeline had dreaded another night spent together because of the tension that remained between her and Henry. He had not pressed her for more intimate sleeping arrangements, which surprised her. Yet, she had felt safe with him in the room and had rested surprisingly well.

He was gone with Sarah before she awakened. After her morning ablutions, she found her husband and daughter on deck. He carried Sarah with one arm and strolled along the deck pointing out things that might interest the eighteen-month-old. Little Sarah hugged her father's neck and chattered to everyone they passed.

Warmth and love spread through Evangeline seeing this glimpse of her family so content and happy. Regret and fear closed in like dark clouds hiding the sun, piercing her heart. Would they ever forgive her abandonment so she could be a part of their close bond? With whispered prayers to the only One who could make that happen, she continued to watch the happy scene before her.

The ship's crew was in equally good spirits and broke out into hearty songs about adventure, whales, and pirate treasure, which delighted her daughter. Billy came out to play for them on a set of bagpipes, and another joined in with a simple hand carved flute. Sarah's giggles were contagious as Henry bounced her in a shuffled jig with turns, dips, and swirls. The song had a few missing words, no doubt eliminated for Sarah's sake, but the tune was lively.

Henry stopped and glanced her way as if he'd felt Evangeline's presence, though she stood in the shadows.

Fear and expectation warred within her whenever she caught his gaze on her. She too heated with restrained passion, which had flared in Henry's eyes when he held her. How long would he wait for her to submit to what they were both feeling?

She straightened, stepped out of the shadows, and walked toward her family. Fear would not keep her from enjoying every moment with them until then.

"Land ho!" The sailor stationed in the crow's nest hollered down his sighting. All singing stopped immediately. The first mate relayed the information to the captain and sent the crew to prepare the ship for docking.

"There be time to eat 'fore we dock." The first mate stepped up to Evangeline, who had taken Sarah into her arms, and motioned them toward the galley below. "The men must focus solely on their jobs and not be distracted by our lovely passengers." He smiled, but his tone was earnest.

Henry ushered her below deck and to the galley, where they met the commander and his men, who stood when they entered.

"We are finished. Please take our seats." The commander waved to his vacated bench and motioned for his men to leave. He honored her with a slight bow before he left.

"Thank you." She appreciated the commander's willingness to help free her and Sarah from their kidnapper and his determination to find the truth about her father, but she found it difficult to make eye contact with him. She feared what he would do if he found out she'd played the Fox.

"We'll be packed and ready to go when we dock, Commander." Henry took Sarah from her and bounced his daughter on his knee. The cook came into the room humming and happy.

"'Ere ye go, little Princess." Cook placed a buttered scone in front of the child. He laughed when she tried to stuff the whole thing into her mouth before Henry intervened. Bowls of hot mush were brought for Henry and Evangeline, then the cook departed leaving the couple and child alone to eat their meal. Drawing the steaming bowl closer, Evangeline toyed with the ground corn, which had been boiled until it thickened and dribbled with sorghum to sweeten it. The ship had very little in the way of supplies, but the captain had been generous in sharing what they had. She must find a way to reward the captain's kindness.

With a frown, she pushed the bowl away, knowing her untouched food would risk offending the cook. Worry had forced a lump against her chest and closed her throat against swallowing more than a sip of water.

"I need to change Sarah and get ready for our journey." She used her napkin to wipe up a dribble from her cup.

"The commander will want to make the journey to Castle Brighton with as much speed as is safe for you and our daughter." He raised his hand to interrupt her before she could speak, leaned in closer, and lowered his voice to a conspirator's whisper. "What he doesn't know is how capable you are with a sword if we should encounter more brigands. Although, I believe we could all avoid bloodshed and fare far better if, when dealing with the commander, you would wield your charm rather than your sword." He smiled, and his eyes twinkled with challenge.

"I will consider your suggestion." She allowed her anger at the commander to dissipate. Perhaps Henry had a point. It had been a long time since she'd been confined to the position of the *charming* Lady Evangeline. After the freedom of the last eighteen months, resuming that role would be like donning a corset pulled too tight to breathe, yet she would do it if it meant protecting her father. She took perhaps her last breath of freedom and made a silent vow. At the first hint of her father in danger, she would don another persona and fight the injustice with whatever means necessary.

~

*T*he ship docked at midmorning, a bit later than the sea captain had hoped. Good-byes were exchanged. Henry made a big production of shaking the captain's hand in front of the onlookers gathered on the dock.

"You saved my wife and child, a heroic act of selflessness as I have ever seen." Henry turned to the crowd. "Captain Fritz and his crew are to be treated as special guests of the king."

Grumbles erupted from a few of the spectators, but the majority cheered. He wasn't sure if the approval would last until the captain's next visit, but he hoped so. He turned back to the captain. "If you ever need my help, send word to Brighton Castle, and it will reach me."

"Aye, laddie, and if ye find yourself in need of a fast ship, leave word with the harbor master. He'll know how to reach me." Captain Fritz clapped a hand on Henry's shoulder. "Remember to take yur troubles to the Good Lord. He'll make things right...even with yur ladyship. Love and patience go a long way to making a bonnie life." With that he turned and started issuing orders for the loading of the goods he'd left behind.

Henry motioned the commander nearer. "I would like to reward the good captain somehow. Do you know of anything he or the crew might be in need of?"

"One thing comes to mind." The commander lowered his voice so only Henry would hear. "But I haven't the authority in this matter."

"Perhaps I do. What is it?"

"Trade goods." When the commander saw the question in Henry's expression, he continued. "The small village where they live is rather poor after so much raiding and battle... with our armies. They raise sheep and are master weavers." He showed Henry a wool scarf he had tucked into his tunic. "I traded a few coins for this fine scarf for my wife." With a look of guilt on his face he shoved it out of sight again. "The king has forbidden trade with the Scots until a proper treaty has been signed. Their village needs the funds to survive and prosper. Do you think you could lift the ban here in this one port?"

"I can, at least temporarily, before we leave. I will also send a missive to my father who can explain the details to the king so that you and I can both keep our heads." Henry chuckled when the commander blanched. "Find the magistrate, and I'll meet with him to sign whatever papers are necessary so our friends here can sell their trade goods and take home a tidy sum of coins and supplies. They've more than earned this small reward on this trip."

One of the commander's men preceded a carriage made of mismatched parts pulled by a team of two stout horses. The older driver wore equally colorful mismatched attire.

"Sorry, your Lordship. The man refused to sell his *carriage* but agreed to take our passengers to Castle Brighton...for a hefty fee." He frowned up at the driver. "I'd be glad to run the blighter through for denying a royal request and drive this contraption myself."

"That won't be necessary as long as the man is capable and does what he's told." Henry cleared his throat to keep from laughing at the shocked expression of the elderly coachman, which changed to one of having been offended.

"I've handled teams of horses, mules, and oxen since before either of you laddies were birthed." He straightened his bent posture and faced forward. "My carriage might not be a looker, but I built her from nothin' and she's sound enough to haul your Ladyship where you're a goin'." He squinted up to the sky checking the position of the early morning sun. "If you want to reach Castle Brighton today, we need to leave now." His tone and stiff posture left no doubt that he was done talking.

Henry walked around the piecemeal carriage, which was as odd as its driver, but it appeared sound. Henry's smile crept into a wide grin. How would Evangeline react to the unusual conveyance?

By the time he met briefly with the magistrate and signed the trade ban exemption for Captain Fritz and his crew, he was tired and eager to leave.

He stopped at the livery and found the horses he and Evangeline had ridden. The merchant they met on the road had left them as promised and had paid in advance for their keep with a note of gratitude for Henry's assistance in stopping his runaway team. The blacksmith had shod Evangeline's horse, replacing the shoe it had thrown, and both animals were well fed and rested. He was relieved, since he had preferred to return his *borrowed* gelding in as good or better shape than when he took it.

He led the horses to the carriage, where he met the commander, who was fastening his gear onto his mount, a powerful grey.

"I take it all went well?" He faced Henry as he approached.

"Yes. The magistrate took some convincing, but Captain Fritz should be welcomed to trade whenever he drops anchor."

"Good. For Scots, they're a decent lot." The commander gave his men orders to make ready to leave. "We've enough supplies to get as far as Castle Brighton. Lady Evangeline and Lady Sarah are settled inside the…" He waved his hand in the direction of the coach.

"Well done, Commander Garrett." Henry glanced into the window of the carriage for reassurance of his family's presence then swung up on the gelding. "Lead on." He would remain close in case of trouble. With God's help, his wife and daughter would never again be out of his protection.

The journey was monotonous and slow compared with the breakneck pace he'd ridden to get to the village.

Evangeline had hardly spoken to him. She must have kept Sarah entertained during the trip, for he hardly heard a peep out his daughter. In consideration of the woman and child, after a few hours, the commander stopped to rest the horses and give the men a short respite. Evangeline took charge of handing out portions of braised beef, bread, and cups of water to everyone, which had been procured for the journey.

Her ease around the commander's men and the elderly driver soured in Henry's stomach. He found he didn't like the looks of appreciation he saw on their faces and heard in their voices. That she even managed a pleasant tone when speaking to the commander displeased him to the point of stirring up unexpected jealousy at his friend's eager response.

He knew his feelings were unreasonable because he had asked Evangeline to be charming, but after all the time she'd spent ignoring his demands during their marriage, did she have to start obeying him now?

His ribs were burning in protest of the constant jostling of their steady pace. It might be best if he rode in the carriage for a while. How would Evangeline react?

After everyone was fed and the food put away, she sought him out.

"I've been watching you, Henry. Your injuries are causing you discomfort, aren't they?" She held Sarah on her hip and stared into his eyes.

As much as he wanted to deny the truth, he shouldn't lie. She would know immediately.

"I'm not as healed as I had hoped."

"Then have your horse tied on the back of the carriage with

my mount and ride inside with Sarah and me." Her smile melted any protest that rose within him.

"Perhaps you're right. I could do with a reprieve." He hated that he was that transparent. Still, the thought of being close to her had a certain appeal. He handed his horse's reins to the nearest soldier. "I'll be riding inside for a time." The soldier nodded and led the horse away.

Reaching out, Henry took Sarah from Evangeline's arms then escorted his wife back to the carriage and helped her inside.

To his surprise, the ugly box on wheels rode remarkably smooth, actually much smoother than his own well-crafted carriage. Maybe the man could be convinced to build him one... using all new materials, of course. He smiled and leaned back against the comfy cushions. The chatter of Sarah and Evangeline allowed him to relax, and the rocking motion of the carriage was as if it were a ship on the water. Sleep captured him.

CHAPTER 23

*E*vangeline had grown impatient with the rest stops that had prolonged their trip to the castle. It was well after midnight when they arrived at the crossroads leading to Castle Brighton. The Black Swan Inn appeared dark and uninhabited.

As soon as the carriage stopped, Evangeline started to step out.

"Stop." Henry grabbed her arm and tugged her back inside.

"Release me. I must check on my friend."

"It may not be safe." He loosened his hold when she leaned back into her seat. "Until we have news that the rest of the brigands who kidnapped Sarah and held us hostage have been captured, you and Sarah are not safe. Stay here until we know who is lurking about."

"Fine." She couldn't help mumbling, "Stay back like a helpless woman."

"We must all make sacrifices when necessity arises." Henry's retort was curt before he stepped out and slammed the carriage door with force enough to rattle the hinges, drawing an angry protest from the driver.

"Commander, would you try to raise someone in the inn to

accommodate us for the night? It would be more prudent to arrive at the castle in the daylight." Henry stepped to the front of the carriage and spoke to the driver. "Calvin, stay alert. If I shout an alarm, be prepared to flee to the castle to protect her ladyship."

"Aye." The driver, Calvin Ledbetter had once served in the King's army until he suffered a leg injury. He knew how to follow orders. A bit of a loner, he had a sound mind that kept him busy inventing. He had become more talkative along the way after he realized one of the soldiers was the grandson of a good friend he'd met while serving in the King's army.

In response to the commander's pounding on the Inn's door, the glow of candlelight bounced with movement through the tavern's thick lead-glass window, as someone carried the flame toward the door. From the stable, two figures emerged, one holding a lantern and the other a sword that glinted in the light.

"Who goes there?"

"Captain Degraf?" The commander stepped forward.

"Yes, sir." The soldier lowered his sword. "I'm glad you're back, Commander."

"Had a bit of trouble have you?"

A jangle of keys turned in the heavy iron lock. The door of the tavern swung open. Helen stood in the doorway fully dressed, as if expecting late night visitors.

"You were not supposed to open the door until I gave you the signal." Captain Degraf chided her, but his tone was filled with concern not anger.

"I listened until I knew it was safe." She motioned toward the open door. "Come in, all of you, and rest. I have a cooked ham and fresh bread to feed you. Finus, show the men where they can house their horses."

The small bent man standing behind Captain Degraf limped forward.

"Come with me, gents. There be room for all of yur fine

animals with plenty of fresh hay and water." The servant turned and motioned toward the barn.

"You were expecting us?" The alarm in the commander's voice set his troops on alert and had them pulling their swords.

"Yes, sir," Captain Degraf said, "We've known you were coming for a couple of hours. Helen...ah, the widow, Oxley, has quite a loyal network of spies along the way that inform her of strangers on the trail. She's made ready to receive you." Pride lit his features as he glanced over to Helen.

"You are quite safe here." She again motioned toward the inn. "Please. I have food prepared and rooms made up for you."

"Helen." Evangeline rounded the carriage, with her wide-awake daughter in her arms, and rushed to her friend's side.

"Evang...ah, Your Ladyship." Helen bobbed a quick curtsy before she enveloped her and the child in a hug and ushered them inside. "You must be exhausted from your adventure. I can hardly wait to hear the details." Humor edged with relief were in contrast to the tears in her eyes. She brushed them away. "Here, I prepared some porridge and cream, for your wee daughter. You can sit and feed her while I care for these men."

Evangeline settled Sarah into a chair built high for children so they could reach the table. Having just awakened when they stopped, Sarah was hungry and insisted on feeding herself. Using both hands, she shoved fistfuls of the thick porridge into her mouth. The warm, creamy mixture of boiled oats and barley topped with honey, cream, and butter was smeared over her daughter's face and ran down her arms, but the child's delight in feeding herself kept Evangeline from intervening.

Helen remained occupied with slicing ham and bread and filling tankards of ale.

The commander shouted orders, which sent two soldiers off to check the darkness for any trespassers. Henry, the driver, and Captain Degraf came inside. Helen handed the driver a plate of meat and bread and a full tankard.

"Thank ye. I'll make quick of this fine feast then bed down near me horses." He took a deep swallow of ale and swiped his mouth on his sleeve. He finished his meal in short order and left.

"I will relieve one of the sentries so he can come in and eat." Captain Degraf nodded to the commander then turned to Helen and winked.

Having made sure everyone had food and drink, Helen laid a stack of clean towels on the table before she sat across from Evangeline.

"Was that the same skinny, shy and eager-to-please Armand that we sparred with as youths?" Evangeline smiled at Helen's blush. "He's grown quite tall and filled out nicely." She used a damp cloth to clean her daughter's face and arms. Sarah had finished eating and was now rubbing her hands through the mess she'd made.

"She's an enthusiastic eater." Helen took the bowl out of the child's reach then swiped a towel across the table to keep Sarah from getting more spilled porridge on her.

"Yes, so I've found. Thank you. She quite enjoyed her meal." Evangeline laughed at the amount of towels it had taken to clean up her daughter and her surroundings. Full, the toddler was ready to play, her voice raised in protest when Evangeline refused to let her down to wander.

"Let me take her." Henry scooped up Sarah and walked toward the door. "Come sweet girl, we'll go see the horses."

Evangeline watched them until the door closed behind them.

"Hmm. By the longing in your gaze, I assume your love for your husband is not dead?" Helen smiled. "Perhaps during your adventure you've had time to reconsider your life as his wife."

"Not all has been resolved, but I believe him when he says he was never Millicent's lover and did not conspire with her to have me killed." She straightened and turned to study her friend. "How are you feeling?"

"My headaches are gone," Helen frowned. "Including Ox, who was buried, while I was resting, by the villagers who were eager to be rid of him for good. Mouse was buried the same day. None attended either burial, except for the gravediggers. It is so sad that their deaths brought no sorrow, only relief to all who knew them."

"By Armand's gazes toward you, it appears as if he still loves you." Evangeline was glad her friend was finally free of the evil man who beat her and, by the overheard conversation between him and Hemming, had every intention of murdering her. The realm is better because of Ox's death. Helen can finally live in peace and have a good life filled with love and joy.

"Armand told me, once things are made right at the castle, he wants to talk." Helen grinned and brushed a stray hair away from her face. She had the glow of happiness, the first Evangeline had seen on her friend, since Evangeline had returned to Brighton. "What say we save our visit for another time? I overheard the commander say he wants to leave at first light. You'll need your rest." She stood and motioned for Evangeline to follow, lighting the way up the darkened stairway to a room at the top. "Surrounded by the king's best men, you should be safe."

"Do I need protecting?" Evangeline's voice rose in alarm. "How is my father?"

"He's fine. Armand stationed two of his men to protect Lord Brighton until that scoundrel Urso Hemming is caught."

"Yes, the fake Earl of Evanwood. I had hoped that menace would be in custody or dead by now." Evangeline would like to see him hanged for all of the grief he had caused.

"I have the wanted poster Ox used to blackmail him. The king put a hefty bounty on the blighter's head." She stopped at the end of the hall and opened the door. "Hemming is still on the run, but his hired thugs have been caught and hung by the Fox, according to the villagers. They sing the Fox's praises for seeking revenge for the terror they've endured at those cutthroat's hands and—" she leaned closer and lowered her voice—"for the murder of the beloved nun, Sister Margaret Mary. Her bloodied cloak was found in the forest."

"The Fox?" Evangeline whispered. Her thoughts swirled with confusion. How was it possible? Had someone found the mask and used it to wreak revenge?

"You mean the Fox still exists?" Henry appeared behind them. "Rubbish. He would be well into his nineties. I've heard of that outlaw since I was a child. It couldn't possibly be the same one." He shifted a sleeping Sarah from one arm to the other arm and went inside the room. "Oh, this will do quite nicely." He entered and paused. "There's a fire in the hearth, a cradle for Sarah...and a sizable bed."

"I also left clean clothes for her ladyship and the baby," Helen said. "There's goat milk in that pitcher on the table, ready for the wee one if she should awake hungry in the night. You will also find a bottle of wine and cheese there on the mantle for you." She pushed the reluctant Evangeline into the room. "I'll talk with ye tomorrow." With that, she closed the door.

Henry settled the sleeping child into the cradle, which had been placed near the hearth for warmth. He turned to Evangeline.

"I trust that there will be no problem with us sharing this bed?" He stood with his back to the firelight, leaving his features shadowed, but she could feel his attention on her. "Unlike the ship's bunk, it's quite large enough to accommodate the both of us."

"I..." She stammered then swallowed. "No problem at all." Grabbing the long linen nightgown that lay folded and waiting at the foot of the bed, she slipped behind the dressing screen and put it on. Dread slowed her movements. She lingered over washing away the journey's dust until she heard Henry get into bed. After the ablution, when her bare feet were cold and her body chilled to the bone, she could no longer put off the inevitable.

A quick check on her sleeping daughter, she walked to the empty side of the large bed. To her relief, the steady sound of breathing meant Henry was already asleep. She pulled back the covers and found a bed warmer filled with hot stones, which she removed and placed on the floor. The feather bed was delightfully warm, allowing her tense muscles to relax in spite of her husband's presence. He mumbled something before the rhythm of his breathing continued. A deep repressed longing surfaced of being held in his arms as they slept. She ignored it and turned to her side, hugging the edge of the mattress farthest away from him.

CHAPTER 24

a tentative knock on the door awoke Henry with a start. The dream of having Evangeline in his arms became reality when he opened his eyes. She was pressed up against him, her back against his chest as she'd once liked to sleep. He drew in her scent and savored the moment. The silkiness of her hair covered his arm. He brushed it to one side, which revealed a nasty scar on her neck. It disappeared down her spine, no doubt the result of the fire that had trapped her and almost taken her life.

The evidence of her suffering sent fury surging through him. He would see that Millicent was marched to the gallows and hung as soon as possible.

"Lord Stanton. It is time we leave." Another rap sounded against the door, this time loud enough to wake the baby.

Sarah whined. Evangeline stirred within his embrace. Henry reluctantly released his wife and slipped out of bed. He walked to the closed door and responded without opening it.

"Thank you, Commander. We'll be down shortly." What he wanted to do was rant at the man for disturbing them. What might have happened if... Henry mulled over the possibilities as he pulled on his clothes. He gazed at his wife and longed for the closeness they'd once shared.

Dawn's rosy blush peeked through the window and highlighted Evangeline's beauty as she stretched. She tugged the blanket higher when she saw him staring.

"It's time to get ready."

"I heard." She yawned and stretched again.

"Da, da, da." Sarah's fussing grew more demanding. "Go!"

"I'll take care of Sarah while you dress." He forced himself to turn away when all he wanted was to climb back in bed and remind her how good they were together. Forcing his thoughts on the present, he focused on his daughter as Evangeline disappeared behind the changing screen in the corner of the room. The nightgown she'd worn was flung across the top. His mouth went dry and his heart thumped loudly against his chest. There had been a time when no gown was necessary. He swallowed the regret that rose like bile in his throat.

"Da, da, da." Sarah reached up and tugged on his tunic, eager to be up and about. "Go."

"Yes, sweet Sarah, we go." He finished changing her, checked the pitcher and poured a cup of goat's milk, which he offered to his daughter.

"No." She fussed, turned her face and pushed it away. "Go."

"Shall we go and find more of that delicious porridge?" He gathered her into his arms.

"I'm ready." Evangeline walked out from behind the screen dressed in a simple dress of linen, her hair brushed until it shone and tied back. Even in a simple unadorned linen dress, a servant might wear, she had that regal air of royalty. "Shall we go?"

"Of course." Henry followed her down the stairs. The odor of fried meat and fresh bread met them as they descended. His stomach growled.

The food was good, but the meal was hastened with an impatient commander hovering over them.

"My men are ready to take charge of the castle," The commander said. "Captain Degraf sent two men there to guard from any trying to enter or leave. The villagers say the castle is free of those who besieged it and held Lord Brighton hostage, however I believe it would be better if I take my men ahead and make sure. You should wait and bring your family after we are assured it is safe." His gaze met Henry's.

"I agree, but…" Henry barely had the words out before Evangeline raised her voice.

"I refuse to be left behind while my father is in danger," Evangeline stood and picked up Sarah. "If the gates are locked and there is any resistance, I know ways into the castle you do not, and I can minister aid to any who are injured."

The commander frowned. "I cannot guarantee their safety, Lord Stanton."

"I know. But she's right. A secret passage into the castle would be a great advantage." Henry hated the thought of putting his family in danger, but he knew once Evangeline's mind was set it would not be easily changed. Hopefully the rumors proved correct.

"I would be glad to care for your daughter while you deal with matters at the castle." Helen hovered nearby. "I will protect her with my life."

"You know that I'd trust you to keep her safe, but as long as Hemming is loose, I shall keep Sarah with me." Evangeline smiled and gave her friend a quick hug.

"I understand." Helen turned as a peasant appeared through the back door and motioned for her. "Please excuse me." She disappeared outside shutting the door behind her.

"The commander insists we leave immediately." Henry gathered Sarah into his arms and put a hand on Evangeline's back to edge her toward the door.

~

*E*vangeline turned back to say good-bye, but there was no sign of Helen. Only something important would have kept her away. Since her return as Lady Evangeline, the wall of separation between royal and servant had once again risen between them. As Sister Margaret Mary she'd been privy to both realms. Now, she would be once again confined to her royal position. Determination rose inside like a battle cry. With God's help, she would do what was necessary to again bridge the gap between the classes and keep her friendship close.

She'd heard the mumble of the soldiers, who feared meeting the notorious Fox along the road. Since she had no idea who now played the Fox, an uneasy feeling of imminent danger kept Evangeline on edge.

CHAPTER 25

*T*he journey to the castle was hard and fast. Evangeline kept a tight hold on Sarah to keep her from being flung around by the hard-driven carriage over the rough road. The clanks and groans of the ugly conveyance gave her concern whether it would withstand the punishment.

She sat close to the window to watch the landscape rush past. No sign of strangers or hidden dangers in the most likely places, where she and her band of women had often hidden in wait for their victims. Where was their little gang? The thought of any one of those valiant women in danger was a great concern with a new Fox on the prowl.

In spite of dealing with her fussy daughter, the scene from the small carriage window spread joy, ousting the dread that clung to her like a stench she couldn't escape. This was her first official appearance as Lady Evangeline since her reported death. How would she be received after she revealed her duplicity of posing as Sister Margaret Mary these last months? She shoved the guilt away. It had been necessary. Her father would be thrilled to declare her presence, which alone gave her enough reason to rejoice.

The carriage slowed. Here the trail descended steeply and wound its final path down to the castle.

Where were the farmers tending their flocks or peasants walking along the road? Warning prickles sparked down Evangeline's neck. Hopefully, the king's guards could handle any trouble that lay ahead.

"We're almost home, sweetie." She tried to console Sarah, whose frustration at being confined had reached her limit, resulting in a demanding squall.

The carriage stopped just before it reached the timbered bridge outside the castle gates, which were open and suspiciously unmanned.

The burning sparks grew more intense. She rubbed her neck but it did little to relieve the sensation. Danger lurked nearby.

"Stay here, driver, while my men check for trouble." The commander issued more orders, and three soldiers, including Captain DeGraf, rode over the bridge that covered the moat and entered the bailey. Henry rode up beside the carriage and stopped, fully alert, sword in hand.

"Why would the gates be opened and unattended?" He swiveled in the saddle to check the surroundings.

"They shouldn't." She hugged a whining Sarah tight to her side. "There." Pointing up to the nearest of the castle ramparts, she watched a woman frantically wave a red cloth of warning.

"Stop!" A multitude yelled and rushed toward them from the thick woods.

Without waiting for the commander's orders, the driver whipped the frightened horses forward and drove the carriage within the castle's courtyard as the horde of people hurried toward them. Henry and the king's soldiers followed closely.

A shouted order and the castle gate lowered to the ground just as the first peasant rushed forward, waving a pitchfork and yelling. The roar of the crowd sounded more like a warning than a threat. She caught the words, "danger" and "trap".

The soldiers dismounted. Two ran up the stone stairs to gain access to the ramparts that would give them the highest vantage. The remaining guards surrounded the carriage to protect the passengers as Evangeline stepped out, hugging Sarah tightly within her arms.

Henry propelled his family toward the castle entrance. A sentry standing nearby stepped forward and pulled the heavy door opened as they reached him.

"Lord Stanton, welcome." The strange man in ill-fitting livery had shifty eyes and avoided Evangeline's gaze. In deference? She didn't think so, since she wore a servant's dress. Her neck sparked with warning like hot embers bouncing against her skin.

"Henry…" She grasped her dagger and stepped closer to her husband.

The door slammed behind them. The guard and another man placed the heavy bar in place from the inside.

"We have men out there." Henry raised his sword and stepped toward the guards. "Open this door immediately and let the commander inside."

"Sorry, yur Lordship. We has our orders." The man smirked and elbowed his companion.

"Whose orders?" Henry bellowed.

Fists pounded against the door, and swords rang against the oak.

"My orders, Love." Millicent wore a regal gown trimmed with hundreds of polished silver beads that sparkled, reflecting the candle light as she walked toward them from the grand hall. A sickeningly sweet scent of lily of the valley intensified as she drew forward. Four guards, swords drawn, surrounded her.

"You!" Henry pointed his sword at Millicent as he stepped in front of Evangeline shielding her and Sarah.

"That's right, Darling. I came as soon as I heard of your tragic loss." She pulled an embroidered handkerchief from the sleeve and dabbed her eyes. With an undo amount of regal aplomb, she continued toward him, her hand extended.

"And what loss would that be?" Evangeline stepped out from behind Henry, Sarah on her hip.

"You!" All color leeched from Millicent's face. She staggered back, bumping into one of her guards, who grabbed her to keep her from falling. Shoving his hands away as if they were dirty, she straightened. "You're dead. I had you..."

"Murdered? Yet, here I am." Evangeline felt Henry's arm encircle her shoulders, uniting them. "Unlike the cutthroats you hired to kill me and my daughter." Her voice lowered from the intensity of her anger. "Your henchmen have met face to face with their maker to pay for their murders, as you soon will." Her husband's embrace tightened to a restraining hold. He knew her too well.

"Guards, take Lady Millicent to the dungeon to await her trial." Henry loosed Evangeline, while his sword remained pointed at the woman who had caused so much misery.

"I think not." Fury laced every word. Millicent's hands fisted at her side, her body shook with the intensity of her unstable emotional state.

Suddenly, a cold look of madness filled her eyes. She relaxed her stance, and a wicked smile lit her face. "Henry, be a love and come with me, away from that wretched woman and that—" she waved her handkerchief at Sarah. "—that abominable brat, or I shall have my guards run their very sharp blades through them both while you watch." Her voice was chillingly calm. "You are to be my husband and no other. My father promised that the king will give me my rightful place in court as soon as you and I are wed."

The door splintered open. Four of the king's guards pushed through and dispatched the two men standing at the entrance.

"No!" Millicent turned and escaped up the stairway, followed by one of her guards. "Kill them all!"

The remaining hired assassins were no match for the king's guards. Captain DeGraf unlocked the door to the servant's entrance. Those held captive poured out holding knives and cleavers. A shout of victory rose once they saw their enemy had been defeated.

An elderly servant, Gertrude, appeared with a kitchen knife in hand and dropped it when she saw Evangeline without her veil. Recognition lit her features. She rushed up and flung her arms around her and Sarah.

"I knew it. Sister Margaret Mary, indeed." Her voice filled with tears of joy. "Here, let me take your wee one. You'll have need of both hands free to protect your father from that witch." She pulled Sarah into her ample arms and was surrounded by her fellow servants, ready to protect the child with their lives. "We'll hide in the pantry until it's safe to come out. Go." She turned and escaped back through the passage leading to the kitchen.

Evangeline grabbed a sword from one of the downed henchmen and sprinted up the stairs after Henry, who had already disappeared in pursuit of Millicent and her guard.

The sounds of boots pounding against the oak floor, raised voices, then steel clashing against steel echoed in the halls before she turned the corner and raced toward her father's chambers.

"God, please protect Henry." There was no sight of him. As much as she wanted to help him defeat their enemy, he would want her to see to her father's safety first.

The sounds receded as she turned down another corridor, drawing closer to her father's quarters. Wafts of lily of the valley lingered along the way. She slid to a stop.

"Father?" The door to her father's suite was open. Where were his guards? She hesitated lest she walk into a trap. Her fingers ached as they tightened around the hilt of the heavy sword. Muscles tense and ready to fight, she stepped inside the room. All appeared untouched, but the cloying scent of Millicent reeked throughout the space. Evangeline hurried through the drawing room to her father's bed chamber.

"Come in, *Lady* Evangeline." Millicent's voice dripped with contempt. She leaned out, then disappeared behind the heavy tapestry that surrounded Lord Brighton's large four-poster bed.

Readied for battle, Evangeline searched the perimeter, checking for any of her adversary's henchmen waiting to attack.

No sign of anyone else, she hastened forward. The heavy curtains that surrounded the four-poster were loosed on three sides effectively blocking her view until she reached the opened side.

At the head of the bed, Millicent sat beside Lord Brighton with one arm tightly around his neck and the other clutching a dagger at his throat.

"Let him go at once!" Evangeline raised her sword and pointed it at her nemesis.

"Stop! Drop that sword or I'll slit him ear to ear." Millicent grinned and pressed the blade against his flesh. A trickle of blood appeared.

Evangeline dropped the sword. Her hand clutched her cross ready to release its blade.

"I will exchange his life for your vow to provide for my free passage away from this vile land. I want a carriage and horses for my guards…well, any that have survived."

"You can't get away. There is no place in all the kingdom where you can hide. The king will issue an edict for your arrest." Evangeline's thoughts raced for a solution to save her father. He remained silent, his body relaxed and a smile curving his lips. How could he be so calm at a time like this? Every scripture for protection she had memorized escaped her. All she could think to pray was, *help us, Lord Jesus*, as she edged nearer. If only she could move fast enough to disarm her enemy without the risk of hurting her father.

"Thanks to my dear departed father's many connections and his ill-gotten gains, I have other countries where I may go and live like a queen." Millicent tugged Lord Brighton closer. "I will need gold and jewels to take with me. Hiring brigands is quite expensive." Her eyes narrowed, and her mouth pinched into an angry line. "If you do not comply, this worthless old man will die before your eyes." She grinned. "Where he will die quickly, my wretched father died slowly and violently from a powerful poison I put into his wine. I watched him thrash about for almost an hour before the end." Lost in her thoughts, she relaxed her grip on the knife. A maniacal laughter erupted from her. "My only regret is that I hadn't learned the use of such potions sooner to rid me of my tormentors."

"Why?" Evangeline shifted from one foot to the other, ready to spring. If she could keep her talking she might…

"I had the misfortune of being born a lowly girl." She tightened her grip again. Her eyes narrowed in anger, and she pointed the knife at Evangeline before again placing it against Lord Brighton's throat. "My father was furious that his firstborn was not a son. As the story goes, in a drunken state, he fled the castle in the physician's carriage to be consoled by his mistress and was nearly killed when the carriage lost a wheel and crashed, pinning him beneath. His injuries kept him from fathering more children. My poor weak mother was so terrified of the man, she could never stand up to him, no matter how many times he humiliated her . . . or me." Deep in thought, her gaze strayed to the bed's heavy coverlet. With the tip of her dagger, she traced the intricately embroidered silk hearts that covered the surface. "She died of a weak heart, or so I bribed the physician to say, but the truth was, I couldn't bear to watch her grovel another day." With a vicious stab, she plunged the dagger into the bedding, but her free arm remained tightly around Lord Brighton's throat. Her voice dropped to the low babble of the insane.

"After that wench stole Henry, my father threatened to sell me like a prize cow to the highest bidder if I didn't marry that stupid brother of his." She glanced up at Evangeline as if she didn't recognize her and edged the blade up and down the coverlet, cutting each heart-shaped swirl of the pattern. "They all deserved to die."

Lord Brighton remained still, his breathing shallow.

"Henry's brother adored me, of course. I might have let poor ole Robert live if he hadn't found my journal of poisons and my list of victims. He was going to have me locked away." With a flick of her wrist, she sliced another vicious cut of the delicate fabric, shredding the coverlet inch by inch. The goose down filler floated out and covered the room like snow. "He died in my arms. Poor man. He looked very much like Henry. I might have learned to love him."

"Loose Lord Brighton at once!" Henry erupted into the room and rushed to Evangeline's side.

"Really, darling, must you be so...hostile?" She waved the dagger in the air then let it again settle against Lord Brighton's throat. "I'll gladly let the old man live...if you kill that wench. Then we can leave the kingdom together."

Three more of the king's guard burst into the room and surrounded the bed, jerking down the heavy curtains, which gave them a clear vantage.

"Now look what you've done. You've ruined our lovely privacy." She pushed up against the heavy carved headboard. "Leave the room or..." With a swift movement, she stabbed Lord Brighton in the arm. He gasped with pain.

"See what you made me do?" She pressed the blood-stained blade against his neck. "I can keep stabbing him until he has no life left, or I can leave the castle with him, and Henry can bandage his wounds in the carriage along the way." She pointed the blade at each of the guards. "If you take another step closer, you will be responsible for Lord Brighton's death."

"Stop! Don't hurt my father." Evangeline touched Henry's arm. "Let her leave." Regret tainted her words even as her body shook with restrained rage. "Please."

"No." A clear command erupted from her father. With a burst of strength, he grabbed Millicent's arm and shoved her away. The guards pounced on the bed. One pulled Lord Brighton to safety while the other two wrestled with Millicent. She fought like a maniac, thrusting her dagger fruitlessly against their chainmail until they disarmed her.

"Let me go at once!" Millicent's screams and curses grew more hysterical. She writhed against the guard's firm hold as they dragged her from the room. "I have great wealth. Loose me, and I'll make you rich."

Henry followed the guards to the door. "I will return after I make sure Millicent is securely locked in the dungeon. I will also make sure no misguided soul is tempted to take her up on her generous offer." Henry met Evangeline's gaze. With that one look, she knew without a doubt she was loved and she in turn had sent him the same silent message. He grinned and gave her a wink of acknowledgement, then followed the sounds of the guards hauling their protesting prisoner down the back stairs toward the dungeon.

Evangeline followed the guard as he carried her father to the outer chamber and eased him into a chair near the fireplace. Expecting the worst, Evangeline was surprised to see, instead of her father anguished with pain, his face was ruddy with excitement. A servant rushed forward to wrap his wound with a linen napkin that had been discarded on a nearby table.

"Was she injured?" By Lord Brighton's flushed cheeks and the sparkle in his cloudy eyes, he had actually enjoyed the excitement.

"She is unharmed and the king's guards have taken her to the dungeon." She reached out to him, and he clasped her hand. "Are you well, father?"

"Useless old man indeed!" His voice was strong and confident. He patted her hand. "I'm fine, child."

"Thank God." Only God could have produced such an outcome with no further bloodshed. Watching helplessly as her father was held by a madwoman was not an experience she ever wished to repeat.

"Other than a minor bloodletting, I'm quite well." He chuckled. "Actually it was quite invigorating."

Evangeline buried her face into his shoulder and clung to him. Drawing a calming breath she wiped her tears and motioned for a young servant to come near. Several hovered in the doorway eager to be of help.

"Rodney, please fetch Elsa and have her bring the herbs." Evangeline waved the young man off to do her bidding. With a nod, he disappeared, his footsteps echoed as he ran down the corridor.

Elsa had been a faithful servant for as long as Evangeline could remember. She had run the household with a minimal fuss in spite of Evangeline's aunt's bitter interference.

"Be gone. Back to your jobs. As you can see, his Lordship is fine." Elsa hurried in with two servants close behind. The last one paused only long enough to close the door.

"Bring that fresh water and set it beside the chair." Elsa waved forward the servant who carried a large bucket, then motioned to a second servant, who carried an arm full of folded cloths. "Now, what have you gotten yourself into this time, milord?" She tsk-tsked, as she removed the napkin tied around his arm, and cut away the sleeve of his nightshirt to reveal the dagger wound.

"Tis only a flesh wound, unless you would like to do the doctoring." Elsa glanced up at Evangeline awaiting her answer.

"Please continue. I don't think I can." Evangeline's voice quivered. She drew a steady breath and leaned in to get a better look.

"Then, I need you to step out of my light so I can do a proper job, Lady Evangeline...or is it still, Sister Margaret Mary?" Elsa glanced up and grinned.

"Does everyone know my real identity?" She shook her head in disbelief.

"No, just Gertrude, me, and a few others, but we've kept your secret." She turned her attention back to treating Lord Brighton's wound. "You look no worse for the excitement, your Lordship."

"I haven't felt so alive since my little girl came back to me." Lord Brighton's voice was strong and vibrant.

"I have a surprise for you, father." Evangeline stood and smiled.

A firm knock sounded on the door, and the servant nearest opened it.

"I have a wee one who is missing her mum." Gertrude stepped inside with little Sarah on her hip. The little girl spotted Evangeline and reached out for her.

"Mum, mum, mum." Her childish demand brooked no refusal.

"Thank you, Gertrude for keeping her safe." Evangeline accepted Sarah into her arms. "Come, my sweet baby." She nuzzled her daughter's neck until she giggled.

"Father, I have someone who wants to meet you." She walked over to where he sat straight and regal, a new bandage wrapped around his right arm. Unable to see them, he tilted his head and listened.

"This is Lady Sarah, your granddaughter." She handed her daughter down into his outstretched arms.

"My granddaughter?" His voice quivered with emotion. "I wasn't sure I would live to see this day." Tears ran down his wrinkled cheeks.

Little Sarah somehow understood the importance of the

man who held her. She patted her grandfather's cheek then jabbered the serious but incoherent language of toddlers.

"You are indeed your mother's daughter." Lord Brighton gathered the child into a hug and laughed.

Another knock sounded, and loud whispers erupted when the servant opened the door. A scuffle ensued, and an intruder pushed his way inside the room. A king's guard stepped forward, sword raised.

"Wait!" Elsa rushed forward. "This is my grandson, Fred." She put a hand on the young man's shoulder. "What's wrong?"

"The crowd outside is threatening to break down the gates unless Lord Brighton shows himself." He knelt beside his grandmother. Fear filled his gaze as he raised his eyes to meet Evangeline. "Please, yur Ladyship, I fear they'll be killed, for they're no match for the armed guards. They be only concerned for Lord Brighton's safety, not to do 'im harm. They want to help."

"Lead me to them." Lord Brighton handed the child to Evangeline and stood.

"Here, yur Lordship." Elsa helped him slip on his finest robe and slippers then ran a quick brush through his wispy white hair.

Evangeline placed her father's hand on her arm to lead him. He held his head high. His gait was slow but steady. Together, they reached the castle's outer gates. The angry shouts of the crowd silenced when Lord Brighton raised his hand.

"My loyal friends, thank you for your support during the long days of this siege. As you can see, I am well, and the enemy has been subdued." Lord Brighton smiled as the crowd cheered. He raised his hand again and waited for the people to quiet. He turned and put an arm around Evangeline's shoulder.

"Let me officially announce the return of my beloved daughter, Lady Evangeline, and introduce my grandchild, Lady Sarah."

The people clapped and cheered.

"I heard she died." Murmurs of agreement continued. "Why didn't she return sooner?"

Evangeline fought the guilt of her deception as the whispers and speculation replaced the cheers and circulated through the crowd at her father's announcement. She couldn't fault them. Hadn't they mourned with Lord Brighton at the news of her death?

There would be much discussion around their campfires this evening as to where she had been all of this time.

Henry appeared and took his place on the opposite side of Lord Brighton putting a supporting hand under his Lordship's bandaged arm.

"And she has brought her husband, Lord Henry Stanton, who has come to put right the injustices that…"

"You be too late. The Fox's done what the royals have not," a peasant shouted from the throng of people. The crowd roared their agreement. Lord Brighton raised his hand again until the crowd calmed.

"I am deeply grateful for the Fox's help in the manner of capturing the real outlaws who have reigned terror over our land. I will issue an order of amnesty for the Fox and his gang." Lord Brighton waited until the cheers died down. "With the provision that they cease their activities immediately."

The crowd's response was a mixture of cheers and boos.

"The King has sent soldiers and will send as many more as necessary to insure order and safety to your land." Henry raised his voice to be heard and stepped forward. "I will remain until this is done. You have my word." He straightened and spread his feet, sword in his hand. "Please, go back to your homes. We will continue to hunt down the last of our enemies to see none escape justice."

The crowd continued to voice their doubts, but began to disperse.

The castle servants came with a chair to carry Lord Brighton back inside. His strength depleted, he eased down and grasped the arms of the carrier, releasing a sigh.

"Please, take me to the garden. I've been captive far too long. I want to breathe in the fresh air of freedom." Lord Brighton raised his face to the bright sunlight and smiled.

The servants turned to Henry, who nodded his approval. That the servants already looked to Henry as the authority sent strange feelings surging through Evangeline. Fear that they thought her father was no longer capable to be in charge, or was it that Henry had stepped in? With the need to ponder the situation more, she adjusted Sarah on her hip and turned to follow her father. Henry placed a restraining hand on her arm, his expression serious.

"I'll be along shortly, Father." She turned to Elsa, who hovered nearby. "Would you take Sarah and stay with them until I join you?"

With a grin and a curtsey, the woman gathered the child into her arms and followed Lord Brighton to the rose garden.

Henry stepped close and placed his arm around Evangeline. He guided her from the gates to a stone bench away from prying eyes. Two guards stayed far enough to give Henry and Evangeline privacy yet remained close enough to protect them if necessary.

"What is it, Henry?" Evangeline saw the worry in his stern expression and furrowed brow, but also the tension and restlessness of his every gesture, a sure sign he pondered a problem of utmost importance. Dread quickened her heartbeat.

"No one has seen nor heard of the capture of that imposter Urso Hemming." As if unable to stay seated, he stood and rubbed a hand over the hilt of his sword. "That man must be brought to justice if we want any chance of regaining the confidence of the people."

She knew him well enough to understand his need to do what was right. A warmth like sweet butter melting on a slice of fresh bread spread throughout her thawing another portion of the hurt frozen in her heart. Placing a hand on his arm, she stopped him.

"He will not escape. With the generous reward you offered for his capture, the fake Earl of Evanwood will find it difficult to flee." She dropped her hand and clasped them before her. "I know of some places that a fugitive might hide in the area." She smiled at his surprise. "I'll send a servant, who is familiar with the area, to go with you."

Henry hesitated.

"Go. I'll stay here and organize a search within the castle walls in case the fugitive is still waiting for a chance to escape."

"Hopefully this matter will be dealt with by the eve, and then perhaps we can finally resolve more private issues." He ran his fingers down her cheek then pulled her into an embrace. A deep longing to regain what they once had stirred within her. She stepped out of his reach, her face flushed.

"Until then." She turned away and headed toward the garden, her heart pounding with the doubt of her decision to remain behind when she'd rather ride at Henry's side and pursue Hemming.

A shout stopped her as she passed the sentry's post.

A familiar voice came from the gates, which remained closed. "Help! He stole my baby."

CHAPTER 26

"*W*hat's wrong?" Evangeline rushed to the gate where Anna stood crying and wringing her hands.

Henry stepped up behind his wife.

"He stole Angus." The young girl's sobs made it hard to understand the rest.

"Open the gates." Henry shouted to the gate guards. Excruciatingly slow, the gates rose until there was room for Anna to duck under and scurry inside. She bobbed a quick curtsey then threw herself at Evangeline's feet.

"Please, your ladyship. My son. He took my Angus." Anna's words came in a rushing raspy plea.

Evangeline put a hand under the young woman's arm and helped her to stand. Henry issued orders and had horses brought forth.

"Who has Angus?" Evangeline patted Anna's hand.

"The earl. Him what stole my baby." Anna's voice rose.

"The *earl* took your child, but why?"

"I be staying at the abbey to take care of the goats and the garden while the kind sister be away." She took a deep breath and wiped her tears with her sleeve. "He burst inside at sunrise. Pale as milk and wild-eyes as if the hounds of hades was chasin' him."

"Go on." Evangeline feared for the child's safety each minute of delay.

"I hid and watched as he searched for food and drank the goat milk I had strained last night." The girl's tear-filled eyes met Evangeline's. "Angus awoke and cried." Anna raised her face, pride lit her eyes. "He knowed that something was wrong. My son be very smart, like the sister said."

Seeing Evangeline's impatience she hurried on. "He reached Angus 'fore me and picked him up. Angus blared out a hardy protest, but the earl just laughed. I come out of hiding and tells him to put my baby down, but he lifts him high and waves my babe around like a prize pig and says. 'this is my ticket to freedom.' He grabbed my arm and demands I help him escape." Anna fidgeted from one foot to the other and wrung her hands. "I pretended to want to help him, but he wouldn't give Angus to me. Just told me to hurry. I gathered cheese and bread into a bag." Tears again filled her eyes. "I offered him the food as trade for my son." Her lips tightened with anger. "He grabbed me arm and said I would have to go with him if I wanted Angus to live." She drew a ragged breath. "He looked at me like the time he…"

She paled as the horror of that encounter flashed across her features. "He led the way jabbering about getting his money. By his crazy talk, I feared he would kill us once he got where he was going. When he released me arm, I ran to the keep for help." Panic edged the rest of her words into an indiscernible rush again. She captured Evangeline's hand and tugged her toward the gate. "Please, I knowed where he be headed. We have to save Angus."

"Then we must make haste." Henry led two horses forward. Three of the king's guards were already mounted. "You can ride with her ladyship and point the way."

Evangeline watched fear light Anna's eyes, but she allowed herself be led to the animals. Evangeline sent a servant to convey her plans to her father and turned toward her mount. Henry handed Evangeline up into the saddle and then reached for Anna, who backed away.

"I never rode afore." Her eyes were wide with fright.

"Anna, this is the fastest way to save Angus." Evangeline reached her hand down and watched the conflict in the young girl's eyes. A moment of hesitation, then she nodded and allowed Henry to lift her up to sit astride behind Evangeline. She clung to Evangeline's waist.

"Hang on tight." Evangeline patted Anna's arm and pressed her heel into the gray's side, which sprung into an easy canter.

Mounted, Henry and the three armed guards followed.

Anna pointed them toward the old mill road that led to an old stone silo near the waterfalls. Overgrown but still visible, they galloped onward.

"Where did you last see him?" Evangeline turned her head so Anna could hear her over the den of thundering hooves. The girl's eyes were shut tight. She repeated her question but this time she patted the girl's hand to get her attention.

"Just afore the turn in the road." Her voice a high squeak filled with fear.

A loud wail rose from a tall patch of grass at the side of the road just ahead. A red-faced toddler stood screaming out his protest at being left alone. The group pulled their horses to a stop. Before Henry or a guard could reach them, Anna then Evangeline dismounted and rushed to the child.

"Go. We'll take care of the infant. Find Hemming before he slips away." Evangeline put an arm around the young mother as she comforted her distraught child.

Henry nodded and ordered a guard to stay behind and the rest of them rode off scanning the path and surroundings for any sign of Hemming.

"The blackheart must have taken the bag of food I left and abandoned poor Angus after I ran off." Anna fumed as she assessed her son for injuries, thankful at finding none.

Wham!

Evangeline whirled around and saw their guard slump to the ground, his face bleeding and his helmet smashed. Urso Hemming stood over the man with a bloody rock in his hand. He threw it down, grabbed the guard's sword, and pointed it at Anna and the child.

Evangeline released the dagger from the cross and edged closer to Hemming.

"I knew the wench would bring someone with a horse if I bided my time." He waved the sword at Evangeline. "Stand back." He pointed it at Evangeline and she stopped. "You will lead us to a place where I can wait until nightfall for my escape from this wretched kingdom." He picked up a heavy bag from the ground where he had hidden it.

"You will not escape." Evangeline's grip tightened on the dagger.

"I have my money and some hostages to guarantee my freedom." His gaze narrowed as if he could read Evangeline's intent. He wrenched the screaming child from Anna's arms. "Back away, wench, or I'll cut the brat."

Anna screamed and Hemming shoved her to her knees.

Evangeline helped her stand. If she could get close enough she could end this.

"Shut up! If you want to keep on living, you'll cease your caterwauling." He pulled the bag's strap over his head and settled it across his chest to keep his hands free then tucked the toddler under his arm. Holding Angus against his side horizontally so that the babe's arms flailed and his legs dangled without support, he reached for the reins of the guard's horse.

Anna kept stepping between Evangeline and Hemming

making it impossible for her to throw the dagger for risk of hitting either the child or his mother.

"You can walk, your Ladyship." He waved Anna to the other horse. "Get up there." He pointed the sword first at Evangeline then Anna. "If you try anything I will kill you all, starting with the brat."

At Anna's expression of horror, he laughed, but his eyes narrowed with intent.

"No!" Anna backed away from the animal. Angus' tears and cries grew loud and demanding.

"Shut up you little brat." Hemming shook the child.

The heat of anger burned with a silent promise of revenge, Evangeline stepped forward ready to strike.

A crash of brush being trampled erupted beside them.

A big man wearing the mask of the Fox burst through and grabbed the child from the surprised Hemming's grasp. The babe was shoved into the arms of his mother before the Fox struck Hemming to the ground.

The Fox stood over the fake earl. There was something familiar about the stance.

"I'll take care of this vermin. You ladies must go." He crushed Hemming's wrist with his boot and picked up the sword loosed from his grasp.

"Griswold." The name slipped out before she could stop it.

"Nay, my Lady. I am the Fox, the righter of wrongs." He grabbed Hemming and jerked him to his feet. The hand he used was missing two fingers. "Dispatching evil and doing good 'tis pleasing to the Lord, is it not?"

Three hooded men in forest green tunics slipped out of the brush, confiscated the bag from the protesting Hemming and hauled him into the woods.

"You have been tried and found guilty by every maiden that you soiled, every family you robbed, and every victim you murdered." Griswold's voice could be heard loud and clear as they dragged their prisoner out of sight.

Hemming's screams of outrage echoed through the woods then suddenly stopped. The knowledge of what that could mean left both relief and concern.

"Please, yur Ladyship. You heard the Fox. We must go." Anna tugged on Evangeline's arm.

"First, I must tend to the guard." Evangeline knelt to assess the man's injury. The blow had knocked him unconscious. After tearing a length from the hem of her dress, she dabbed it against the wound on his forehead. He groaned. The wound had bled a lot, but he would live.

At the sound of pounding hooves headed their way, she stood.

"Quick. We must restrain the horses. Survival instinct will cause even a well-trained horse to flee if it hears other horses running for fear of being chased by predators." Evangeline stood and captured the reins of the guard's horse. Anna fisted the reins of the gray. The skittish horses pawed the ground.

Appearing from around the bend, Henry and the two guards raced toward them.

"We had not gone far when we heard the screams. What happened?" Henry dismounted as his gelding slid to a stop, reaching Evangeline in three strides. "Are you injured?" Fear hardened his tone. He touched her face and rubbed blood from her cheek. "I should not have left you."

"'Tis the guard's blood, not mine." She turned from Henry's touch as the other two guards approached their comrade. "He will be fine, but we must get him back to the castle to tend his wound."

"The Fox saved us and captured the earl." Anna's voice rose in admiration and excitement.

"The Fox?" Henry drew his sword and scanned their surroundings. "It might be prudent that we leave this place." He assisted Evangeline to mount her horse then helped Anna up behind her. A guard held the child until the two women were settled, then handed the fussy toddler up to Anna, who tucked him between her and Evangeline.

The men helped the injured guard onto his horse. The ride back to the castle would require a slower pace to accommodate the wounded man and the child.

Anna explained her version of the kidnapping up to and including the Fox's intervention.

By the stiff posture and grim expression on Henry's face as he listened, there would be much to discuss about the dangers of her riding out after outlaws.

At the cross roads, Evangeline pulled her mount to a stop.

"Take Anna and her son to the abbey and guard them." Evangeline motioned to one of the guards to come near then took the baby so Anna could be helped down. "She and her child have had a very trying morning. No reason for her to travel all the way to the keep when the abbey is so much closer." After Anna and the child were on the ground, Evangeline said, "I will come to visit you and Angus soon. Until then, please continue taking care of the abbey."

Henry helped the young mother to remount behind the guard and handed her the child.

"I'll be safe. No need to have a guard. My da and brothers are coming today to enlarge the paddock for the goats. They'll protect us. I will pay them with milk, cheese, and vegetables from the garden. Do you think the Sister would approve?"

"I am quite certain Sister Margaret Mary would be very pleased with your plans."

The remaining guard led the horse and the injured man as Henry and Evangeline rode toward the castle. They had not gone far when they came across an angry crowd of about twenty peasants standing in the road spewing curses and throwing rocks and sticks at something hanging from a tall sycamore tree a few paces from the road.

As her group drew closer, Evangeline recognized the object of their hostility.

Urso Hemming. His judgment had been swift, but the sight repulsed her.

"The blackheart is quite dead. Get along with ye." The guard waved his sword at the crowd. With grumbles of displeasure, the peasants dispersed into the woods and along the road in both directions, no doubt eager to spread the word of Hemming's demise.

"Stay here and guard the body until I can send a wagon back to bring him in for burial. I fear others will come who also have reason to stone the dead man. Not that the blighter doesn't deserve it, but his body must remain recognizable to officially confirm his death by the regents and Lord Brighton and his servants." Henry reached for the reins of the injured man's horse. "I'll take your friend on to the castle and see that he receives care."

They had to take it slow because of the injured guard. The time it took to travel the remaining distance to the castle was more than enough for the villagers and farmers to spread the news of Hemming's capture and death. Land that had remained fallow because of the siege now had farmers inspecting and clearing the fields by picking up rocks that had come to the surface. Soon they would be plowing the ground to ready it for fall crops. Their grins and cheerful waves to Evangeline's group confirmed an atmosphere of hope, as if a terrible storm had finally passed lifting the oppression from their land.

Except for the occasional moan from the injured guard, Henry and Evangeline rode in silence.

Her one attempt to engage Henry was met with a scowl and a clipped, "We will speak in private."

When they came in sight of the castle Evangeline breathed a sigh of relief.

"I will ride ahead to have everything readied to receive our patient." Without waiting for Henry's agreement, Evangeline kicked her mount into a canter, and, when she was far enough away not to hear Henry's protest, she pushed her mount faster and raced down the hill to the keep. The wind in her face was invigorating. Justifying her breakneck speed with her mission to prepare for the injured guard and eagerness to check on Sarah and her father was secondary to getting away from Henry's dark mood.

"Open the gates!" A sentry had spotted Evangeline and called to the guards. The gate was opened by the time she slowed her horse to cross the bridge covering the moat. A servant met her to assist her dismount, then took the winded horse to the stable.

With a few clipped orders, she sent other servants to prepare a comfortable place to receive the injured man in the guard's quarters. She would check on her father and Sarah and then assist Elsie in doctoring the guard.

After tending to the guard, she was relieved that he would be fine with a little rest. With lighter steps, she proceeded to her quarters to clean up. She pondered the feeling of usefulness and contentment which seemed to relate more to her persona as Sister Margaret Mary than that of her role as the overly confident, pampered Lady Evangeline.

Still, the prospect of facing the officials and curious gentry who would soon arrive, no doubt with their many questions, filled her with dread. Her slow but determined pace was reminiscent of her youth when she had to face up to one of her many transgressions. She would need God's grace and mercy to get through it all.

Evangeline headed toward her quarters to clean up and dress for dinner, her first official appearance at Castle Brighton as Lady Evangeline since her marriage over three years ago. The castle hummed with activity preparing for the celebration of her return and the end of the reign of terror for her father and the region.

Using the servants' stairs to avoid unnecessary contact, she made it to her room unhindered. She slipped through the door and closed it behind her with a sigh of relief.

"You're late." Henry stood at the window, washed and handsomely dressed in a finely woven tunic. He turned to face her, arms crossed, expression stern.

"I'm tired and in need of a bath." Anger filled her tone at being addressed as if she were a tardy child. "You must go." She stiffened and drew her tired frame to full height.

A tentative knock came at the door.

"Come in." Evangeline was relieved at the interruption.

The door opened, and two servants carried in a copper bathing tub and placed it before the fireplace then started a roaring fire. They left as an older woman came in.

"Lord Stanton." The older woman bobbed a curtsy before she turned to Evangeline. "We are all glad at yur return, m'Lady. If there is anything we can do—"

"You can leave." Henry's curt demand drew instant contrition and the servant backed toward the door, her face aghast.

"Henry!" Evangeline's stern rebuke brought a frown to his face. She ignored the thundercloud brewing in his countenance and stepped between him and the servant. "Please, forgive his lordship's bad manners and continue preparing my bath, Helga." Evangeline barely restrained the offer to help the old servant, who now used a cane to aid her in climbing the many castle stairs. Helga had been another faithful servant Evangeline had known since her youth. A flutter of guilt welled up within her at Helga's joy in her return. After many months experiencing servitude as a nun and visits to the keep, Evangeline had gotten to know the castle servants as hard working people with their own hopes and dreams. They would never again be the invisible nobodies whose sole purpose was to fulfill her every whim.

"Thank you, m' lady. We won't be but a minute." The older woman flushed and returned to her duties directing the servants who waited beyond the doorway for their command to enter.

"In with ye." Helga clapped her hands and pointed the direction to the empty tub.

Six more young women entered, each carrying a steaming bucket of water, which they emptied into the tub. A tall intricately carved screen was brought out from a closet and extended around the bath to keep in the heat and provide privacy.

Evangeline and Henry stood silently as the servants completed their jobs. Evangeline's handmaiden poured in rose scented oils that permeated the air.

"Yur Lordships." Helga gave them a stiff curtsy, accompanied with popping joints, then hustled the remaining young girls out of the room and closed the door.

Henry ambled over and slid the door bolt in place with a loud and determined click.

"Finally." His voice was calm, but his stance, feet apart and his arms crossed, expressed his determination.

"'Tis late. You need to leave. I must bathe and dress." Her tone came out curt to cover the dread squeezing her insides. She had given Henry the basics of her disappearance while being sequestered in Captain Fritz's cabin. His anger was stirred by what she didn't tell him. They knew each other well enough to know when one or the other withheld something important.

"We'll leave the discussion about the danger and what could have happened today for another time." He walked toward her. "I know you are reluctant to finish our discussion of your whereabouts these last eighteen months, but I refuse to wait any longer. I demand you tell me where you've been and why you were in hiding."

"You demand?" Evangeline's voice, raspy with exhaustion, rose in defiance.

"You are my wife and as your husband, I demand the truth." His tone softened as he reached Evangeline. "I thought I'd lost you forever." He held a steady gaze as he sought her reaction to his touch.

"There isn't time to get into all of it now. My father will send someone to fetch me soon if I don't make an appearance." She allowed him to capture her hand. The gesture cooled the anger and fear of his demands.

"The commander has already dispatched a messenger to the king with his report. He believes the king will send Lord Alfred Gilfried, the king's current viceroy within a week or two at the latest, to confirm the report." He rubbed a thumb across her cheek. "Try not to worry. Gilfried will find the report to be true and accurate and your father will have no need to fear punishment from the realm."

"That is my prayer." Evangeline touched his hand. "Thankfully, we will have a small intimate meal with just our immediate family tonight."

"Shall we discuss what we'll say when anyone asks?" He searched her face with his gaze.

With her nod, he relaxed his stance.

"For tonight, to stem the rampant rumors of your disappearance, I made a brief statement to the staff. I told them that you had narrowly escaped an assassin's attempt and, at my insistence, went into hiding at a secluded nunnery." He searched her gaze. "That much you've told me."

"Except for the part of being there at your insistence, what you say is true." She gave an exhausted sigh. "The nuns of The Sacred Heart Order did find me after the fire and took me in."

~

*H*enry glanced down at his wife and rubbed his thumb across her fingers, once soft as silk, now rough and calloused. "Last year, at the anniversary of your death, I visited..." He closed his eyes and cleared his throat of emotion. "I ran across a nun on the road not far from the burned out cabin. When I questioned her, she refused to tell me where her order was located. Through some connections in the church, I finally located the remote abbey and demanded to speak to the abbess in charge, I found her just as evasive." He watched the emotions flicker across Evangeline's face with the facts he had uncovered. "I assume once you were well enough to travel you returned here."

"I had heard that my father was ill and wanted to use the knowledge the nuns taught me to help him." She stared at the floor. "I wore a habit and veil to keep from being recognized."

"You used the name Sister Margaret Mary and lived in the old priest's crumbling abbey."

"Margaret was my grandmother's name, and I found solace in that rundown abbey." She paced to the window. "When I arrived at the castle, Hemming was masquerading as an heir, all the while keeping my father prisoner." There remained an air of sadness about her as if something still grieved her. If he was patient, perhaps in time she would share the rest.

"Even with my explanation of your disappearance, those who saw me after your disappearance won't be deceived, for my grief at your loss was very real." He cleared his voice. "Does that story meet with your approval m'lady?" He smiled and drew her into his arms when she didn't resist. "Or do you still wish to tie me to the stake, flail the skin from my body, then burn me alive for my past stupidity?" He leaned back and searched her face when she remained silent.

"I'm thinking." She couldn't keep humor out of her voice. He laughed and tugged her tight against his chest.

"I love you, Evangeline. Always have and always will." After a deep kiss, he released her. "Now I shall leave you to get ready… unless you wish me to stay and help." His voice was husky, and his eyes lit with challenge.

"I have been raised, as have you, Lord Stanton, to attend to the duties of the court before personal pleasures." She stepped out of his embrace and waved him away. "Go. Spread your version of my disappearance to the curious. I will join you in the great hall as soon as I'm presentable."

CHAPTER 27

A little over two weeks later, the castle was filled with guests. After the commander's thorough report, the king sent the viceroy as expected, however, with viceroy came six officials interested in other affairs of the realm bringing their wives, at their insistence, if the rumors were correct. Probably to see for themselves that the Lady Evangeline they remembered was indeed alive.

Assured that Sarah was content and protected by guards and the servants tending her, Henry was free to concentrate on the evening.

The servants had prepared rooms for their overnight guests, which he sincerely hoped would not prolong their stay more than a night or two at most. He and Evangeline were still in the process of getting reacquainted.

The king had also sent papers officially declaring Henry Lord of Brighton Castle and surrounding region. He was to take charge immediately, a surprise that he hoped to share with Evangeline later. He looked forward to raising his family in this place far removed from the politics and dictates of court life in London.

So far, tonight's banquet had gone far better than Henry could have hoped. He, Lord Brighton, and Evangeline had prepared for this evening over the weeks by answering every question they could think that might be asked, until they could mask any indignation and answer with calm and discretion.

His beautiful wife glided from guest to guest with royal dignity and decorum. Stuck in a group of men discussing trade issues with Scotland, he watched Evangeline's posture stiffen, lips thinned in anger, and her fists clinched at her side. A gesture he recognized as the calm before the tempest. Before he could go to her side, she smiled. Instead of a full out explosion of temper, she ignored their guest's persistent inquiries for details of her disappearance and expertly turned their attention to the latest court fashions. While praising her father's part in capturing Millicent, Evangeline gathered the sympathy and admiration of even the most ardent skeptic, the same gossips Henry had overheard over the months of Evangeline's disappearance, who had speculated a number of outrageous reasons for her being gone so long and allowing everyone to believe she was dead.

A deep respect warmed his heart for her. She had matured in the time they were apart. Yet, he couldn't dismiss the feeling that she was hiding something. Would she ever be able to forgive and fully trust him again so they could resume their life together?

~

*E*vangeline's gaze was drawn to a small crowd of women standing near the food table. The wife of the king's viceroy, a busty blonde dressed in silk and dripping with expensive jewelry, stood in a corner with other bejeweled matrons. Once, not so long ago, these pompous overindulgent biddies would have been relieved of their wealth by the Fox.

Their bobbles would have helped the suffering of many less fortunate. To her shame, but for her tragedy, she might have acted just like them.

Evangeline had escaped the constant barrage of questions and the women's frivolous conversation of fashion and gossip of the king's court by hiding behind a large marble column. A quick glance confirmed Henry was involved in a deep discussion of commerce and trade with the women's husbands. She overheard her name mentioned and for curiosity's sake edged closer to the women's circle staying in the shadows.

"Do you think there is any truth in the rumors that Henry beat her, which caused her to run away?" A plain woman with a large mole on her chin used a lace fan to hide behind and emphasize her question with its rapid flutter.

"I heard from a very reliable source that Henry had become bored with her and taken his brother's widow as a lover, and that was why she fled the marriage."

"That may have been true, because I heard she joined a nunnery."

"You are both wrong." The skinny brunette leaned into the group and whispered, making it hard to catch her words. "I heard she left for Spain with a foreign lover whom she jilted to return home."

"Oh, Bertie, the Spaniard wasn't her lover but her kidnapper."

Henry captured Evangeline's elbow and steered her away from the gossips.

"Amazing how facts can become so distorted in such a short time." His breath feathered her neck as he followed through with a brush of his lips, sending chills down her spine.

"Not so surprising when those facts are distorted on purpose for the pleasure of the old hags who prefer lies to the truth." Evangeline rubbed a hand discretely across her neck to try and alleviate the tingle that refused to dissipate from his kiss.

"You can't rid yourself of my touch, for I shall be ever touching you and reminding you of my presence." His eyes were full of humor and promise which loosed warmth within her.

~

*H*enry remained at her side, ready to intervene if necessary, but she appeared to have no further need of his gallantry. She had put a retraining hand on his arm when he would have slain the intoxicated Lord Alfred Gilfried, the king's viceroy, for his improper advances. Even an hour after the servants and his wife whisked Gilfried away to his chambers, Henry's face still flushed with anger.

"Did that popinjay think your husband would stand by and ignore his impropriety?"

"Henry, let it go. He will feel awful tomorrow when he learns from his very angry wife of his actions." Evangeline captured her husband's arm and drew him near. "Besides, he will leave on the morrow for London. He will report back to the King that all is well and confirm that my father is not, nor ever has been, a traitor to the crown or his people." She glanced up, smiled seductively and fluttered her eye lashes at him, an action she once used to humor him out of a foul mood.

He leaned down to whisper, "Does this mean you will follow through with the rest of my reward for not pounding that fool into a bloody pulp?"

Evangeline grew flush and pulled away.

"I...ah. No. Not tonight." She turned and walked away to sit beside her father, leaving Henry standing alone and frustrated that she had shut him out again.

"But soon, my love." His whispered vow grew in determination to find out what caused the fear in her eyes. What secrets did she hide from him? His mind swirled with horrible possibilities. He paced the hall until he was able to calm his thoughts. It took all of his control to keep from throwing her over his shoulder and hauling her to their chamber where he would lock the door and remain until she revealed whatever she kept from him. For she did withhold something and it was time he knew it all.

~

*I*t was well after midnight before Evangeline was able to leave the celebration, which seemed destined to go on for hours yet. Exhaustion made every step a focused effort. Two handmaidens met her at the door of her chambers and whisked her inside. Never was she so grateful for their help. She crawled onto the feather bed and fell fast asleep.

Loud pounding rattled her door. She tried to focus, but everything remained a muddy blur. Dawn blushed the stained glass of her window with a translucent glow.

"Who is it?" Her voice was a raspy whisper. She tried to sit up, but her head pounded from not enough sleep.

"Your Ladyship, the prisoner has escaped!" The male voice grew more demanding and the pounding increased.

"Millicent escaped?" Evangeline threw off her covers and pulled on her robe as she stumbled to the door and unbolted it.

Rodney, a downstairs servant, pushed open the door, grabbed her hand, and tugged her toward the back stairs.

"Where are we going?" Fully awake now, danger prickled against her skin. Something was not right. She planted her feet, jerking her hand out of the startled young man's grasp. "Where are the guards? Where is Elsa?"

"I'm the boss so come with me." He reached for her hand, but she stepped back. Anger flushed his face red. "We have your child."

"Impossible." Evangeline turned and ran for the stairs to prove him a liar. "Guards!"

"Stop." He grabbed the back of her robe.

With one tug, she freed the robe's silk belt and slipped out of the heavy garment. Her plain cotton sleeping gown swished around her legs with every stride.

"Guards!" Her hoarse cry echoed throughout the halls. She took the marble stairs two at a time, but the castle's spy and her would-be kidnapper was right behind her.

The sound of voices raised in alarm and the clangs of armor echoed along the corridors.

"Got you." Bony fingers grabbed the back of her thin gown, ripping the fabric.

She seized the torn fabric in front and turned in time to see the stunned horror on his face a moment before Henry jerked him off his feet and threw him down the stairs into the waiting arms of two castle guards.

"Sarah?" Evangeline backed away.

"She's safe. She is surrounded by guards at the door of the nursery and servants who are as intent on protecting her as we are." Henry stepped up the stairs to her level and covered Evangeline's bare shoulders and exposed back with her discarded robe. "Come. Let's get you to your room."

"Millicent?"

"She was found in the stable trying to escape but is once again safely locked away. The commander and his men will take her to London to stand trial. They leave tomorrow with the viceroy and the others."

A new dread pounded in her chest. Had Henry seen her back?

They arrived at her chambers and were met by Evangeline's chamber maid.

"I have set warming stones beneath the blankets and prepared strong tea for M'lady."

"And you are?" Henry stepped between his wife and the servant.

"Hilde." She bobbed a curtsey and smiled.

"Thank you, Hilde but you can return to your quarters now." Henry's tone brooked no refusal. "I will take care of my wife."

"Yes, M'lord." The maid frowned but nodded and left.

Henry closed and locked the door.

"What were you thinking unlocking the door and rushing about this time of night without escort?" He paced from one end of the room to the other as if unable to settle in one spot.

"Henry." Evangeline touched his shoulder as he passed by.

He turned and gathered her into his arms and sobbed. Great racking waves of grief poured out of him.

Emptiness carved out her heart. His reaction to her disfigurement was far worse than she could have imagined.

"I understand." She soaked up his last embrace. No man could be expected to accept such disfigurement into his bed.

"What?" Henry drew back but did not release her. The misery on his countenance was a mirror image of her own.

"I must repulse you…"

"Repulse?" His question was sincere.

"The scars."

"My grief is not about your scars, but for your suffering and my stupidity that caused them." He turned her around and tugged the robe off of her shoulders leaving her back bare. He rubbed his hands down her back then gently traced each puffy scar with his fingertips.

Even the light touch ignited the memory of being trapped and alone. But then she felt him kiss each ugly ridge. His actions burned away the past and ignited a different fire within her, a fire of love and passion that could only grow between the life commitment of a husband and wife.

After a lengthy exploration, he stepped around to meet her gaze.

"You could never repulse me." He drew her close and kissed her with such passion they were both left breathless. "You are the best part of me." He pulled back the covers and set the bed warmer on the floor. "Did you realize that the scars are in the form of a tree?"

"A tree?" She knew the scars started at her spine and spread up toward her neck and across her shoulders. Dropping her shredded gown to the floor, she climbed beneath the warm covers, no longer fearful of her husband seeing all of her.

"Yes, a tree. It's like a symbol of God's tree of life or…" He shucked his clothes and followed her onto the bed. He tugged her within his arms. "It could be our family tree."

"There are a lot of branches." Her voice drew husky within his embrace.

"I know." His chuckle rumbled against her neck.

CHAPTER 28

Six months later

*E*vangeline sped across the meadow with her hair flying in the wind. She was determined to enjoy this last bit of freedom before Henry forbade her from riding in her condition. Being pregnant didn't mean she was fragile. As much as she loved him, he could be a bit overly zealous in his vow to protect her. If he watched from their quarters, she would be in store for a stern lecture when she returned.

After much struggle with her conscience, she had finally forgiven Millicent, not because the wicked woman deserved it but as an act of her will. She released her anger to God and prayed for the woman's salvation two days ago. It was a relief to break that tie that bound her to the past. Evangeline felt as if a heavy burden had been lifted.

A messenger had arrived at Brighton Castle early this morning with the report that Millicent was dead. Found guilty in her trial, she had cheated the court of her beheading by taking poison the morning of her execution. With that bit of news, Evangeline vowed to never give the dead woman another thought.

Her mount eased into a gentle rocking canter. The morning sun burned off the last of the fog and shone brightly across dew-kissed fields that would soon be ready for harvest. Wheat, barley, and corn had grown in abundance after the soil's long rest, as if eager to share its stored up wealth.

From a distance, a small horse-drawn cart approached. Evangeline waved and leaned down against her horse's neck.

"Go, Misty." The white mare stretched out and ate up the ground with her long strides.

Evangeline eased back the reins and slowed her mount when she reached the road. She stopped when she reached her friend.

"Evangeline you mustn't... Oh, never mind." Helen had blossomed too since her marriage to Armand. After he resigned his commission in the king's army, they married and ran the inn together. Expecting their first child in a few months, her friend looked happier than Evangeline had ever seen her. "Dismount and ride with me so we can talk on our way to our meeting."

"Fine." Evangeline dismounted, tied Misty to the back of the cart and joined Helen. "Did you know the king has suspended taxes in this region for three years?" At Helen's gasp of delight, she grinned. "It might be because of all the gold and grain recovered from Hemming's thievery. The king still got his tax money, just all at once. The bulk of the grain was distributed fairly to the people and kept them fed through the winter and spring." The tax burden relieved from the peasants and farmers shoulders would provide a great incentive to plow as many fields and raise as many crops as they could manage. Even immigrants were welcomed to come and find employment with promise of an allotment of land for those willing to work hard. It was good to see so many happy people.

With everyone eager to put the past behind them and willing

to work hard, a great deal had been accomplished in such a short time.

"It's wonderful to know the restoration on the building is finally complete." Evangeline glanced over at the abbey as they passed by. The money Evangeline had hidden in the wall had been put to good use toward that effort.

"And with the many generous donations, the workmen were also able to enlarge the chapel." Helen shifted positions to get more comfortable.

"Everything has worked out better than we could have hoped, Amen." Evangeline smiled, knowing even the money Henry had hidden in the carriage had been recovered. Besides contributing to the work done on the abbey, a good portion of those funds were needed to repair the castle from neglect and replace the lost wages of the servants who had become unpaid slaves during Hemming's occupation. The castle was once again a happy place to work and live.

"How are all of our friends?" Hope warmed Evangeline's heart.

"Busy as us, but eager to have the gang together again one last time. So much has happened since *The Fox* and *his* gang retired." Helen turned the cart down a well-used lane toward the old mill.

"We went from a feared band of outlaws to peace-loving, law-abiding citizens. God is good." Evangeline had a rush of gratitude for the better-than-could-have-been-expected outcome. Only the traitor, Mouse, had died. The rest of their gang had done well in the region's new era of peace and prosperity.

"Wren, her mother and younger brother moved from living in the cellar beneath the old Danby farm house to occupying their home again. Their farm has flourished since a young farmer was hired to help them rebuild the barn, repair the house and plant the land. He and Wren have grown close. I predict before the wheat is harvested the two will wed. The new priest, Father Benjamin has stayed busy announcing marriage banns and performing marriage ceremonies since he arrived." Helen laid a hand on her protruding abdomen. "I never knew life could be this good." She glanced at Evangeline with a glow of contentment.

"I know what you mean." Evangeline leaned over to give her friend a quick hug. She hoped one day their children would become as close friends as she and Helen. "How about Owl and Sparrow?"

"Owl has also remarried. Her husband is younger than her by a decade, but has earned her respect with his hard work and is shaping up to make a fine blacksmith under her mentorship."

"The old mill is working!" Evangeline pointed to the water-wheel turning.

"I cannot remember when last it ran. It's hard to imagine how fast they repaired it." Helen kept the pony pointed toward a newly built addition to the smaller mill doubling the space.

"Henry thought it important to have a working mill nearby to accommodate the farmers and their harvests." Evangeline turned to check on Misty, who plodded along behind the cart. The mare shook her head with impatience at the sedate pace.

"Since her late husband once owned the mill, Sparrow supervised the repairs with the help of an apprentice, a Scot from Glasgow, someone Henry recommended. I heard the Scots' first few weeks were a bit rough, including very loud and heated discussions between him and Sparrow about how to repair and improve the mill's mechanics." Helen laughed. "I think they are getting along much better now. Who knows? Father Benjamin may be called to wed them or bury them after it is all said and done."

Evangeline joined in her laughter.

"The rest you will have to wait and find out for yourself. We are here." Helen drove the cart into the clearing next to the Mill and stopped under the shade of two towering oaks.

The door of the mill opened, and her friends poured out leaving no doubt that the gang had survived and flourished since they had last been together.

The Fox's gang had been thrown together by necessity and forged into a sisterhood by a righteous cause. Their connection would be forever bonded by friendship far stronger than the restriction of class between servant and high-born. At least in this place and at this moment they were all equal.

After Evangeline's lengthy confession to Father Benjamin, he had strongly advised she refrain from mentioning her part as the Fox to anyone, including Henry or her father. She had agreed it was indeed a secret part of her life best left buried in her past. Only these brave women knew each other's real identities, and they had all sworn a vow of silence on the matter. Her secret was safe with them, for they had proved themselves trustworthy. They had as much to lose as she, if the truth of the matter ever came out.

The legend of the Fox had grown with the rumors he had put to right the wrongs of Castle Brighton. With the resurgence of the Fox, no one would ever guess the part these women had played in setting things right here. If rumors were correct, Griswold, as the Fox, had continued righting wrongs, making him and his gang welcomed by villagers wherever they went. Even songs were sung in his honor, no doubt something Griswold would appreciate in his quest to fulfill his new calling.

It was time she left her secret life behind and wholeheartedly embraced her most important role of Lady Evangeline of Castle Brighton, wife and mother.

After she left this place today, she would no longer be associated with the Fox...unless.

She frowned and shook off the thought. Only God knew what tomorrow might bring.

Did you enjoy this book? We hope so!
Would you take a quick minute to leave a review where you purchased the book?
It doesn't have to be long. Just a sentence or two telling what you liked about the story!

Receive a FREE ebook and get updates when new Wild Heart books release: https://www.wildheartbooks.org/newsletter

Don't miss *The Sword and the Secrets*, book 2 in the Secrets series!

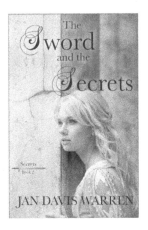

Chapter 1

1209
ENGLAND

"*A*arrgh!" A second too late, Lord Henry John Stanton III pivoted to the left, and swung his sword in a tight arc to deflect the sharp blade that grazed his midsection. The coppery smell of blood and the sting of pain triggered the battle rage of the warrior he once was.

Using the flat of his blade and a heavy downward thrust, he aggressively disarmed his sparring partner. The rush of the fight surged through his veins, driving his every instinct to strike harder. Attack with lethal force.

No! Shaken, John threw down his sword and took three steps back. "I..." But for God's grace, he had almost delivered a killing blow. How could he have let the fight take hold of him so?

John swiped his hand across his eyes. Too many sleepless nights from fighting the relentless dreams. Those nightmares plunged him into never-ending bloody battles and kept him exhausted. His last encounter with the enemy, ten months ago, had left him near death and ended his two year service in the king's army. Memories he would give anything to forget. So much death and destruction and...

The large, raised scar on his side burned with fresh intensity.

"By the saints!" His best friend, William, rubbed his bruised knuckles and released a string of unsavory curse words. His gaze met John's, then dropped to John's torn tunic with its growing stain of fresh blood. William motioned to the crimson-stained tear with an expression of horror and regret. "I tripped." He ran his uninjured hand through his hair and hung his head in defeat. "Is it bad?"

"No." John growled, raising his tunic to examine the wound. He swiped away the blood, then cleaned his hand against the ruined fabric.

"I'll replace your tunic."

"Hang the garment. A hair's breadth closer and you would be explaining to my family why you killed their only son." John's voice rose in anger, not because of his wound, but at how close he'd come to ending William's life. He retraced his steps, picked up his sword, and with a shaky hand shoved it into its battle-scarred scabbard.

"That would not be a conversation I'd likely live to finish." William paled as he swiped the sweat off his brow. With a groan of frustration, he bent down, retrieved his fallen sword, and gave it an angry swing, lopping off the tops of a patch of tall weeds. "It's all the fault of..." He didn't finish his thought and, instead, pushed his sword into its war-worn sheaf, and then picked up a woven bag from the ground. "I must not be the only one distracted to allow my blade to come so close."

"Aye." John slapped his friend on the back to show there were no hard feelings. Neither were of a mind to continue their sparring, so they shouldered their equipment and ambled back toward Brighton Castle. "I'm glad the glen is far from prying eyes, or the whole village would be ablaze with embellished details of our swordplay." John glanced around to confirm there were no witnesses.

"Your sister..." William waved his hand at John's torn tunic. "I should have never yielded to her last request."

"I assume you refer to Elise." He checked his wound and found the scratch had stopped bleeding. "I am more inclined to blame our injuries on our equal lack of focus." John's desire to help William keep his skills honed was the only reason he would wield a sword again. Boastful pride and arrogance on the battlefield had cost many unnecessary deaths, including the hostages they'd sought to free. Their screams still tormented even his waking thoughts.

"John?" William raised his voice to get his friend's attention.

"What?" John rubbed his hand across his brow to erase his thoughts, then glanced over at William to show he was listening.

"I said, certainly 'tis Elise I'm speaking of." William sent him a look as if John were daft. "Your eldest sister, Sarah, is long married and lives near London, and I cannot imagine someone with aught against quiet, little Hanna." He loosed a deep sigh. "How can three sisters be so different?"

"So what has Elise done now?" John adjusted his pace with William's slower, more awkward, gait. His middle sister always seemed to have her hands in something.

"This." William tapped his right leg with his scabbard, receiving a dull thump. They had met at the glen, and John had been so consumed with his own problems he hadn't noticed until now. William's pant leg was usually tied just below his knee, exposing a pine peg, but now the garment fell to his ankle where a shoe appeared.

He stopped and raised his pant leg. "See?" A carved wooden leg, with an attached foot enclosed in a leather shoe, was visible. "It's heavy and awkward. This thing caused me to stumble, and is the reason my blade came close enough to strike you."

William's limp became more pronounced the longer they walked. He stopped at a tree stump and sat. "I can't stand it another moment." He unstrapped the wooden leg, held it up, and pulled off the shoe to show John.

"Hmmm." John barely suppressed his laughter at the detailed sculpting of the foot with individual toes and toenails. It must have taken his sister weeks to carve such a life-like foot. "'Tis a work of art. What don't you like about it?"

"It's too heavy and, in spite of the padding, it rubs a blister when I wear it." He lowered his bag and pulled out a simple, lighter-weight piece of carved pine, which was wide enough at the top to fit his stump, then narrowed to a dull point. It was scarred and discolored from daily use, quite a contrast from the smooth and polished limb he'd removed. The pine peg had a hollowed out top, lined with a thick pad of wool to cushion his stump.

He folded his pant leg and used the straps to attach the well-worn peg leg in place. "I know she means well, but why she insists on trying to invent a better leg is beyond me." He tapped the wooden peg. "This works fine and I'm able to do most anything I did before."

"She just wants to help. Besides, I think she's a bit smitten with you since you saved my life." He waited while his friend stuffed the carved masterpiece inside the bag and stood.

"Smitten?" He shook his head and walked on. "She's destined to marry someone with a title, a lord or maybe even a prince. Not a low-born, crippled soldier." His protest hinted at his regret.

"You earned your knighthood in battle. I heard the commander give the scribe orders for your commendation." John wondered if those orders had been lost, since no mention was made about a ceremony after the commander was killed in battle shortly after.

"It doesn't matter. I don't think anyone thought either of us would live long enough to receive such honors after our last battle." William adjusted his bag to his other shoulder. "Such a title still wouldn't make me a noble."

"I don't think my parents are as determined to find a suitably royal husband for Elise as you apparently are." He sympathized with his friend's dilemma, but he knew of his parents' concern that Elise's unorthodox interests and refusal, as she put it, *to being bartered off to a stranger in an arranged marriage,* had already made the process of finding her a suitable husband a challenge.

"When I think of what I heard happened to the last candidate who came to court her...something about singed hair and beard." John's humor could no longer be withheld, and it bubbled out in undisguised laughter. "Elise's version of the matter was simply that the pompous windbag got less than he deserved after he tried to take liberties with her while she was in the middle of a volatile experiment."

"If I'd...*we'd* been there, the scoundrel would have suffered far more than singed hair." William's angry tone and scowl confirmed John's suspicions.

His friend was indeed in love, or at the very least, in danger of falling deeply in love with Elise. The thought lightened John's mood. The man who saved his life would make a worthy husband for his unique and creative sister.

"William, we grew up together, and are close as brothers, but I still do not understand your fascination with Elise. I love my sister, but she has been taking things apart and inventing contraptions since she was able to use tools." John allowed another chuckle to escape. "My parents never knew if the furniture would hold together after she'd been around."

"Aye. I remember an incident involving a visiting dignitary." William's scowl was replaced by the crinkle of laugh lines.

"I think that was when she was twelve. After the wheels came off the king's magistrate's carriage, she confessed to the vandalism. All because she wanted to see how the blacksmith had fashioned the new brackets that attached the undercarriage. That cost my father a new carriage to replace the broken one and a lot of futile promises of keeping my sister in hand in the future." John smiled at William's lighter gait. "My mother finally insisted Elise be given a tutor to direct her inventive passion and a shop of her own to experiment to her heart's desire, safely away from anything in and around the castle."

John stopped as the sound of thundering hooves headed their way. "Looks like we're about to have company."

Two riders galloped toward them, slowed, and then stopped a short distance away. His mother, Lady Evangeline, and the subject of their discussion, Elise, waited as the men approached.

"Good day, gentlemen." Lady Evangeline nodded to William, then focused on the bloodstain on John's torn tunic. Her gaze met his, and he smiled with a slight nod of assurance for his wellbeing.

She frowned, making it clear there would be further discussion as she examined and doctored his wound when he arrived home. "Son, we must start for London first thing in the morning. The girls are almost packed, but your servants said you've done nothing in preparation for the trip. They said you've decided to travel later. Is that true?"

Her expression of disapproval stirred John's conscience, but did nothing to dissuade him from his decision.

"I've decided to wait and leave in week or so. Before I leave, I'll help William track down the predators killing our sheep." It wasn't exactly a lie, for he had intended to offer his help with the hunt. A glance at William showed he was avoiding eye contact with either woman. As an honest man, he wasn't a good liar, and John had not discussed his decision to leave later, or about helping him with the hunt, something he would address once the women had gone.

"I heard you have a gift for me?" John turned his attention toward his sister, hoping to avoid being questioned further. His mother had an uncanny way of knowing when her children were hiding something from her, and he wasn't ready to discuss his decision with his family just yet.

"Hanna told you?"

When John confirmed with a nod, Elise smiled. "I wanted it to be a surprise, but that's all right. It's my latest invention. I'll give it to you when you get home." Excitement edged her tone, but Elise couldn't keep her eyes off of William. She frowned when she spotted him wearing the old peg leg, sending her gaze up to the carved foot sticking out of the top of his bag. Her mouth opened, and then closed without speaking as she glanced from William to their mother.

"This trip is supposed to be a family outing. I know Sarah will be disappointed when you don't arrive with us." Lady Evangeline was not to be deterred by idle conversation.

"Sarah will have much more important things on her mind with this being her first child. She needs you, not me, to be there to hold her hand when her time comes."

"Your father is not going to be pleased to be trapped in close quarters with three talkative females for such a long journey." Lady Evangeline smiled and straightened in the saddle. "We'll discuss this further once you are home." She gave them both a dismissal nod. "Gentlemen."

"Mother, I could keep them company." Elise turned to her mother for approval.

John frowned and shook his head.

His mother caught the gesture, and sent him a smile understanding before she turned to his sister. "I'm afraid not. You've neglected the last of your packing and need to finish. That means bringing nothing you can not wear. Understand young lady? No tools, no—."

"But I..." Elise gave a big sigh, but then submitted to the lecture.

His mother was still talking as they rode away. He dreaded keeping something this important from his parents, but it was necessary if he were to fulfill his plan.

"What's this about you needing to help me track down whatever is killing the sheep before you can leave?" William continued to watch Elise as she rode away. "I don't *need* your help for a job I've done plenty of times, but you're always welcome to join the hunt." Being the gamekeeper for the castle and surrounding two hundred acres kept William busy training the men in his charge to guard the estate against predators and poachers, a serious crime that would result in the death of man and beast if caught. "What is the real reason for not going with your family?"

"I have decided..." John rubbed the sweat off his brow and quickened his pace.

"Decided what?" William drew his attention from Elise to John.

"I'm going to become a monk."

"What?" William caught up to his friend and took John's arm to halt him. "You cannot! You're the sole male heir of your family line. You have a solemn obligation to marry." He smiled and released him. "Your mother will not allow it." As if the subject was closed, he turned and resumed the journey to the castle.

"I am serious." John walked beside his friend, his voice lowered to assure his words wouldn't carry beyond them. "I vowed that if you and I lived after being struck down in battle, I would devote my life to serving God and the church."

"I appreciate your earnest prayer on my behalf, and I am most grateful to God for His divine intervention, but don't tie *me* to your vow. I plan to marry and have many children to carry on my father's line." He slapped John's shoulder and laughed. "You would do well to follow my example."

"Would you marry to forget Elise? Or are you planning to marry her in spite of your lack of title and numerous other objections?"

"Let's leave your sister out of our discussion, please." His laughter was once again replaced by a scowl. "I know she'll be waiting to pester me about this fool leg. There will be endless questions and demands to try it again after she does one thing and then another."

"Your protests are exaggerated. You're a free man who could say no without penalty. I suspect you love every minute of her fussing over you, simply to be in her presence." John's comments were met with continued murmurs of denial until they arrived at the castle, where William hurried off to the stables to escape Elise until he was ready to be found.

John slipped inside the castle by the servants' entrance to avoid running into his mother, then sought the sanctuary of his room. He would need to spend time in prayer before he met his family for the evening meal.

Deceiving his parents was not his intent, but the truth of his plan was his to keep until the right time.

And this was not that time.

GET FOR *THE SWORD AND THE SECRETS* AT YOUR FAVORITE RETAILER.

ABOUT THE AUTHOR

Jan Davis Warren is a mother, grandmother, and a young-at-heart great-grandmother. Her wonderful husband passed away the same year she won the ACFW Genesis Award for Romantic Suspense. That win and many others are encouraging reminders that God wants her to continue writing even in the tough times.

Learn more at www.janwarrenbooks.com.

ACKNOWLEDGMENTS

I love learning about different periods in history and the people that lived them. My research, using several avenues, books and internet for information on the year 1186 England, left me frustrated by the vague, often contradictory and unverifiable facts. The world-wide pandemic made it impossible to personally travel to the region and research the area first hand. Therefore, The Secret Life of Lady Evangeline is written intentionally as a work of fiction. Any errors you devout historians find in the content are strictly mine and I ask for your indulgence and forgiveness.

Medieval Historical Romance is not my normal genre, although I enjoy reading them. Lady Evangeline's story would not leave me alone until I wrote it, thinking one and done, even after several of my beta readers suggested I write a sequel. No way. (Famous last words)

After I submitted The Secret Life of Lady Evangeline to Wild Heart Books, the publisher, Misty Beller asked if I could write two more and make it a series. Book 2 and 3 were already whispering to me, stirring my imagination with the promise of unique characters and adventure, which I had no plans on pursuing until her request. Secrets became a three book series, which I hope will bless many readers. Thank you, Misty and Wild Heart Books, whose professional staff helped this book to shine, from cover to content.

Writing is a solo journey that requires a village to teach and hone the craft of storytelling. I found this out over the years as I grew from newbie to published. The amazing process that starts with the first stirring of the imagination to the finished book, still awes me.

I must acknowledge my wonderful family, Shelley, Paul, Whitney, Kent, Kayla, Cole, and Arin for their continued encouragement. Many thanks to my first critique group, Inspy Crits, Margaret, Vickie, Gloria and Therese. You are such talented writers who have generously shared your knowledge, wisdom and encouragement with me and so many others. You continue to inspire me to be a better writer. To my Fantasy-for-Christ, online critique group, you are such a blessing. Thank you! To my beta readers, thank you ladies, your excitement over this story blesses me beyond words. To my good friend, Berta who is always willing to listen to a problem passage so I can polish the edges, thank you.

My biggest thanks goes to the One who started me on this journey, who also saved me, filled my heart with His love and continues to stir my imagination to overflowing, Jesus, my awesome Lord and Savior. You are the ultimate love story. John 3:16

If you love historical romance, check out the other Wild Heart books!

Marisol ~ Spanish Rose by Elva Cobb Martin

Escaping to the New World is her only option...Rescuing her will wrap the chains of the Inquisition around his neck.

Marisol Valentin flees Spain after murdering the nobleman who molested her. She ends up for sale on the indentured servants' block at Charles Town harbor—dirty, angry, and with child. Her hopes are shattered, but she must find a refuge for herself and the child she carries. Can this new land offer her the grace, love, and security she craves? Or must she escape again to her only living relative in Cartagena?

Captain Ethan Becket, once a Charles Town minister, now sails the seas as a privateer, grieving his deceased wife. But when he takes captive a ship full of indentured servants, he's intrigued by the woman whose manners seem much more refined than the average Spanish serving girl. Perfect to become governess for his young son. But when he sets out on a quest to find his captured sister, said to be in Cartagena, little does he expect his new Spanish governess to stow away on his ship with her six-month-old son. Yet her offer of help to free his sister is too tempting to pass up. And her beauty, both inside and out, is too attractive for his heart to protect itself against—until he learns she is a wanted murderess.

As their paths intertwine on a journey filled with danger, intrigue, and romance, only love and the grace of God can overcome the past and ignite a new beginning for Marisol and Ethan.

∾

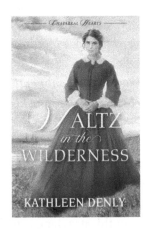

Waltz in the Wilderness by Kathleen Denly

She's desperate to find her missing father. His conscience demands he risk all to help.

Eliza Brooks is haunted by her role in her mother's death, so she'll do anything to find her missing pa—even if it means sneaking aboard a southbound ship. When those meant to protect her abandon and betray her instead, a family friend's unexpected assistance is a blessing she can't refuse.

Daniel Clarke came to California to make his fortune, and a stable job as a San Francisco carpenter has earned him more than most have scraped from the local goldfields. But it's been four years since he left Massachusetts and his fiancé is impatient for his return. Bound for home at last, Daniel Clarke finds his heart and plans challenged by a tenacious young woman with haunted eyes. Though every word he utters seems to offend her, he is determined to see her safely returned to her father. Even if that means risking his fragile engagement.

When disaster befalls them in the remote wilderness of the Southern California mountains, true feelings are revealed, and both must face heart-rending decisions. But how to decide when every choice before them leads to someone getting hurt?

∾

Lone Star Ranger by Renae Brumbaugh Green

Elizabeth Covington will get her man.

And she has just a week to prove her brother isn't the murderer Texas Ranger Rett Smith accuses him of being. She'll show the good-looking lawman he's wrong, even if it means setting out on a risky race across Texas to catch the real killer.

Rett doesn't want to convict an innocent man. But he can't let the Boston beauty sway his senses to set a guilty man free. When Elizabeth follows him on a dangerous trek, the Ranger vows to keep her safe. But who will protect him from the woman whose conviction and courage leave him doubting everything—even his heart?